After Ninety, What

After Ninety, What

more stories
from Rhoda Curtis

ISBN 9781453704394

Cover painting by Robert Holdeman
Book design, layout, and back cover photo by Cathleen Maclearie

Printed in the U.S.A.

DEDICATION

To my ancestors;

To my immediate and extended family;

To Ric, Remi, Ade, and Aba;

To my Support Group, members of which range far and wide;

To my teachers and mentors;

To my students, from whom I have learned so much.

Table of Contents

INTRODUCTION

This new collection includes stories, a play, musings, stories, teaching and travel, and a bit of poetry. It's an assemblage, rather than a chronological story, which is what most of us look for in a memoir.

I've added expansions of some stories from my first book, *Rhoda: Her First Ninety Years,* as well as a brave venture into drama. Poetry is sprinkled generously throughout the book, and the Stories section includes two stories for children. The book is loosely organized under different headings; you can skip around in it at your pleasure.

Reflection on seminal events in our lives changes with time, and memories change too. In this collection I reconsider the lives of my parents, my brother as well as my sisters, trying to imagine their lives from their own point of view. That stretches memory, and demands a kind of improvisation that goes beyond memoir. Sometimes I combine memory and fantasy, and I tell you when this happens.

As you read the various sections of the book, you may remember events in your own life that match mine, and you may find my reflections encouraging you to visit your own.

We all grow up with tapes in our heads that we didn't make. Those are tapes that echo reprimands, warnings, compliments, joy, and there are other tapes recording action that surprises us. Have you ever heard yourself yelling at your child or your loved one in a voice that doesn't seem your own? Have you ever said to yourself, "Oh, my god, I sound just like my mother (or my sister, or my brother, or my father)?" and you wonder, "Where did that voice come from?" I know this has happened to me, and in this small collection of material in different genres, I try to put those voices where they belong—in the past, at a different place and time.

Gabriel Garcia Marquez, in his memoir, *Living to Tell the Tale*, uses nostalgia in a gentle, forgiving way, but in my poem, "Nostalgia," I give it short shrift. Here it is.

The Land of Nostalgia

> The Land of Nostalgia
> is a dangerous place.
>
> Its roads are poorly maintained,
> full of pot-holes, mud-holes,
> dips and bumps and crumbling walls.
>
> They lead you into bogs, fogs,
> swamps, dead ends, and even
> quicksand, where you might disappear.
>
> The buildings have a mottled patina
> from the pigeon droppings
> hardened into greenish crusts.
>
> And the people, walking here and there,
> in and out of the crusted buildings,
> shudder in ghostly shimmers.
>
> It's best not to venture
> into that unstable place;
> that Land of Nostalgia.

Family

—part one—

Pa

PA: A LOVER OF LIFE

Pa was fifty when I was born, and when I think of him, I smell his bay rum aftershave lotion and hear his resonant singing voice.

TO MY FATHER
Hello! You red-haired ghost!
Your blue eyes twinkling at me,
twirling the waxed, curved,
cactus-pointed ends of your mustache —

You still smell of bay rum.

I think of midnight snacks of
green pickled tomatoes, home-brewed wine
and brown-paper-wrapped cheese —
you and me at the oilcloth-covered table,
Chicago west side kitchen, second-floor flat.

I conjure you up,
and hear the murmur of "shana maidele" —
my back prickling even now
from the stroking of your gentle hand.

So, my father, what are you telling me?
Live it up Enjoy! Enjoy!
Smell! Taste! Dance! Sing!
Love! and Love! and Love!

You smile and wink, twirl your mustache;
come again, friendly ghost,
stroke my hair, whisper in my ear,
sing me a song.

Pa had red hair and an exuberant mustache, whose ends he waxed longingly and carefully. His skin was so fair, he had to wear a hat outdoors, and his blue eyes held a hidden inner smile. Pa loved music, good food, good wine, and he loved to play cards.

He played poker with his friends, rummy and casino with me, and he also loved the Yiddish Theater. I remember seeing Polly Picon and other great Yiddish artists when the Theater played Chicago, and I copied some of those elaborate gestures when I recited poetry.

Pa used to warm my long underwear on the dining room radiator in the cold Chicago winters, handing it to me as I came out of the bathroom, and I hugged those drawers to my chest as I walked down the hall to my bedroom. I still remember the feel of those warm cotton leggings on my thighs.

Although Pa and Ma were observant Jews, and Pa prayed every morning facing east with a prayer shawl over his head, he would take me out on Sunday mornings for forbidden treats like bacon, lettuce, and tomato sandwiches, and sometimes even ham and eggs. It was always understood that I wouldn't tell Ma about these transgressions.

Pa loved a good story, and he was a great storyteller. I know that

Sara, Al, Fay, and I inherited our love of drama and our storytelling ability from Pa. I didn't inherit his singing voice, but that ability skipped a generation and manifested itself in my son, who has perfect pitch. When Ricky was two or three, I used to sing Brahms's "Lullaby" to him, and one night he put his hands over his ears and said, "Please don't sing, Mommy; tell me a story instead." So I did, and never tried to sing anything again.

Pa never had an inflated sense of himself, which made it so hard for him to deal with my brother Al, whose sense of self-importance was overpowering. For Pa, the cup was always half-full, and he could always find something positive to say about people or even the weather. If we planned a picnic, and it rained, Pa would say, "Well, at least it's not snowing!" When it came to betrayal, like when his partner in the roof repair business ran off with their roof repairing truck and all the tools, Pa found a way to excuse Irving. Pa said that the truck was old and that he always hated the business anyway. He acted as if Irving had done him a favor. Perhaps he was secretly relieved.

Pa made his own wine in the basement of the duplex we lived in, and the process demanded several trips down the back stairs to sample the contents of the various barrels: sweet red wine for the women and children, a clear, dry red and a dry white for the men. This wine graced our Friday night dinner table and all the Jewish holiday festivals. On holidays like Passover, my father would get happily drunk, and proceed to sing some boisterous songs. Some of them were a bit off-color and satirical, and some of them were "skat" songs which I heard Danny Kaye sing, many years later. Cab Calloway sang "skat" also—it requires snorting and sniffing and rapid-fire singing, without losing a beat.

Pa knew that Ma was the driving, disciplinary force in our household, but he always made a brave show of pretending to be boss. When conversation at the dinner table would get out of hand, with some of us shouting at the tops of our voices, Pa would bang the table and call out, his voice rising above the din, "One at a time, please! Let's have some order here!"

When I was twenty-one and had left Chicago for the University of California at Berkeley, I wrote him to tell him that I had decided to marry Jim Pack, a non-Jew. Pa was so hurt that he wrote me to say he considered me dead to him, and that I shouldn't come to his funeral. That was difficult to swallow, especially remembering those wonderful Sunday morning outings, but tradition dies hard. When my mother died, I was thirty-four, and I went back to Chicago for her funeral. I talked to Pa, and he had apparently forgotten that he had disowned me, because he was genuinely upset that I had divorced Jim after twelve years of marriage. Pa was eighty-two and frail. He and Ma had been married for more than fifty years, and I saw clearly that his love for Ma was deep, even though they had fought vigorously and often during their married life. He told me not to come back for his funeral, because he expected to be dead within two months. And he was.

Ma

MA: A FRUSTRATED WOMAN

I learned early on that Ma was a passionate woman, and it must have been hard for her to say "no" to my father. My sister Sara was nineteen when I was born, Jeanne was fifteen, Al was twelve, and Fay was nine. My mother was forty and my father was fifty. My mother was surprised and appalled when she found herself pregnant again.

Ruth Esther Hoffman, my mother, was born in Braila, a small enclosed Jewish settlement on the outskirts of Bucharest in 1879. Ruth Esther was the fourth daughter of an impoverished widow, and her village was hardscrabble poor. After her marriage to my father in 1898, they moved to Marseilles in August, 1899, with their first daughter, Sara. Five months later, in January, 1900, they made it onto a freighter bound for Montreal. They traveled in steerage, and Mayer, my father, was seasick most of the time, but Ruth man-

16

aged to find a place for them to sleep near the steps leading to the deck, so that every time the hatch was opened, there was a breath of fresh air for them. Sara was ten months old, and quickly captivated one of the stewards, who slipped them leftovers from the crew's mess.

In America, Mayer and Ruth settled in Chicago, where I was born. My mother always said she wanted some kind of independence, a small shop of her own, a dressmaking or alteration shop, but there was never enough money to put a down payment on a location. I often saw her pick up a small engraved ceramic pitcher she and my father had bought on their honeymoon in Vienna in 1898, look at it for a moment, heave a deep sigh, and then put it down. Perhaps she was wondering how she had ended up with five children, struggling to make ends meet, resentful that the charming man she married was not as good a provider as she had thought.

When I was in grammar school, in 1926, I enrolled in a Home Economics class, and I was supposed to make an article of clothing as a final project. My mother had sewn all my sisters' clothes and many of mine, when I outgrew the hand-me-downs. Here was my chance to make something by myself. I chose the simplest thing I could think of, a slip. One day, as I labored on the foot-pedaled Singer sewing machine in our flat, my mother looked over my shoulder, and suddenly put her hand on the wheel, stopping the machine.

"Here," she said, "give me that." She pushed me off the chair. "You're making a mess of it. You're hopeless. I'll finish it." She ripped out my stitches and started over.

"But Ma," I remember wailing. "It's *my* project! I'm supposed to do it by myself!"

"Never mind. This way you'll get a good grade." She continued sewing for a few minutes, whipped the now beautifully stitched garment off the sewing machine, and handed it to me triumphantly.

I didn't realize how long I carried that sense of humiliation until

17

I stood in my own workroom in San Francisco in 1950 and decided I could, and would, make a suit for myself. I called a friend, and we went downtown to buy a pattern and fabric. My friend Eileen wanted to know if I really wanted to make a suit as my first sewing project, and suggested that I start out with something easier. I needed a suit, and I insisted that it was a suit or nothing.

We bought tightly woven tweed and a simple Vogue pattern and came back to the shop to work. Poor Eileen! I fought her every step of the way. "Why do I have to baste it? Why can't I just pin the two pieces together and pull out the pins as I go? Why does it have to have five-eighth inch seams? It seems like such a waste of material!" *I didn't realize I was fighting the ghost of my mother during the entire endeavor.* However, I managed to finish the skirt, complete with zipper and button closing, as well as the jacket, struggling with the shoulders and the set-in sleeves. Eileen did the hand-bound buttonholes, and I found some bone buttons that I liked. *Completing the suit was a triumph, and my mother's ghost retreated.*

I never really understood the demons that drove my mother. I came closer to those demons in 1942, the year my first child died, ten days after being born. I stopped over in Chicago to see her on my way to Washington, D.C., where my husband, a first lieutenant in the Navy, was stationed. I had been living with friends in Los Angeles, and I left for Washington shortly after being discharged from the hospital.

When I arrived at my parents' apartment, my mother did not greet me with enthusiasm. Sitting at the kitchen table, we tried to talk. "So how is Pa?" I asked. I knew he had had a stroke, and I wondered how she was coping.

"All right." She paused. Then, without preamble, she looked at me over her tea and said, "Be glad the baby died."

I froze, my own cup halfway to my mouth.

"Children are a nuisance," she continued, in a flat, even tone. "No matter what you do, they always disappoint you."

What is she saying? "Didn't you want me?" I could hardly get

18

the words out.

"I never wanted you. Tried to get rid of you." Her voice didn't change. "But nothing worked. I threw myself down the stairs. Nothing happened. Not even a broken bone. I drank vinegar. Nothing. You came anyway."

I'm cold. I'm not really here. I am above this table. Who is that down there? That's my mother, in her print housedress, sitting at the oilcloth-covered table; that's me, my cup halfway to my mouth; there's my father, snoring in his rocking chair in the small living room, the newspaper dangling from his limp hand.

I put down my cup. *No way to answer her. I have to get out of here.* Standing up, I said, "I'd better go now, Ma," leaned over and pecked her soft, wrinkled cheek. Her lips were a thin tight line, her small black eyes fixed on my face, challenging me. *I don't know what is in your head, Ma. I wish I did.* "Bye."

Staggering down the steps to the street, I stood for a minute, taking deep breaths. *What was her message? Was it her kind of "tough love"? Remember the acts of love, Rhoda. Remember the way she made apple strudel, stretching the dough over the cloth-covered table, spreading apples and cinnamon only, no nuts, because she knew I was allergic to nuts. Remember the holiday strudel, made with candied fruit, and a special bit for me with no nuts. Was that not love?*

I took a taxi back to the station, and stumbled onto the train. Still feeling numb, I crept into a corner of the compartment and fell asleep. I was twenty-five years old. I was seventy when my sister Jeanne told me that Ma really didn't want any of her children except for Sara and probably Al. Ma had told her that men were no good, they only wanted sex and that their love was a trap. I asked Jeanne, "Do you think Ma was a passionate woman and that therefore it was hard for her to resist Pa?" Jeanne said, "Maybe." However, my asking the question clarified my understanding, and in the course of that conversation, I finally heard my mother weeping. I wrote the following poem:

19

FOR MA

I hear you weeping
bitter, bitter tears
that the searing, leaping
pleasure of love
should bring such lasting pain.
I hear you weeping
bitter, bitter tears
that plans and dreams
should disappear
without a trace.

I hear you weeping
tears of anger
and frustration
that love and passion
bring forth unwanted pregnancies.

In the autumn of my life,
I hear you weeping, and
understand, finally,
why you wished me dead.

Sara

SARA

Sara, nineteen years my senior, was the first of my three sisters to die. I didn't know her very well, but her influence on me was the strongest of the three. Sara was nineteen when I was born, Jeanne was fourteen, and Fay was almost ten. I was always the kid sister, on the outside, never part of their lives. Even so, they had a potent influence on the way I grew up. Sara gave me a sense of the connection between the beauty of the body in movement and in stillness. She taught me to be aware of my body and to be proud of how I moved. Since I was the tallest in the family, I was afraid of being gawky.

In 1931, we moved to Van Buren Street, a different part of the west side of Chicago. It was not a Jewish neighborhood, but my family was fiercely determined to become integrated Americans. At thirteen, I wanted to go to ballet school with our next door neighbor, and Sara heard me pleading with my mother for lessons. She noted Ma's disapproving expression, and she intervened with Ma, saying that she would pay for my lessons for three years. The seed she planted lasted

21

all my life. Dance is still part of me. Sara encouraged me to walk with grace, my head upright. "Think of a string from your head to the sky, reaching down your back to your feet."

When I was fifteen, in 1933, Sara's first marriage hardly registered, especially since she and Harry left immediately for California. Unfortunately, Harry died of pancreatic cancer within two years, and Sara returned to Chicago in 1935, a widow, accompanying her husband's coffin in the baggage car. I was just graduating from high school, but I remember Sara, slim and beautiful, holding her grief to herself.

Coming home, she announced that she was applying for a secretarial job with the Army in Puerto Rico, and immediately started to study Spanish, confident that she would get the job. What bravery and resilience! My mother was horrified, but Sara was practical. There were very few jobs in Chicago in the depression years of the thirties, and the U.S. government was one of the rare places to get a job. Sara left for Puerto Rico in 1936, but not before making sure that I would attain my dream of attending a four-year university.

The odd thing is that, although we corresponded intermittently, I didn't see Sara again until 1979, forty-five years later. When I left Northwestern in 1939, at the end of my junior year, for the University of California in Berkeley, I severed ties with my family. After graduating in 1940, I married Jim Pack, a non-Jew, and Sara was shocked. Perhaps she felt betrayed; I don't know. Yet without my being aware of it, there was an invisible thread that connected me to her. Our lives were very different; she lived in Knoxville, Tennessee, and I lived in Berkeley, California. We lived in two very different worlds.

By 1979, at the age of eighty, Sara was a widow for a second time. She had met and married Lou Sackron, a physicist and an engineer, while she was in Puerto Rico. They moved to Knoxville, where Lou worked for the Atomic Energy Project. They had no children, but Sara became a mentor for teenagers through her community activities. Sara and Lou started a hobby shop, specializing in model trains, and Sara loved managing that shop, pouring out her nurturing nature on the Knoxville teenagers who hung out at the shop. She also drove a library mobile van, which became a reading classroom on wheels. Between her activities at the local synagogue, the library mobile van, and the Hobby Shop, Sara was a vital force in the community. She was well known, loved and respected.

All my siblings, including my brother Al, moved to the Bay Area after I did, except for Sara. She was the only one who continued to live away from the rest of the family.

I decided to give a party for Sara on the occasion of her eightieth birthday in the garden of my house in Berkeley. I knew she was going to be in Chicago that summer for a convention of hobby shop owners, and I suggested that she come to the Bay Area before she went back to Knoxville.

Jeanne and Fay had both moved to Palo Alto in 1972, and I thought it would be a rare occasion for all four of us to be together, a first since my teens. I was now sixty-one and had just finished my master's degree at San Francisco State University. I was celebrating a return to academia after having been out of the classroom for forty years.

I had seen a show by Judy Chicago at the San Francisco Museum of Art, called "The Dinner Party." It was a show of ceramic plates set on a formal table covered with a lace tablecloth, candles in silver candlesticks, silver place settings, wineglasses, and linen napkins. The large colorful plates were all variations of vulvas. It was a stunning and disturbing show. Judy Chicago had posted a statement urging all women who saw the show to give dinner parties (for twelve) and to send her a telegram or letter telling about the party.

We had our dinner party in my garden, and, using ordinary plates, I invited twelve women, including my sisters, Sara, Jeanne, and Fay, my niece Alice and a few friends. I asked my guests to bring a significant totem and to be prepared to tell us all about a turning point in their lives. We taped the conversation, and sent the tape with a letter to Judy Chicago. I never heard from her, and don't know if she ever used the tape or letter in other shows. However, Sara was thrilled with the party, and I had achieved my purpose. We had come together as adults, and I finally felt as if I belonged — I was no longer "just the kid sister."

Sara went back to Knoxville, and I went to Korea in 1981 for two years, on a Fulbright Fellowship, specifically to create a teacher-training program for Korean teachers of English. Fay wrote, telling me that Sara was ill, after an operation for colon cancer, and I went to Knoxville from Korea in 1983 to take care of her. I worked with her and her physical therapist to help her recover. We took short walks, and following the therapist's suggestion, I encouraged her to take longer steps, to walk with more confidence, to recover a sense of bodily strength. It

Sara

was almost as if our roles were reversed.

I stayed with her until January, 1984, and I tried to persuade her to come back to Berkeley with me and settle in Palo Alto where she could be near Jeanne and Fay, but she didn't want to leave her friends and her close connections with the Knoxville community.

I took off again in 1985 to go to China, on another teacher-training program, and returned in the spring of 1986. That was when I heard that Sara

was back in the hospital, this time terminally ill. I went to Knoxville to be with her as she died. On the plane, I allowed myself to fall into a reverie, remembering Sara at different times in my life. I remembered especially one of her comments about distributors at the convention she attended in Chicago in 1979. "Oh!" She had said, disdainfully. "Those salesmen! They thought I was a pushover. But I knew what would sell in our community and what wouldn't. They were so... so...." she hunted for the word, "arrogant, I guess would be a good word for those... those gangsters!" She grimaced in distaste. I could just see her, five-foot-two, firmly defiant, saying "no thank you" in a "don't mess with me" voice. That was an inner force in Sara that I recognized.

I knew I would find a different Sara this time. I went directly to the hospital from the plane and Sara, in her hospital bed, greeted me enthusiastically.

"Rhoda! I'm so glad to see you!" She stretched out her arms, her face lighting up.

"Hello, Sara. Yes, I'm here, and I'm going to stay a while." I sat down on the chair in the room and started to take off my boots.

"Oh, don't take off your boots. We're going to California."

I laughed. "Well, not tonight, Sara. It's raining outside, and I'm kind of tired. I just got off the plane."

"Oh, yes, well... tomorrow then." She lay back, sighed, and closed her eyes. Then, stirring, she sat bolt upright. "You won't go back without me, will you?"

"Of course not. Just relax." I embraced and kissed her, gently putting her back down, drawing the covers over her. "Time to sleep now. We'll talk tomorrow."

I went out into the hall to talk to the doctor. I said, "We've been trying to get her to move to California since the last time I was here. What is this talk about going to California now?"

The doctor, direct, answered, "The cancer has metastasized. We don't know how long it will be. She's heavily medicated, and she dreams."

"I think you're telling me that she's dying, am I right?" The doctor shifted from foot to foot, and then finally looked directly at me. He said, "She's as comfortable as we can make her, but she's very ill." He wouldn't allow me to put words into his mouth.

"All right," I said. "I'd like some sort of cot or sleeping chair set up in her room, so that I can be here as much as possible. I'll go to her house and pick up a tape recorder and some tapes, and then I'll come back. She liked to listen to James Galway's flute playing. Music might help her." Her doctor nodded and I left.

When I walked into Sara's house in East Tennessee, I came full circle, re-entering the scenes of my childhood. Paintings on the wall that I always thought belonged to me, on the walls of our Chicago flat during all my growing-up years, obviously belonged to Sara. Here they were! A familiar Whistler landscape, prints of European folk dancers, gay figures in colorful costumes dancing through the feverish dreams of my childhood illnesses. Instead of the red brick two-story houses of my childhood, I looked out on a rainy scene of falling leaves, drippy trees weeping autumn tears, an East Tennessee November. A country road wound down from her clapboard cottage to a main road leading to the town mall.

I scanned the room, looking at my sister's walls, crowded with her own paintings. I didn't know, until then, that she was such a good artist. Her paintings described a rich, active life. Portraits she painted of friends and models peered at me, her watercolors and oils hung helter-skelter on the pale blue walls. I caught a glimpse of myself in the mirror over the fireplace mantel at my sixty-eight-year-old body and face. Suddenly, I saw myself in Sara. Both Sara and I were the only siblings with auburn hair, having inherited reddish, curly hair from our father. Now her hair and mine were about the same color, gray flecked with black, and still curly. We both had deep brown, almost black eyes, and we both threw ourselves into whatever task engaged us at the moment.

Sara died two days later, and I went back to her house to air it out. I called my niece, Alice, who agreed to come to Knoxville and help with the funeral arrangements. Walking into the woods, after talking to Alice, I found Sara's well-traveled path winding through birch and thin elms, nothing like a California rugged forest. An old log beckoned me. Sitting on the log, I lifted my head, absorbing the dripping rain, the wet leaves falling on my face, and welcomed the part of me that was forever Sara.

Jeanne

JEANNE

Jeanne was fourteen when I was born. I knew her as the mysterious one, the most beautiful and the most distant. She was slim, and her high cheekbones gave her a different look from others in the family. Her soft brown eyes had a melancholy look, but when she smiled, her whole face lit up. She was about five-feet-three, but she carried herself as if she were taller. Jeanne teased Sara, five years her senior, and would find ways to make fun of her. She would report that Sara talked in her sleep, and that she was privy to Sara's secrets, but Jeanne never said what they were. She would just look mysterious, smiling in a self-satisfied way.

Jeanne was a writer, and all of us, Sara, Fay, Al, and I knew that she was working on the Great American Novel, which we called GAN. Jeanne also instituted what we called the Friday Night Drop-In, which Jeanne intended to be an evening of "cultured, informed conversation." Jeanne liked to invite friends whom she considered "intellectual," and tried to steer the conversation into discussions of music, plays, movies, art exhibits.

However, most of the time those evenings turned out to consist of parlor games, including Charades, and other guessing games. I remember those evenings, when I was about ten or eleven, because I would creep out of bed and eavesdrop from behind a door leading to the living room. Whenever I was discovered, I would pretend to be walking in my sleep, my arms outstretched, my eyes half closed.

Jeanne had changed her name from Tillie (a name she hated) to Jeanne, when she was in her teens. My mother took Jeanne's name change with a shrug. Changing names was not a surprise to her. Jeanne, like Sara, didn't finish high school; they had to quit and work at menial secretarial jobs to help support the family. Over time, both Jeanne and Sara became executive secretaries with important jobs, but Jeanne always felt tainted somehow by not having finished high school. She was an avid reader and in addition to the novel she was working on, she wrote poetry, which was published in the *Chicago Tribune*. For Jeanne, the cup was always half-empty; for Sara, it was always half-full.

Jeanne married Arthur Quadow in 1932 and they went to Palestine in 1933 to find a better life than was available to them in Depression-shrouded Chicago. Arthur had graduated as a lawyer, but could find no work anywhere. Arthur was also an idealist, and he had an idea about going to Palestine to grow tomatoes, make tomato juice and sell it to the Jews and Arabs. He was so convinced that his idea would work that he and Jeanne stopped in Czechoslovakia and bought tomato-crushing machinery on their way to Palestine. They joined a kibbutz and planted their tomatoes with seeds they'd brought from the United States. Unfortunately, the soil of Palestine did not welcome the American seeds, and the tomatoes that grew were too full of pulp to make into juice.

The years between 1933 and 1936 were relatively quiet in Palestine, during the period when Britain governed Palestine under a mandate granted by the League of Nations in 1920. The mandate language included the provision that Britain "shall facilitate Jewish immigration under suitable conditions and shall encourage, in co-operation with the (Jewish Agency), close settlement by Jews on the land, including State lands and waste lands not required for public purposes." Arabs rioted in 1929, demonstrating against Jewish immigration, and the Hope-Simpson Commission was set up to calm the situation. There was uneasy peace in Palestine between 1933 and 1936.

Jeanne hated life on the kibbutz, and they soon relocated to Haifa, where Jeanne got a job working for a British company, and Arthur languished. Jeanne was not really satisfied with life in Haifa either; life was not safe for Jews. They kept a loaded gun in their refrigerator, where they felt no one would be inclined to look for a weapon. The British had allowed uncontrolled Arab immigration from Egypt, Transjordan, Syria, and North Africa, but put restrictions on Jewish immigration. A serious Arab revolt erupted in April, 1936, and Jeanne and Arthur returned to Chicago.

I regarded their return to Chicago as truly fortuitous. Jeanne and Arthur moved into my bedroom, and I had a perfect excuse to move to the Northwestern campus, instead of commuting from home.

While they lived in Chicago, Arthur went back to the University of Chicago, where he acquired another degree in Economics and Political Science. He got a job as an administrator in the State Department, and he and Jeanne moved to Washington, D.C. Arthur worked on the Marshall Plan after World War II ended, and Jeanne became an executive secretary in the Personnel Department of the Navy.

Between 1936 and 1943, I didn't see much of Jeanne and Arthur. We traveled totally different paths. I connected again with Jeanne in 1943, when Jim and I came to Washington. My first husband, Jim Pack, was drafted into the Navy, in 1942, and later was assigned to Officers Training School. We were both post-graduate academics at UC Berkeley in 1941 when the United States entered World War II, and our plans for a peaceful married life disappeared. By 1943, Jim was transferred to Washington, D.C., and I left my teaching job in Oakland to join him there. I had always wanted to be a journalist, and decided to look for a job in the Office of War Information. Neither Jim nor I expected him to be sent to sea. He was very near-sighted and wore heavy, strong glasses.

Unfortunately, two weeks after I arrived in Washington, Jim was assigned to a destroyer in the Pacific, and I, alone in a strange city, tried to create a relationship with Jeanne, but she still considered me the "kid sister," somewhere outside her adult friendships.

Searching for a place to stay, I left my name at numerous rental agencies, and finally found one on DuPont Circle. However, it wasn't going to be available for about a week, so I brought up the dilemma one evening at dinner.

Jeanne, Sara, and Fay

Jeanne gave me a cold look, and remarked, "You know the saying: 'Guests and fish begin to smell after five days,' but I guess you could sleep on the couch, just for a week." It wasn't the gracious invitation I was looking for, but I had little choice. Actually, at the end of the week, she told me that I could stay another week if I needed to. Happily, I was able to say "No, thank you," and move to my own apartment. After that, I saw Jeanne and Arthur infrequently during the two years I lived and worked in Washington. They didn't invite me to any of their parties, and after that initial rebuff, I didn't try to get closer to them.

Jim came back to Washington from the Pacific as a patient on a hospital ship in 1945. By that time, Jeanne and Arthur's lives had also shifted. When Eisenhower became president, there was a general shift of personnel—Democrats were out, and Republicans were in. Arthur was again without a job.

A mutual friend in Philadelphia had created a new business dealing in plastics, and he invited Jeanne and Arthur to join his company. They did, and I think Jeanne was happier in Philadelphia than in any other place they had lived. Philadelphia provided her with the cultural stimulation she had always wanted. She studied art at the Phillips Gallery and took classes in painting. She made sure that they subscribed to the Philadelphia Symphony Orchestra, to the ballet, and to the theater. They became part of a select group of intellectuals and artists, and she felt she was living and breathing the kind of intellectual life she had always wanted.

That satisfying life came to an end when Arthur became ill with cancer. He fell into a coma that lasted several months, and finally Jeanne was asked to authorize the removal of life-sustaining equipment. That decision haunted her, and she became very depressed. Both my brother Al and sister Fay rescued her from being institutionalized, and Fay agreed to become responsible for her. When Fay and her husband, Henry Bauling, moved to Palo Alto in 1972, Jeanne came with them.

Fay and Henry and Jeanne and Arthur had taken trips to Europe together almost every summer for at least ten years, and there was a close bond between them. Jeanne moved into an apartment next door to Fay and Henry, and she slowly regained her equilibrium.

In 1983, my third marriage, to Bob Holdeman, was starting to fray, and I invited Jeanne to travel to Europe with me. I was teaching at the Berkeley Adult School at the time, and I had created a plan for myself. I would teach year-round for two years, and then I would clean out my savings account and travel for the length of the summer term. I invited Jeanne to travel to Europe with me. I told her that we would not be traveling first class, but that we would be visiting students, and possibly staying with some of them. I was hoping to lay down some other memories for Jeanne.

We spent a couple of days in Belgium with students, in between staying in hotels, and then we had a week in Paris during August, when most Parisians flee the city. My student had arranged for us to get the key to her apartment from the concierge, since she and her husband would be in the country. We had been traveling for about four weeks at that time, in close quarters, and the prospect of being in an apartment for a week was enticing.

Walking into the flat, we noticed a hall leading from the living room, and that there were bedrooms opening off the hall, similar to our flat in Chicago. Without a word to each other, we each fled into a different room, closing the doors without a loud snap. When we emerged several hours later, we were ready for conversation again. That apartment was a real refuge. We were able to shop at the local market for a leisurely breakfast, take lunch and dinner wherever we chose.

We took the underground to the museums and art galleries we wanted to visit, and we roamed around Paris to our hearts' content. Jeanne wanted to explore areas of the city she hadn't seen with Arthur and Fay and Henry, and I was all too happy to oblige. We went to concerts at small churches, to the Opera Comique, and to the Folies Bergere, where Jeanne declared herself shocked at the nudity.

We traveled together for six weeks, and even though there was a gap of fourteen years between us, we managed to become closer. She had a good sense of humor, and during our trip, she finally treated me as her equal and not as a kid sister. We had fun. Apparently, each of us, in our own separate ways had decided that Washington, D.C. was another life. We had a chance to start a new relationship, and we took it. We became friends.

After returning from Europe, Jeanne moved from her apartment next to Fay to a condominium in Palo Alto, and I used to visit her at least once a month. She had a one-bedroom apartment, and I slept on a couch in her living room. We played Scrabble and talked. Jeanne liked to have a cocktail before dinner, and sometimes we would get quite drunk. At those times, I would try to get her to open up about some of the things that haunted her, but at the last minute, she would pull herself up and stop talking, saying instead, "There are some things I will never talk about. The psychiatrists kept trying to get me to talk more, but there are closed doors that I will never open."

Jeanne died in a nursing home in 1992, at ninety-four, silent to the end.

Alexander

ALEXANDER MARTIN CURTIS, My Brother

I never understood my brother. We all knew him as Al, and I always wondered where he got his name. It certainly didn't seem like a Jewish name to me. My sister Jeanne, I knew, had chosen her name when she was a teenager, changing it from Tillie, a name she hated. Where did Alexander Martin come from? Did he choose the name himself? I never found out.

Al was twelve when I was born, and he was terribly disappointed that I was not a boy. He had bought a baseball glove for me before my mother went to the hospital; he was so sure that he wouldn't be stuck with another sister. He already had two older sisters, Sara and Jeanne, and a younger sister, Fay.

Al always seemed to have a chip on his shoulder. He felt aggrieved, because he never had a bedroom to himself. In a three-bedroom flat, one bedroom would belong to Ma and Pa, one to Sara and Jeanne, and one to Fay and me. Al would end up sleeping on a cot in the dining room or on the covered porch off the kitchen.

I remember ironing his underwear and handkerchiefs, and wondering why he got such special attention. My mother always treated him as if he was special, and he accepted all the extra favors as his due. My father treated him as an enemy. Pa, a member of the International Workers of the World (the Wobblies), was an ardent Socialist and a strong supporter of all unions. Al became a conservative Republican, and to my father, he was incomprehensible. He couldn't understand how a son of his would have political and social opinions so different from his own. I remember stormy arguments when my father would leave the room, fuming, because Al always managed to get the best of him.

Al was a small, thin, wiry man, bandy-legged, with piercing black eyes. He tried very hard to boss me around. He taunted me about not being as smart as he was, and he kept telling me that he and Fay had graduated from high school when they were sixteen, saying that I would never be able to catch up to them. He denigrated my interest in the Drama Club, and had no interest in any plays or poetry I wrote. He said Jeanne was the only true writer and intellectual in the family.

Al enjoyed control, and I resisted being controlled, so there was always a silent war between us. He had promised that I would be able to go to a four-year university, and that he had put money aside for that purpose. When I was graduating from high school, in 1935, and was ready to apply for a scholarship to the University of Chicago, Al informed me that he had gambled the set-aside money on the stock market and lost.

I went to work after graduating, but in 1936, Sara and Fay helped me realize my dream. They knew how strongly I wanted to go to university, so they proposed to Al that each one of them put up one thousand dollars to pay for my first semester, with the understanding that I would get a scholarship and a part-time job and go the rest of the way by myself. Al reluctantly complied, and with that money, I did go to Northwestern. Neither Fay nor Sara approached Jeanne, who was then living in Palestine with her husband, Arthur. Jeanne and Arthur had gone to Palestine in 1933, at the height of the Depression. Fay and Sara knew Jeanne and Arthur would not be able to afford any kind of contribution. However, Al was a successful practicing lawyer by that time, and that was the reason they approached him.

With the three thousand dollars from Sara, Fay, and Al, I was able to pay the tuition for one semester, and also take advantage of the WPA (Works Progress Administration) support for students in 1936. I earned twenty-five cents an hour as an assistant to a political science professor, and I worked summers for Mandel Brothers, a department store in Chicago. During one semester I worked as a maid for my room and board, and managed to get full scholarships for the following years.

I transferred to the University of California in 1939, and went on to establish a life for myself outside the confines of the Chicago area. It was odd, the way my siblings all followed me to the Bay Area. Fay's daughter, Alice, came first, in 1964, followed by Fay and Henry, then Jeanne, then Al. Al married an Austrian woman, Edith, and they had two daughters. They settled in Tiburon, in Marin County, California.

I remember a party my brother gave for my sister Sara in 1980, at his home in Tiburon. We were sitting on the patio, our shoes off, comparing the similarities in our feet when Al reached over and pushed my foot out of the group. "These feet don't belong," he said. "Look at the hammer toes." I was so furious I tried to drown him with a garden hose. I felt as if I were a teen-ager again, fighting with a brother, twelve years my senior, who considered himself a father figure.

At one point, during the same party, Al brought up the money he had advanced in 1936. He said he thought it was a loan, and the three of us, Sara, Fay, and I, looked at him with such withering contempt that he closed his mouth, and changed the subject abruptly.

Socially, my brother was a great success. He was a good storyteller; he had a good sense of humor, and he would have made a good stand-up comedian. He made friends easily, and entertained lavishly. Al loved a good argument, and he invited confrontation. The high point of his

35

life was when he argued a civil case before the U.S. Supreme Court. t didn't matter that he and his firm lost the case. It was the argument that he enjoyed.

Because of Al's constant challenges, I too became adept at confrontation and at logical argumentation. Al and I met again, ten years later, at his daughter's home in Mill Valley in 1990. Moments after we said hello, we were engaged in a verbal fencing match. It was as if sixty years fell away, and we resumed the kind of sparring that was our pattern. My reaction was different this time. I remember catching myself on the edge of a really cutting remark, and I was able to say, "Okay, you win," changing the subject. After all, I was in my seventies, and my brother was in his late eighties! When Al died, at the age of ninety-one, I spoke at his funeral, speaking mainly about his wit, his easy sociability, and the dramatic way he told a good story.

I learned many things from my brother Al. I learned how to tell a good story, how to interrupt effectively, how to be careful about accepting a basic premise, and I also learned never to make a promise I couldn't keep.

Fay

FAY

How many people do we know who have the opportunity to relive one of the best parts of their lives? My sister, Fay, at one hundred and a half, did just that. She moved from Palo Alto to Israel at that age, and, ensconced in her grandson's house, became a live-in teacher to her five great-grandchildren.

Whenever Fay talked about the best part of her life, her face lit up and she would talk about the time she was a young mother, in her thirties, spending the summer months at the Sand Dunes of Indiana, sixty miles from Chicago. Our family rented a small cottage on the beach, and Fay, a kindergarten teacher, created a program that she called "The Play Club."

Fay gathered all the children on the beach and assembled them in front of our cottage. With the children (and her two small daughters) around her, she told them fairy tales. Then she assigned roles and created an environment in which the children felt free to express

37

themselves creatively. I was a teenager at the time, and I used to watch her, enthralled at the way she inspired the children to dance, sing, make costumes, and create magical scenes.

During the brief time Fay lived in Israel, she relived that wonderful part of her life. David, her grandson, called to tell me that Fay gathered his children, ranging in age from twelve to two months, around her, told them stories, and encouraged them to act, sing, and dance.

She was a rejuvenated person, using her walker more than the wheelchair and was animated, having come out of the shell into which she had retreated in Palo Alto. She felt needed, loved, and revered. What a wonderful way to end one's life!

David had invited Fay to move to Israel to live with him and his family shortly before her hundredth birthday on June 14, 2009. She was a little uncertain about whether or not she should go. Fay told me about David's invitation, asking me if I thought it was a silly idea. She said, "If I go to Israel in October, I will already be one hundred. Do you think it's a dumb idea?"

I said, "No! I think it's great! Are they going to move to a bigger house, to accommodate your wheelchair? And will the house be air conditioned?"

"Oh, I guess so. But I won't be coming back, will I?"

"No, does that bother you?"

"Well, no, but I've already paid for my cemetery plot next to Henry."

"Ah," I said. "You could always have your body shipped back to California so that you could be buried next to Henry."

"What for?" she said. "Henry isn't there. It's just dust. I might as well be buried in Israel. Easier for everybody."

"You're right, Fay," I said, reassuringly. "I think that's the best idea." I reached over and hugged her. My dear pragmatic sister. We hung on to each other for a long time. We shared a long process of saying goodbye. On October 25, she moved to Israel to live with David, his wife Naomi, and their five children. The move was not occasioned by a sense of desperation or real disaffection with her life in Palo Alto; she was simply excited by the prospect of change, and also about the possibility of being useful. She looked forward to being helpful in the home-schooling her great-grandchildren are receiving from David and Naomi. I found her attitude remarkable, and felt uplifted by the thought that we shared similar genes.

Her Day of Discard, in her apartment at Palo Alto Commons, was illuminating. She sat in her wheelchair near Alice, her daughter, who was sitting at Fay's desk, going through piles of paper and other things. I was sitting on a couch near her, and watched Fay's offhand discard of various objects. Alice held up one of Fay's stone sculptures: "Do you want to take this with you?"

"No."

"Do you want it, Rhoda?"

If my answer was "yes," it went into one pile; if it was "no," it went into another pile, destined for someone else in the family, Goodwill, or the Salvation Army.

Sometimes Fay's answer was a shrug. And then Alice demanded, "Yes or no?"

Shrug.

"Yes or no? Decide! Yes or no?"

Shrug.

They eyed each other. Alice wisely put the item aside. We went through books, paintings, magazines, piles of paper, and Fay seemed most happy when the wastebasket was full. I leaned over and spoke into her good ear. "This is fun, isn't it? Throwing things away? It's something you always liked to do, isn't it?" She nodded, smiling, and made a grand, sweeping gesture. She beamed at me.

I always thought Fay had inherited the best parts of both our parents—she had Pa's sense of humor, enjoyment of love and music, and she had Ma's sense of practicality. She was a pragmatist. I loved the way her mind functioned; I hear her voice in my mind whenever I am unsure about a course of action: "Will it work?"

When Fay and her accountant husband, Henry, moved to Palo Alto in 1972, to be near their daughter Alice, we had to make a change in how we related to each other. I answered the phone at home in Berkeley one morning, and encountered the bossy elder sister I had known during my childhood. When she began to lay out a program for my coming to Palo Alto, and in general giving me firm directions about many things, I interrupted her.

"Fay," I said. "I'm now fifty-four years old; I am an adult, and if you persist in treating me as the kid sister, we will not be able to have a decent relationship. If you want to know me as a friend, and not as your kid sister, it will work; otherwise not."

There was an extended pause on the line, an intake of breath, and then she said, "Okay, when will you be able to come down?"

Her response told me that she had heard what I said, remembered much about the contacts we had established during the years between 1939 and 1972, and accepted the boundaries I established.

Fay and Henry had stayed in contact with me during my life in California. They had visited me in Berkeley, and bonded with my son, Ricky. Both of them had been loving and supportive in a way that was nurturing and not condescending. I was surprised to hear the bossy sister reasserting herself, and I was reassured by her quick retraction of that attitude.

Fay was really the practical one in the family. She was the balanced one, the sensible one, a giving, caring person. She was a natural mother figure, yet she was also a practical older sister. I was a child when she was taking courses studying to be a kindergarten teacher, and she felt free to use me as a guinea pig for psychology course experiments. One of the experiments included strapping a blood pressure cuff on my arm, and then reading off a list of words. Changes in blood pressure indicated which word associations caused that change. I thought those experiments were fun; I got intimate attention, and I liked being part of her research.

Fay also took me to symphony concerts, where we sat in the gallery, listening to the Chicago Symphony Orchestra under the direction of Frederick Stock. The cost of a seat in the gallery was twenty-five cents. She took me to the Art Institute, to the Field Museum, to the Aquarium, and each visit was accompanied by pointed questions as to how I felt, what I learned, which exhibits made an impression on me. She was a good teacher. Fay tried to teach me to play the piano, but I never practiced enough to satisfy her, and we finally gave up. I did learn to read music, however, and later, in my fifties, took piano lessons again.

As my parents aged, they became frailer, and Fay became the care-giver. She visited them frequently in their small apartment in Chicago, and she made sure they were comfortable. Fay also took responsibility for everyone in the family.

After Jeanne's husband, Arthur, died, Fay was the one who brought Jeanne to Palo Alto from Philadelphia. She took care of Jeanne, and she also made it her business to look after our brother, Al, when he was hospitalized in Marin at the age of ninety-one.

In addition to feeling responsible for all the members of her family, Fay was an accomplished sculptor. Earlier in her life, she worked in clay, stone, wood, and marble, and her fig-

Fay at 100 years old

ures are alive and sensuous. She was a leader in the Head Start program in Chicago, and a docent at the Palo Alto Museum of Art, leading groups of children on tours of the museum, encouraging them to make art in special programs that she led. She was an avid reader, and we shared an affinity for the *New Yorker* magazine, as well as "novels with substance," as she put it.

During the years that Fay lived in Palo Alto, we remained strong friends. After Jeanne and then Henry died, Fay moved into the Palo Alto Commons, an assisted living complex, and I came to Palo Alto from Berkeley to visit her at least once a month. Most of the time I stayed overnight, sleeping on her living room couch, but over the years, I drove down in the morning and returned in the afternoon. Every time I visited, we played Scrabble, and she won.

Saying goodbye was not easy; I miss her deeply, but all the dynamics around this move were positive. Fay looked forward to the change in her life; she was excited by the challenge. She knew she would have round-the-clock caregivers in Israel, as she did in Palo Alto, and in addition, she would have the loving attention of her grandson and her great-grandchildren. She moved forward, at the age of one hundred, into a milieu suffused with a sense of security, love, and affection. In addition to all the reassurances, she herself had no fear.

I received a telephone call from my nephew-in-law at seven thirty in the morning on November 26. Rich was calling from Israel to tell me that Fay had died a few hours earlier. Later, when I spoke to Alice, the story she told me was as beautiful as Fay's final weeks.

Fay was having trouble breathing, in the wee hours of Thursday morning, and Alice and Rich drove her to the hospital. Fay didn't want to stay in the emergency room and insisted on going home. A doctor, who lives across the street, said that she should have medicine called Lasix and apple juice. After Fay was back in bed, Alice sent the caregiver to get the medicine, and she went to get apple juice. Chana, the two-month-old new addition to the Stiebel household, was in a crib next to Fay. Fay was looking at Chana and smiling when Alice left. When Alice returned with the juice, Fay was dead. Alice thinks that Fay waited until everyone was out of the room and then left. That was the kind of person she was. When she decided something was over, finished, that was that.

She died as she lived, calm, peaceful, at one with the universe.

The Curtis Family, June, 1918

FAMILY VOICES
a one-act play in verse with music

PLACE: Chicago
TIME: 1929 to 1936
CHARACTERS: Ma, Pa, Rhoda, Sara, Jeanne, Fay, Al

(scrim behind which stand shadowy figures)

RHODA

Someone made a pattern for me.
In fact, several someones
made a pattern for me. The problem was,
none of them fit. I tried adjusting them.
A tuck here, a nip there;
saying yes when I meant no;
still they weren't right.
I began making patterns of my own
adjusting them, shaping them; molding them to fit
a changing me.

Those attempts to shape me lingered as voices; conflicting, pushing, pulling. I listened and chose my own path.

SCENE ONE

*Stage Left is lit, revealing **Pa**, holding a poker hand (five cards), cigar in one hand, his handlebar mustache well trimmed, the ends pointed. He is looking intently at his cards, but lifts his head and speaks to stage right, dimly lit, with Ma stirring something on a stove; **Young Rhoda** foreground, not lit, on her stomach, reading a book.*

PA

Nu, why not? Why not?
Poker with the boys on Saturday night?
Beer and cigars on a green felt table…
Saxophone with Pa's theme ("Bei Mir Bist Du Schoen")
Light shifts to Ma, stage right

MA

How will we pay the rent? *She stops stirring the pot, looks up as if asking help, clutches her head.*
Every month I worry,
My head hurts.
I hate this worry.
Violin with Ma's theme; her action is suspended as light shifts back to Pa

PA *(looks across the stage)*

I work, work hard. Ach, Ruchelle, we don't
live to work, we work to live. Why not
dance with the widow Kaufman on the
table, five a.m.? New Year's Eve, after all.

44

(Dances a polka around the stage; Pa's theme played as a polka; light shifts)

MA *(looks across the stage)*

Act your age, Mayer.
Never enough money;
I'm tired of cooking, cooking, cooking,
English I must learn.
(Tossing the spoon aside, she looks intently at the book she is holding; violin)

PA

A businessman I became, a roofer with a
partner. So Irving ran off with the truck;
Not such a disaster. I'm a union man.
(Straightens his shoulders, puffs on his cigar defiantly.)

MA

My own shop I want.
Then I the boss could manage the money.
That I know how to do.

PA

Come, talk, talk, share with me,
Wine and cheese, fresh baked bread.

MA

Strength I have, but no power.
It gnaws at me, eats my heart.

PA

Life is to enjoy! To eat and drink!
To dance and sing! To love and love and love!

MA

Sewing dresses, darning socks,
Counting pennies, no time to dance.
(Lights dim on Pa and Ma, lights up on Young Rhoda, center front.
She sits up, and holding her knees, she looks first in Pa's direction, then at
Ma)

Pa, holding me on your knee, you whispered, "shana maidele,
dance, sing, have fun. Take a chance. Failure not such a disaster."
Ma, scolding me, you warned and warned,
"Work hard, you could fail.
People lie and cheat. Keep the day job."

(Pa and Ma step forward)
Your two voices in my head, always in my head; I tried, Pa;
I failed, tried again. Because of you, I leapt into the unknown.
Ma, you were right. I kept the day job; kept teaching.
That's how I managed to take chances, anyway.

(Music: trio with clarinet, saxophone, oboe; blending three voices)

END OF SCENE ONE

SCENE TWO: *(on a lake beach)* The Sisters

SARA

I hike the hills, mountains beckon,
music or no music, I dance,
Isadora Duncan, are you there?
(Clarinet)

JEANNE

(Looks up from the pad of paper in her hand, brushing hair out of her face)

> We dance, my brother and I,
> flying across the floor,
> other partners not the same.

SARA

(Stage left, she continues to dance in an exuberant fashion and speaks)
Let me teach you my secret. Reach out,
reach in. Talk and listen.
When I travel, strangers tell me stories,
teach me songs. Life is a pulsing wave.
I swim, float in a rushing stream.

JEANNE

(Stage right; tears pages from her notebook, crumpling them up as she speaks)
I smile, wanting to please,
I do as I am told. Duty calls; I write in secret,
waiting, reaching deeper into silence,
knowing more, telling less.

SARA

(Standing at an easel, stage left)
Now I paint, colors flowing from my
brush; familiar faces never lost,
dream landscapes come alive.

JEANNE

You will not know my thoughts,
the novel finished, torn pages
float in the lake.

SARA

(Clutching her throat, one hand on her heart)
Must I go? Too soon to die.

JEANNE

What's left for me? Does it matter? I am alone.

FAY

Ma, you named me bird, but gave me
no wings. Sisters, you taught me
courage, trust, hope.
Museum trips, concerts every week.
Flying low, my head cocked,
(She moves across the stage as if flying)

I looked, listened.
I married early. It was safe and happy.
We held each other lightly, whirling
through sixty plus years.
(She dances a waltz with an imaginary partner)

Now, at ninety-nine, solitary but not alone,
cushioned and cocooned,
my carved figures comfort me.
(Holds a sculpture of entwined figures in her hand, lovingly)

I am at peace. *(trio of three instruments: clarinet, saxophone, violin)*

RHODA

Oh, my sisters! How I hung around, hoping to join your lives!
Always on the outside, never belonging. I was the kid sister.
Over there.

END OF SCENE TWO

SCENE THREE

MA

(Ma and Al step forward)
At last, a boy child. Three girls, enough.
Now a boy. For you I want the best.

AL

(Seated on a cot in front of scrim/ flat with painted interior of dining room)
I'm the only one, you said.
Special, I don't feel special.
(Stands, gestures around the room)
Never a private place to sleep,
on a porch, in the dining room, wherever.

MA

Here, the best cuts of meat, the
girls will iron your clothes, we
walk on tiptoe where you sleep.

AL

Clothes in a hall closet, on a chair…
(Picks up a shirt and tie, draped over a chair, disgustedly)

MA

Go to school, hot chocolate when you come home.
Lawyers make good money.
Work hard, be rich.

49

AL

Ma, I see you struggle,
day after day, making do
with less, able to do more.

MA

Don't worry about me. As long
as we can pay the rent, we'll
get along. Save for yourself.

AL

I will not be poor, I promise you.
Power counts, no matter how
you get it. Money one sure way.
(Hands grasping lapels, he struts around the stage, as if addressing a jury)

MA

You come first.

AL

Control fills the hungry void. *(A discordant duet)*

RHODA

Yes, Al, you tried to control *me.* Ordering me around
as if you were my father. You lied and cheated me, gambling
my money for college on the stock market. I fought you
for control of my own life…
(Lights go down, up on Pa, center stage)

PA

Who is this boychick?

Always angry, what's wrong?
He talks, talks, talks
like a Philadelphia lawyer, always arguing.
No respect for me,
a money-grubber, surface
talks for social justice.
Does he understand unions,
my life? Only cares about
"working the angles."
Fah! I don't know him.
(Lights dim, come up on Ma and Sara. Sara does not speak)

MA

Sara, we're going downtown.
You have the pencil? The paper? Good.
Growing girls need clothes; no money.
I must sew, new shapes,
new hems, new collars.
We look at shop windows,
you like that one, Sara? So draw.
No? How about the other one?
O.K. we go inside. Look, how about that one?
(To a clerk) No, thanks, we're just looking.
(To Sara): This one? Quick, into the room.
Draw, Sara, draw quick. The waist,
the buttons, the neck, the length.
The sleeves, draw, draw.
Now for fabric. No, not Marshall Field,
the basement, the cheap discount store.
Here, this plaid? *(To a clerk):* Yes, how much?
What I could do with my own shop!

RHODA

I know, Ma, I know, how sweet it is!
Your talent flowed through my head, my fingers.
Twelve years I worked; finally went broke, but, oh,
the beautiful clothes I made!

END OF SCENE THREE

SCENE FOUR

RHODA

(As she speaks, each shadowy figure steps forward)
   Oh, Pa, I lived and loved, wildly and happily;
   I danced on many tables;
   And the failures were not disasters.
   Ma, I kept the day job,
   But escaped your trap;
   Had the shop you wanted,
   And the success was lovely.
   Al, You fought me for control;
   I fought for independence;
   We fought to a forever draw.
   Sara, Dance became my mantra;
   You taught me the beauty
   of a body in motion.
   Jeanne, You were the model
   I didn't follow; your inward
   self was alien.
   Fay, How I envied you, your

firm consistency; imagine,
A partner for sixty years?
And so, with many voices in my head,
I chose my own path;
Six careers, three husbands, many lovers;
I learned how to love to live and live to love!
L'Chaim! To Life!

THE END

— part two —

REFLECTIONS ON FAMILY

In the Introduction to this collection of writings, I refer to the tapes in our heads, and how the voices on those tapes influence the ways in which we view our worlds. My view of my parents and my siblings was affected by the distance between us — I was always on the outside, looking in, and wanting to belong. In the next series of stories, I connect various memories with particular events, allowing you to see how reactions to events in our lives are affected by how we grow up.

DREAM/MEMORY

We lived on Millard Avenue on the lower west side of Chicago from 1918, my birth year, until 1930, when I was twelve, and I have had this recurring dream many times.

In my dream, I get off the streetcar on Twelfth Street, walk two blocks west to Millard, passing the Jewish butcher, the drugstore on the corner where it's possible to buy, for "two cents plain," a soda glass of nose-tingling seltzer water. (Five cents bought me flavored syrup spritzed into my glass while I twirled around on the counter stool.) On the next block, I pass the grocery store where the Jewish grocer sold me hard candy or chewing gum for a nickel. I can hear the song in my head as I walk down the street, *"My ma gave me a nickel to buy a pickle. I didn't buy no pickle, but I bought some tsooing gum, tsooing gum."*

I turn left on Millard, and suddenly I'm running, past the duplexes, red brick with slanted red-tiled roofs sheltering the porches. Each narrow house has a small flight of steps leading down from the steps to a concrete walk. No fences, sometimes a small patch of grass to one side of the walk. I run and run, but my house, on the left, about one-third of the way down, eludes me. I try to see ahead, to the lower end of that long block, down to Cicero Avenue, but it's dark and vaguely ominous.

Suddenly, I see my house, and I become myself, on my knees, my chin resting on the windowsill, looking out over the slanted tile roof, across the street where my friends, Irving, Harry, Bessie, and Tillie, are playing under the street lamp on a hot, humid night in July.

At that age, I seldom played outside at night, and on this particular night, I am in my small bedroom off the living room at seventhirty. I feel this to be a vastly unfair time to go to bed, when it was still light outside and the voices of my friends playing under the streetlight just opposite taunt me with their chanting happiness.

All the windows in the flat ware open to catch whatever breeze interrupts the smothering humidity. My bedroom window opens onto slanting red tiles, with a drainpipe anchoring the right-hand side of the roof. I kneel on the floor in front of the open window, my elbows resting on the sill, just a few inches from the roof, watching the activity across the street, consumed with envy.

Suddenly I see my parents, my sisters Sara, Jeanne, Fay, and my brother Al troop out of the house and amble up the block. They are going to visit a neighbor whose father has died recently. My mother is carrying the family's offering — a chocolate frosted sponge cake.

They are gone! Quickly, I shuck my pajamas, put on pants and a shirt, and step through the open window onto the sloping roof. Moving cautiously to the right, I grab onto the drainpipe and shinny down to the street. My friends greet me happily.

"Hey, Rhoda! You made it! We were just going to play 'living statues.'"

"OKAY! Let's go! Are you first, Harry?" I jump up and down.

Harry leans on the lamppost, his back to us, covering his eyes with his hand. He begins to count... "one, two, three..." As he counts, we run off in all directions, trying to get out of sight before he says, "ten!" Then we freeze in as many funny positions as we can, and Harry looks at us carefully to see if any of us moved at all. If he sees anyone moving even the smallest bit, that person is out. Then he turns around again, and we run and hide. The game is for Harry to try to find anyone he can, and then race that person to the lamppost. If Harry gets there first, he is still in the game, but if one of us gets there before him, Harry is out and we start over again. After that we play "Kick the Can."

We are in the middle of "Kick the Can," our version of soccer, when

Irving shouts, "Hey, Rhoda! Here come your folks around the corner! Better go back!"

I scramble up the brick steps to the porch, grab hold of the pipe, but my hands keep slipping. Irving and Harry run up the steps; Harry bends over and Irving boosts me onto Harry's back. I clutch the eave and pull myself onto the roof. Scrambling through the open window, I duck into bed with my clothes on, pulling the light cover over my head, closing my eyes, trying to slow down my heavy breathing. I hear Fay come into our room briefly and then go out again. I know I will have a few minutes while she spends some time with the rest of the family gossiping about who was at the Beckers' that night. That gives me enough time to get out of my clothes, throw them in the closet, slip on my pajamas, get back into bed, and turn my face to the wall.

My dream changes, and I find myself jolted awake. I am in my comfortable small bed in the mother-in-law apartment built on the patio of my house in Berkeley, California. The year is 2008 and I am ninety years old. Getting out of bed, I open the blinds and look out on the garden, flooded with full moonlight. I sit on my carpeted floor, wrapped in a blanket, and gaze out through the floor-to-ceiling windows. Although the dream reminded me of that particular hot night in Chicago, when I was seven years old, now other memories come flooding back. I close my eyes and the flat on Millard Avenue swims into my mind's eye. The garden disappears, and I remember the tiny bedroom that my sister Fay and I shared. Even though we called it a bedroom, it was really just an alcove, curtained off from the living room by a heavy blue velvet drape. The bed took up almost all of the space, making it necessary to move sideways to get to the small closet behind the bed.

Our flat was a long, "railroad car" style, with several windows in the living room facing the street. The living room led to a long hall which passed the entry door and proceeded down to the dining room, from which a kitchen on the left led to a screened-in back porch. Two bedrooms on the left and a single bathroom on the right opened off the hall. My parents had the larger of the two bedrooms; Jeanne and

Sara shared the other one. Al slept on a couch in the dining room, keeping his clothes in a hall closet. Mornings were shouting bedlam. With only one bathroom for seven people, Al was the only one to get the bathroom all to himself. There was much pounding on the door and shouts of "What are you DOING in there? Your ten minutes were up five minutes ago!"

When I open my eyes again, and gaze out on my quiet, moonlight-flooded garden, I find myself relieved to be alone, no longer living in a crowded flat in a hot, humid, dirty city. Now, at ninety two, I relish the quiet singleness of my life. I go back to bed to finish the night, the dream played out, never to return.

LOOKING BACK: THE CHICKEN

In 1926 I was eight years old and walked six blocks to Delano Elementary School. Sometimes I cut through alleys and backyards to get to school, and sometimes I walked along Twelfth Street. I always took shortcuts to get home for lunch and then back to school, but I took the long way back after school. On a day in late April, the week before Easter, I passed a florist's on my way home. There in the window were about a hundred fuzzy little yellow chicks, chirping madly. I stood watching them, mesmerized. The sign said, "Fifty cents each." I fingered the two quarters in my pocket, milk money for the week, and sighed.

I knew my mother was adamantly opposed to pets of all kinds. A city was no place for animals, she asserted. I knew a cat or a dog was out of the question, but maybe she would accept a chicken. After all, it wouldn't require much food, and it wouldn't take up much space... I palmed my quarters, and went into the shop.

Our flat was on the second floor of a red brick duplex. It had a pillared porch and a foyer with two doors. The door on the left opened to stairs, the one on the right opened to the landlord's apartment. I went up the stairs, holding my chick inside my coat, feeling its heart beating against my hand, and opened the door to the flat quietly, not flinging it open in my usual exuberant way. Calling out to my mother,

I announced that I was home and walked down the corridor to the kitchen at the back of the flat, hiding the chick in the pocket of my sweater. But nothing escaped my mother's vigilant eye.

"What have you got there?" she said, suspiciously. I opened my hand and there sat my chick, blinking in the light. "What? A chicken? What are you going to do with a chicken? This is not a farm we live in!"

I hastened to explain that I would put the chick in a box in the bathroom, where it wouldn't bother anyone; I would feed it and take care of it; she didn't have to worry about the chicken upsetting the family routine. Talking very fast, I kept stroking the soft feathers of my chick. My mother shrugged and turned back to the stove, stirring whatever it was she was cooking. She said, over her shoulder, "Look in the pantry. Maybe you'll find a good box in there. And if that chicken makes any noise or any fuss…" She left the rest of the sentence up in the air.

I set up the box in the bathroom, lining it with crumpled-up newspaper, put some cornmeal in one corner and water in the other. The name Bettina suddenly came to me, and I was proud of the way the chicken adapted to her new home. I didn't know whether I had a female or male, but remembered something about roosters having a set of red feathers on their heads. Bettina was all golden and soft, so I decided she was female.

The only problem was that as Bettina grew, she learned to hop out of her box, which she especially liked to do when my mother took a bath. For some reason, Bettina was entranced by my mother's feet, and as soon as those feet came into view, Bettina was out of the box, investigating the toes. My mother yelled; I rushed in, picked up Bettina and scolded her. After that, I made an excuse to take the box out of the bathroom whenever I saw my mother heading for the bathroom.

Bettina seemed to recognize me when I came into the bathroom after school; I thought her chirping was different, and she would stop whatever she was doing and hop over to my side of the box, cocking her head to one side, her beady eye fixed on me. I wondered whether chickens had intelligence we didn't know about, and decided to try an experiment. We had a salt shaker in the shape of a chicken, and I put the porcelain chicken into a corner of Bettina's box. She eyed the false chicken warily, then hopped over to it, stopped, cocked her head, pecked at it, and turned her back on the fake bird. Then she scratched at the crumpled-up newspaper, and paid fierce attention to the cornmeal.

Fridays were cleaning house day, and my mother engaged a Polish woman named Mrs. Varshing to help her with the washing and cleaning of our apartment. After lunch, I paused in the bathroom to say goodbye to my beautiful, plump, and healthy pet before running down the steps, back to school.

That afternoon, as I opened the door to the flat, I sensed an ominous quiet, and when I opened the door to the bathroom, I found a scrubbed, clean empty space. No box, no Bettina. "What happened to my chicken?" I demanded of my mother, who was sitting at the kitchen table, peeling potatoes.

"I gave her to Mrs. Varshing," my mother said calmly. "It will make a nice soup for her dinner. That chicken was getting too big for the apartment."

Stunned, I turned away quickly, trying to hide my tears. Pets had no place in my mother's view of the world.

REMEMBERING 1930, the Depression Years

My world in November, 1930, included my sixty-two-year-old father, a man who waxed and twirled his luxuriant red mustache after smiling at his shaved face in the mirror every day; a man who burst into song after a few glasses of wine; a man with boundless enthusiasm for life, as well as my gloomy, introverted fifty-year-old mother, who suffered from psoriasis and migraine headaches. That world, from which I felt excluded, even invisible, also included my widowed thirty-one-year-old sister Sara; my self-absorbed, moody twenty-eight-year-old sister Jeanne; my arrogant, opinionated twenty-five-year-old brother Al, a lawyer; and my twenty-one-year-old kindergarten teacher sister Fay, who acted as a stand-in for my mother. All of those people were deeply involved in their own lives; they were not really interested in me. I felt that I was a mistake that just appeared one day in 1918 and never seemed to fit in. At twelve years old, I desperately wanted to be seen as a full, participating member of the family, not just as someone to be scolded for all sorts of things, like not standing up straight, or not doing all my chores on time.

I came home late as usual on that Chicago bone-chillingly cold Monday in February, 1930, to the flat on Van Buren Street. I always stayed at high school as late as possible, where I was an editor on the school paper and very visible. I was in the habit of reading everything

I could get my hands on. When I was a child, I walked around reading a book as I was dusting, and fully described my mother's assessment of my work as a "lick and a promise."

As I walked down the long hall from the entry foyer of the flat, I heard loud voices from the kitchen.

"What do you mean, Scrip? You're going to be paid with a piece of paper instead of dollars? I don't understand!" Ma's voice was a high-pitched wail.

I paused outside the open swinging door to the kitchen. I strained to hear Fay's soothing murmur.

"It's okay, Ma. We can use Scrip to buy food; it's like a voucher, and the school district representative said that grocery stores and meat markets will accept it. He said that it's sort of like play money, but it works like real money."

I took a breath and walked into the kitchen. My mother turned a baleful eye on me. "So, she's finally home. Miss Always Late. How come you never come home early enough to prepare dinner? Fay never used to come home so late." She ran her hands through her short grey hair dramatically, her small brown eyes already drifting from me, her apron-clad small body hunched over the kitchen table. "Who knows where our next meal is coming from?"

I clamped my lips shut, knowing my mother didn't expect a reply. I looked at Fay. "What's happening?"

"The Chicago School District is broke, and so is the city of Chicago. There's no money to pay the teachers, or the school employees, or city workers. The administration is going to pay all the city workers in Scrip, a kind of imitation money. Since the stock market crash last year, the money has been slowly disappearing. Ma is scared, and so am I. But at least we'll have Scrip."

"Will they close the schools?" My eyes widened at the awful thought that I might be stuck at home, away from my beloved newspaper and the Drama Club, let alone away from Mr. Schwartz, the history teacher on whom I had a crush.

"Oh, I don't think so." Fay, deliberately upbeat, moved to the sink and dumped a bag of potatoes into the running water. "Take off your coat and start peeling the potatoes, Rhoda. I've just put the meatloaf into the oven. Ma, why don't you lie down for a while? Rhoda and I will finish preparing dinner."

Ma lifted her glasses, wiping her eyes with a corner of her apron, and got slowly to her feet. "That's a good idea," she said wearily. "I'll just take a little nap."

Standing at the sink while Fay fussed over the oven behind her, I desultorily began to peel the potatoes. What if we didn't have enough money for the rent? Ma was always complaining about not having enough money to do anything she wanted to do, outside of paying the rent and the utilities. Ma kept saying she wanted a shop of her own, which would give her an independent income, and she fretted over her limited resources. I knew that Ma depended on everybody in the family to contribute to the cost of running the household. Would I have to quit high school and go to work, as Sara and Jeanne had had to do? I had heard plenty of stories about those bad times, which had happened before I was born. My hand, holding the paring knife, trembled.

Fay turned around and looked over my shoulder at the pile of un-peeled potatoes. "Good Lord! You don't have to massage the potatoes! Just peel them!" She grabbed another knife and quickly pared one. "Look, it's easy." With a few deft movements, she skinned the potato and dropped it into the bowl on the counter. "You're the slowest mov-ing person I ever saw. Move over, I want to rinse the lettuce for the salad."

We both heard the front door slam, then the closing of Sara and Jeanne's bedroom door, and the click of high heels along the corridor. Sara appeared in the doorway. "Where's Ma?" She ran her fingers through her bobbed red hair. "Lying down?" she guessed. "Just as well. I've had an awful day. We're in for some rough times." She stared around the kitchen, her glance skimming unseeingly over Fay and me, standing frozen at the sink. We had never seen our ebullient sister Sara, who had inherited her sunny disposition from Pa, look so depressed. Then, wagging her head from side to side, her eyes cleared and she went

65

over to the icebox and opened it. She stood there, lost in thought, as if forgetting why she had opened the icebox door, and finally took out a pitcher of water. Fay and I waited. Sara poured herself a glass of water and drank it down in one gulp.

"Jeanne's lying down. She had an awful day too. I don't know how we're going to tell Ma. I thought things were bad last year, but this is worse. LaSalle Street is like a graveyard. How soon is dinner?" Sara had a way of skipping from subject to subject without warning. But Fay was used to this.

"We'll be ready in about half an hour, as soon as the potatoes are cooked." She glanced at the bowl. "Looks like they're ready to go. Rhoda will set the table. Pa and Al ought to be here by then. It's almost six o'clock."

Sara turned. "I'll go check on Jeanne and wash up."

My heart felt heavy in my chest. I wasn't sure exactly what was going on, but the atmosphere in the room was almost as dark and threatening as the glowering skies outside the windows.

Just as I was setting out water glasses, the front door slammed again, and Al pounded down the hallway. He threw his briefcase onto the cot in a corner of the dining room and declaimed, "Court adjourned early today. Rumor is there's no money to pay the court clerks. God knows what's going to happen. Anybody listen to the news yet?" His face reflected bewildered panic, and I felt my stomach clench.

"Ma's lying down," I said, trying to assume Fay's calm, "Jeanne's also lying down; Sara's in the bathroom; Fay is fixing dinner; and Pa isn't home yet. I don't know what's going on either."

Al sat down on the cot, which was also his bed, his hands hanging listlessly between his knees. Our flat had three bedrooms, and since he was the only male outside of Pa, he never had a bedroom to himself. Sara and Jeanne had one bedroom; Fay and I shared another; and Ma and Pa had the third. In fact, Al considered himself the odd man out and paradoxically, felt that he deserved whatever extra privileges he got as his just due. He liked having his underwear and handkerchiefs ironed by Fay or me; he liked getting the best cuts of meat; liked being fussed over by Ma; and he ignored Pa's cutting remarks because he'd voted Republican at the last election.

Ma walked into the dining room just as Pa came home. She looked at him as he came toward her, his slumped shoulders telegraphing defeat. He put his arm around her and kissed her cheek. She drew back slightly, and looked up at him. "What? What?" her body registering preparation for another bout of bad news. He just gave her shoulder a squeeze, and settled himself at the head of the table.

Fay brought in the meatloaf and vegetables, I followed with the potatoes and the salad, then Fay poured water for everyone. Sara and Jeanne came in, sitting down at their regular places, and an unquiet silence descended on the dining room. Usually there was a loud buzz of conversation, laughter, a hum of connection. But tonight there was nothing, just an oppressive silence. I tried to swallow some water and almost choked over the lump in my throat.

Ma said, "Well, let's eat before everything gets cold. Fay, pass the meatloaf to your father. I'll start with the potatoes. We'll talk later."

This was also a strange departure from the usual pattern. I twisted uneasily in my chair. Usually everyone talked right through the meal, sometimes with their mouths full of food. I often thought of witty things to say so that when I jumped in with a comment I would get the attention I craved. My mind jumped around from topic to topic, trying to think of a joke or something to break through the silent noise in the room, but I came up with nothing. The family chewed and swallowed in silence.

Finally, Pa put down his fork, took a sip of water, and wiped his mouth. "I have some bad news, Ma," he said, looking down the table at her, "Irving ran off with the truck and all the tools. Not only that, he cleared out the petty cash drawer, too. I know, I know," raising his hand to ward off her I-told-you-so response, "you never liked Irving. But we worked together for five years, and after I fell off the roof... no, it wasn't Irving's fault... he still treated me like a full partner." Pa hurried on, ignoring Ma's sputtering protests. "I know I got the jobs, and Irving and Pete did the work, but still and all, he was fair. I really didn't expect him to steal everything. He must have felt desperate for some reason."

Ma snorted in disgust. "That no-good! He had a sneaky look from the beginning. I never did trust him. Desperate? You're making excuses for him? Who's making excuses for you?" She turned to Al. "I heard you shouting something…what was it? Fay says the city of Chicago is broke; is that what you were yelling about?"

The dining room erupted. Al began talking about court adjournments; Fay was telling Sara about Scrip; Jeanne and I sat silently, looking from one to the other. Pa knocked on the table. "Enough! One at a time! Fay, what about the city of Chicago going broke? How can a city go broke? Impossible!"

"It's not impossible," shouted Al. "In this corrupt city, anything is possible!"

Fay interrupted. "It's my turn! All I'm saying is that the Chicago School District is paying all its employees in Scrip! It's kind of like vouchers instead of money. We can buy groceries and meat with it, just not clothes or shoes."

"What?" Jeanne and Sara spoke together. "You mean the city of Chicago is printing money?" Sara exploded. "Like what happened in Germany after the First World War? This is America! We haven't been attacked! What's happening to us?"

Jeanne, who had been brooding silently through the hubbub, finally spoke up. "I don't know about the rest of you, but Mr. Sloan, who's a one-man insurance broker, tried to kill himself today. Like a lot of people on LaSalle Street, he'd been living on promises and borrowed money, and when the bills came due, he just didn't have the money. I came in this morning just in time to grab him by the knees and pull him back into the room. He looked at me as if he didn't want to be saved. Kept crying and saying he was ruined." She began to weep, hiccuping as the tears streamed down her face. "He thinks his life is finished."

Suicide because of debts? I thought about that. In all the reading I had done, none of the characters contemplated suicide because of debts. Dickens's characters went to debtors' prisons; Zola's heroine,

Anna Karenina, threw herself under a train because of unrequited love; and Camille never considered suicide because she couldn't support herself. I tried to think of any examples in Dumas's writing or the Bronte sisters; Steinbeck, O'Neill, Tennessee Williams, Arthur Miller; the list could go on and on. None of the characters in any of the books I was reading currently contemplated death connected to money. No, death was connected to honor or social status or love, but not debts. This was a new concept.

Ma's voice seemed to connect with my thoughts. "What? He'll kill himself because he can't pay his debts? Stupid! Stupid! Sara, is your broker boss stupid too?"

"Brokers are gamblers, Ma. They hang on until the very end. I really don't know what his reserves are, but I think I'll get a paycheck this Friday. After that, I can't say. What about you, Al? Will your office stay open, and is there any money coming in?"

Al got up and paced the room restlessly. "We have a couple of personal injury cases coming up, but if those companies are broke, we can't collect. I feel as if nothing is solid anymore, as if I have no control over anything." He stopped behind Ma and put his hands on her shoulders. Then, looking at Sara, he said, "Actually, our office rent is paid for a year, and Molly said she'd put her salary on hold for the time being. I don't know what will happen next week, let alone tomorrow."

Ma patted his hand. "Go sit down, Al. We have to figure out what to do. Rhoda, clear the table. Everybody, go get your bankbooks; we'll add everything up and make plans." She was a general, marshalling her troops.

"Me too?" Fay complained. "What about my savings for my wedding?"

Ma gave her a look that would wither a plant. "Yes, you too. Are you part of this family or what?" Everybody scattered, while Ma got up and went to the kitchen. She brought back the stewed fruit and pound cake that was our standard dessert. She nodded approvingly as I brought in dessert plates and spoons. *Ah, Ma really sees me; I guess I'm not invisible after all.*

After the bankbooks were assembled in front of Ma, she motioned to Al to sit beside her. "I'll read out the numbers," she said, "You write them down, and add them up. We'll see where we are."

I regarded my mother admiringly. *She's not complaining about headaches or anything; Ma knows how to take charge, all right.* My shoulders and back straightened as my spirits lifted.

Al gave Ma the total. She regarded it thoughtfully and spoke to the hushed family. "We have enough to pay rent for four months," she said. At three hundred dollars a month for a duplex on Chicago's west side in 1930, that amounted to a grand total of twelve hundred dollars from the combined savings of five adults. "If Fay is right about Scrip, and whatever comes in from who knows where, I'll be able to put food on the table. No more steak on Sunday." There was a collective whooshing sound as the family let out the breaths they were holding.

Ma looked at Fay. "Fay, wipe your eyes. June is a long way off. We just have to see what happens." Then to Al, she said, "Suppose we went looking for Irving. Could we get the truck back?"

Al laughed. "Ma, we aren't living in a detective story on the radio. We don't have the money to hire somebody to go looking for Irving, and the police don't care. He didn't really steal the truck; he only took Pa's half, and that doesn't count!" Turning to the rest of the family, he said, "Okay. I suggest we give Ma next month's rent right now. That way she'll feel better." Everybody nodded.

I felt as if a sweet wind swept the room. *I won't have to quit school and go to work!* As I started to wash the dishes, I made a silent resolve to do whatever it took to go to a four-year university. I was not going to have to follow Sara and Jeanne's model, quitting high school and going to work. I would not follow Al's program either, working during the day and going to night school. As it turned out, I had to work for a year after graduating from high school, but with the help of Sara, Fay, and Al, I got through the first semester at Northwestern and went the rest of the way on scholarship and part-time work.

We made it through the worst of the depression, scrounging and saving every penny. Scrip helped, and so did Ma's alterations of my sisters' clothes.

STORIES FROM LATER YEARS,
1936–1939

Immigrant families are governed by a formula: everybody works, teenagers as well as fathers and sometimes mothers. My family was no exception. My parents had emigrated from Romania with my oldest sister, Sara, in 1900. Sara and Jeanne had both quit high school to go to work. My brother Al worked during the day and went to law school at night. My sister Fay was given the special privilege of going to a teachers' college during the day for two years, because she would end up with a steady job and a steady income. When I graduated from high school, my mother assumed that I would get a secretarial job and go to night school, but I had other ideas. I was determined to go to a four-year academic university and pursue a career in journalism. My father was a Socialist, a member of the International Workers of the World, also known as the Wobblies. Perhaps his long dissertations on justice and injustice, particularly against the working class, had an effect on the choices I made.

I knew that the only way to go to a four-year academic university without a family subsidy, then as now, was to get a scholarship and work part-time. I enrolled at Northwestern University in Evanston, Illinois, in 1936. One of my most influential professors was Dr. Ernest Lauer, head of the Department of European History. Dr. Lauer was a native of Germany, and he hated Hitler. He pegged Hitler correctly as a dangerous man, but when he tried to tell a university audience that Hitler was "not a madman at all," that he was very sane, he was booed off the stage. Evanston, Illinois, a small university town north of Chicago, was full of isolationists in 1936. Milwaukee, Wisconsin, close to that part of Illinois, was the headquarters of the American branch of the German Bund.

The administrators of Northwestern, a conservative Methodist college, didn't like Lauer's outspoken points of view. There were other reasons that the administrators didn't like Professor Lauer. As a rational, creative teacher, Lauer didn't believe in the grading system as set up by Northwestern. He was supposed to give a certain percentage of As, Bs, Cs, Ds, and Fs. Lauer felt that this arbitrary system put an unfair limitation on his ability to evaluate his students, and in 1936 he rebelled. I was privileged to be part of that class.

Lauer warned us that the coming final exam was going to be the most difficult we had ever taken or probably would ever take. He advised us to study, study, study, and we all took him at his word. When we arrived at our classroom, quaking, full of anxiety, we were surprised to see, in a corner, instead of the usual pile of bluebooks, a pile of brown paper bags. Professor Lauer instructed us to sit in alternate seats, "so that we wouldn't be tempted to cheat," he said, and when we were seated, he passed out the brown paper bags. They turned out to be full of peanuts in the shell.

"Open the bags," he instructed. "Now eat the peanuts. This is your final exam."

We hooted, of course, and began to eat the peanuts, throwing the shells on the floor. Lauer walked among us, his hands behind his back, and stopped at one student's desk.

"Ah," he said, "Why are all your shells piled up on your desk? All the other students are throwing their shells on the floor."

"This is the way my mother taught me to eat peanuts in the shell," the startled student answered.

Lauer raised his hand, and his voice. "This student has demonstrated that he is the only civilized person in the room. He will receive an A. All the rest of you will receive a B, since I am sure you have learned as much as you will ever learn from me. Class dismissed." We accepted Professor Lauer's decision, even though some of us were hoping for an A or an A-.

Northwestern suspended Professor Lauer, and the entire class marched on the administration building, staging a sit-down. Representatives from the History Department came out to talk to us, people from the president's office also attempted to get us to go home, but we didn't. It was a cold Chicago autumn day. One of our class members went inside the building for a private conference with Professor Lauer and the various members of the administration. He told us later what happened.

"It was obvious," he said. "Everybody wanted this thing to be over. They wanted us to go home, but I told them that Professor Lauer was the best professor on the campus, that his classes were always oversubscribed, and that we were all willing to be suspended."

There was a lot of shifting around when Ben said this, but we waited.

"The president's representative told Lauer that he had to give a certain number of As, etc. if he wanted to keep his job, no ifs, ands, or buts. And then I was asked to leave. I think Lauer will come out and talk to us."

Sure enough, pretty soon Professor Lauer came out, his jaw clenched, his face red, and asked us to go home. He said we should bring our final papers to class the next day, and he would explain what he was going to do. I remember how deflated we felt. We felt we had lost, but we underestimated Professor Lauer. In class the next day, he asked us to evaluate our own work, and put grades on our papers that we thought we deserved. But we also had to write an analysis of why we graded ourselves the way we did. He also told us that no one would fail the course.

What a brave man! It helped, I suppose, that Dr. Lauer had tenure, and probably the university would have had difficulty firing him, if they'd wanted to.

73

In 1936, I was a tall, skinny eighteen-year-old with a chip on my shoulder, and I immediately joined the leftist groups on the campus. Those were the days when the newly formed Congress of Industrial Organization (C.I.O.) battled the American Federation of Labor (A.F.L.) for union control of workers and staged sit-ins in Chicago and elsewhere. Those were also the days of the Spanish Republicans in their war against Franco, and I became the secretary of the League Against War and Fascism.

I took jobs wherever I could, working as a maid for upper-class Evanston families, and working as a writer for a political science professor for twenty-five cents an hour. Since I was self-supporting, and not living at home, my mother couldn't really object to my lack of monetary support for the family, although she didn't approve.

In 1938, when I was a sophomore, the turmoil on the campus was intense. I remember hours of anguished aggression in all parts of the world. All of us had friends who had either died in Spain during the rebellion against Franco, or had trouble getting back into the United States after going to fight in Spain. Many of our friends had been stigmatized as being members of the Communist Party (whether or not they were) and had their passports revoked, resulting in their being stuck in Mexico for several years.

During that year, the Political Science Department at the University of Chicago organized a Mock League of Nations conference and invited Owen Lattimore, who was a guest lecturer at the university that year, to moderate the conference. The students in the Political Science Department at the University of Chicago allocated the countries to be represented to the various universities, public and private, in the immediate vicinity of Chicago. Actually, these universities represented the "Big Ten" of the annual football contests.

The assignments I remember are: the University of Chicago representing the United States and Spain; Northwestern got Germany and the Union of South Africa; and Wisconsin got Ethiopia and Italy. I don't remember the countries assigned to other universities, since the drama in 1938 lay in the conflict between the Italians and Ethiopia,

Germany and Spain. Spain was still in the middle of the ill-fated revolution against Francisco Franco, and the Italians were engaged in their attempt to conquer Ethiopia. Owen Lattimore was the guiding spirit behind the Mock League of Nations project.

Robert Oppenheimer was also there. We had all met Dr. Oppenheimer when he gave a lecture at Northwestern a few weeks before the conference. He was a handsome, charismatic man, and in my journal I noted how impassioned he was, no matter what his subject. One of the things he talked about was his trip to Tibet, when he disguised himself as an itinerant native, traveling on a donkey. My journal from those days describes the story he told about darkening his skin with juice from almonds, and squirting lemon juice into his eyes to change the color from blue to brown. I never knew if he was joking with us, but I believed everything he said, and could easily visualize him hunched over his mule, dressed in rags, bouncing along with his head down.

I had joined the Political Science Club, and I was invited to go with the seniors and graduate students for the weekend experience at the University of Chicago. Of course I was thrilled to be allowed to go along as an observer, never dreaming that one of the senior members would become ill, and I would actually take part in some of the discussions.

We met every day in our dorm rooms to discuss strategy. During a particularly acrimonious meeting called by the United States and Spain representatives, I, the representative of Germany, was asked about the status of German troops in Spain. Coached anxiously by one of the graduate students who hovered behind me, I said, "We have no troops in Spain. We have observers and advisers, requested by Generalissimo Franco. We are neutral."

I thought the University of Chicago student, representing Spain, would have a fit. The argument went on until two a.m. I wouldn't budge, but there was some sort of vote that was supposed to come out of our committee meeting. Professor Lattimore pleaded with us to compromise, and I remember saying to him, "Dr. Lattimore, you told us that we were supposed to behave as representatives of these countries would behave if this were a real conference. Do you want us to act as if this were an ideal situation, or a real one?" Lattimore paused and said, "As if it were a real situation."

So I said, "Then I deny everything. Germany has no troops in Spain, just observers and advisers." Lattimore declared an impasse, and the next day, Germany and Italy walked out of the conference, in effect saying that they withdrew from the League of Nations.

The host student from Chicago was furious, and accosted me in the hallway the next day. "I might have known someone from Northwestern would behave like that!"

"Just a minute," I replied. "We're here in a simulation, and we're following the rules. Besides, you don't know who I am. I'm a Jew, and I'm also secretary of the League Against War and Fascism. You guys set up this conference, and Lattimore made the rules. You can't change the rules in the middle." I walked away and joined the rest of our delegation. Not only was I secretary of the League, two of my high school boyfriends were currently fighting in Spain and I was actively engaged in trying to find housing for German Jews fleeing Hitler. Yet here I was, trying to act like a representative from Germany in a Mock League of Nations meeting, and doing my best to swallow my distress.

I wanted to remind him that the German-American Bund had its headquarters in Milwaukee, and that the isolationists in Congress were doing their best to prevent Roosevelt from coming to the aid of Britain. But I didn't. When we returned to the campus, I wrote a story for the *Northwestern Journal*, but it was cut to the barest minimum; just a brief story about the Political Science Club participating in a conference run by the University of Chicago. Students at Northwestern in 1938 were not particularly interested in world affairs.

There were strong forces working against Franklin Roosevelt in 1938 that prevented him from joining Britain and France in fighting Germany. In order to help Britain, Roosevelt created a program called "Lend Lease" by which he was authorized to send arms to England using the Merchant Marine. The United States did not enter the war against Hitler until December 7, 1941, after the Japanese bombed Pearl Harbor.

Whenever there was a protest or demonstration against injustice of any kind, I was part of the march, carrying a banner proudly on my shoulder. Sometimes it seems as if I've been marching in protest demonstrations all my life. I wasn't particularly comfortable in the upper economic atmosphere of Northwestern University. In fact, one of the ways I supplemented my twenty-five cents an hour WPA job, working for a Political Science professor, was to write papers for wealthy sorority women who were having trouble in their English classes. The word got around that I could write essays to order, and I began to write essays on various topics for different students. I made sure to get copies of the essays they had already submitted. It wouldn't do to submit an A quality paper on behalf of a C student. Since I couldn't get on the newspaper staff, I honed my writing in this way. It was fun.

On one particular morning in May, 1939, I joined a group of friends at Charlie's Café, a hangout near the campus for a discussion about what we were going to do that summer. We all knew it was the last summer of peace, and that it would be only a matter of time before Hitler invaded either Poland or Belgium; we weren't sure which.

Harry was talking as I walked in. "Let's take a ship to Europe and bicycle through France and Spain," he said.

"Spain?" Sylvia practically spit out the word. "You're nuts. The Spanish Republicans lost, remember? England, France, Switzerland maybe, but not Spain, and not Italy, either. Not with Mussolini as head of the government!"

"Okay, okay," he demurred. "But what about the idea of staying in hostels and going around on bicycles?" Much head-nodding and happy murmuring. "I'm restless," he said, running his hand through his red hair. "If this is really the last summer of peace, I want to go to Europe now." He began to pace up and down the room.

There was a heavy silence. We all knew war was in the air. My roommate Peg and I, both juniors, were the only ones on scholarship and

77

working twenty-five hours a week in order to pay our fees. I looked at her, and stood up, saying, "Hey, guys, I have to go now. Quiz tomorrow. See you." Peg stood up also, and we both walked out.

"Yeah," Peg said on our way back to our dorm, "Bicycle through France. Heck, we don't even have bicycles, let alone money for the ship."

I thought about what my friend Alvin had said to me a few nights before. He was from Stockton, California, and was working on his master's degree in music. We had had long talks about my attitude toward the rich debutantes of the North Shore and the privileged young men in my classes. He thought I would be happier at a public university and had urged me to transfer to the University of California at Berkeley.

"Listen, Peg," I said, "My friend Alvin, who lives in Stockton, California, says I ought to transfer to the University of California at Berkeley. His idea is for me to go to Yellowstone National Park, work for the summer as a waitress, save up some money, and go on to U.C.B. He said he'd pick me up on his way back to Stockton after summer school and drive me to Berkeley. Are you interested?"

"I don't want to transfer to UC Berkeley," Peg said, "but I like the idea of Yellowstone. Do you think we could get jobs as waitresses?"

"Maybe. Charlie, at the Café, might lie for us, and say we worked for him. It's worth a try."

Peg said she would check out Student Employment services and see if she could find out anything about getting a job as a waitress at Yellowstone. On our way back to our dorm, walking through the quiet, tree-lined streets of Evanston, the air seemed cloying, even suffocating.

I don't want to graduate from here. If I do, I'll probably end up marrying a nice boy of my mother's or my family's choosing, and never get to be a real journalist. I'm sure we can get jobs as waitresses. Alvin had the right idea. I could save up my tips and go on to Berkeley. I guess I'll have to send my credits off to UC Berkeley Admissions. Excitement coursed through my veins like an electrical current.

The next day I saw Peg waving at me as I left my English class, and she ran to catch up with me. "Guess what! There was a sign on the bulletin board asking for people who wanted a ride to the West Coast! And I got all the information about Yellowstone!" She was jumping up and down. "All we have to do is get a recommendation from a restaurant or cafe owner saying that we have experience, and I think we'll be okay. Here are the application forms that I got from the employment bureau."

We filled them out immediately and went over to talk to Charlie at the Café. "Okay, girls," he said. "I don't think they'll check. The places that hire college kids for the summer usually train them anyway. Good luck." He grinned at us. "Don't take any wooden nickels!"

I sent off my credits to the University of California, and we called the boys who had advertised for riders. They had signed up with a company that hired drivers to ferry cars from Detroit to California, to save shipping charges. They warned us that we would be driving night and day in shifts, but they did agree to drop us off in Yellowstone.

I went home to pack, and thought about what to say to my family. *How could I explain the force that was pushing me?* If I told them my plans, I would be asking for permission to leave. *No, I couldn't do it.* I would simply say I was going to Yellowstone Park to work for the summer and leave out any future plans.

Here was a real fork in the road. I knew I could work in Chicago for the summer and save up money for the fall term. Then after graduation, I would probably settle down close to my family. *If I transferred to Berkeley, they might never forgive me for running away. Was I willing to take that chance?*

The answer was yes. I went to Yellowstone, then on to California and a new life. It took years for the family to accept the different path I chose.

CHICAGO REVISITED, 2003

Between 1939 and 2003, my life in California and other places in the world was so rewarding that I never regretted leaving Chicago. However, in 2003, my granddaughter, Adeyemi Omodele-Lucien, was a freshman at the University of Chicago, and I decided to visit her at the end of her first year. Not only did I want to reconnect with her, I wanted to see how Chicago had changed. Ade and I had developed a grand rapport during her childhood, but by the time she left for college, we were spending less and less time together. Eighteen-year-olds don't want to spend all that much time with their grandmothers!

I wanted to revisit the places I lived in when I was growing up in Chicago, and I hoped Ade would have time to go with me. As it turned out, she was too busy with end-of-term chores, and I went on my odyssey alone. My visit in 2003 was an attempt to go back in time.

I wondered how different Millard Avenue would be, and also how much Van Buren Street and the area around my high school, John Marshall, had changed. I wanted to see if what I remembered of Chicago, the place where I grew up, matched reality in any way. I remembered that Thomas Wolfe, the author of *You Can't Go Home Again*, says emphatically that it's not possible to go home once you've left, but I needed to go back, at least once, to connect memory with reality.

Did that house on Millard really have a sloping roof down which it was possible to slide on and connect to a drainpipe? Did I imagine that story? Could it have happened? I was driven, not so much by nostalgia, but by a need to validate my memory.

I hired a taxi driver and asked him to come to the hotel on Friday to take me around, not certain about what I would find. I had had a dream about a long narrow street named Cicero that cut at an angle across Chicago's west side but I wasn't sure if it was a real street or a dream. When I told the driver I wanted to go to Millard Avenue, I found myself on just such a street as in my dream. I sat forward on the comfortable seat in the car, feeling excitement and anticipation in my throat. "Yes!" I cried as we approached the intersection of Cicero and Millard. "Yes! I remember that corner. But there used to be grass there and several trees. It looks so bare and neglected. That patch of dirt is full of trash."

We turned onto Millard, and the stately elms I remembered were gone. But there were new trees, and the neighborhood was still full of the two-story red brick houses with porches that I remembered. Millard had not yet been gentrified. I told the driver I was looking for 1647 Millard and we drove up and down the block slowly. Suddenly I found it. I found the house in which I had been born. It now had a fence around it, but there was the second-story window and the sloping tiled roof down which I had slid to play with friends under the lamppost. My scalp and spine tingled with the memory. I took several photographs and showed the photos to my elder sister Fay to see if she also recognized the house. (She did.)

The street was quiet. It was a residential neighborhood, and the few people on the street were black women, chatting on their front porches, looking at me curiously. I'm sure they were trying to figure out who I was, an elderly white woman taking pictures of different houses. Maybe they thought I was a buyer or a developer. Twelfth Street, at the end of the block, was also different. Instead of Jewish butcher shops, grocery stores, and a synagogue, there were still grocery stores, supplemented by liquor stores and several store front churches. The old synagogue on the corner was now a Baptist church.

Other streets parallel to Millard had been gentrified; the old red brick duplexes torn down and upscale condominiums built instead; no trees, just concrete. I wondered where all the old residents had gone ... would they be able to afford those fancy new buildings? Those other streets seemed impersonal and dead to me.

I was afraid that my neighborhood had been erased. The streets were still there, but the neighborhood had changed. It was comforting to see that Millard Avenue had avoided gentrification for the time being, but I sensed that it would only be a matter of time before 1647 Millard Avenue disappeared, along with the neighborhood.

We crossed Twelfth Street and made our way to the area near Garfield Park, to Van Buren Street, where I had lived while going to high school. Garfield Park was completely different. My driver said it had been "upgraded," and most of the neighborhood had changed. The old red brick duplexes had disappeared here too and in their place were by now familiar looking condominiums, some with carefully manicured front lawns. The elevated train tracks I remembered had disappeared, and in their place were broad boulevards.

I fell into bed that night satisfied that I had revisited my past, and found that part of it was still there. The infrastructure of Millard Avenue was intact. Although the old elms had succumbed to elm disease in the forties, people there had replanted the trees. The houses were still well cared for; the lawns were neat; the people were different, but the street looked as if it was still populated with working class families, and that was reassuring. The years between 1918 and 2003 had been kind to Millard Avenue. I had "gone home" and was reassured that enough was left to reinforce part of my remembered childhood.

Now I could revisit other places in Chicago that also held potent memories. Before I left Berkeley I had surfed the Web, looking for a relatively inexpensive hotel on or near Michigan Avenue, and found one on Michigan Avenue. However, when I arrived from the airport, I discovered that this hotel was the last holdout in a strike by hotel workers, and picketers marched up and down in front of the entrance. No wonder the rates were so low! Gritting my teeth and keeping my head low, I walked into the hotel. I hated walking through picket lines, even to reside in an old hotel which had hosted the Democratic Party nomination

View from Michigan Blvd., looking toward Lake Michigan

of Franklin Delano Roosevelt in 1932.

The hotel was being slowly remodeled, and I managed to secure a large room overlooking Michigan Avenue and the lake in one of the re-modeled towers. After settling in, I started out on another journey back through time. My first stop was the Art Institute, two long blocks north of my hotel. As I walked out of the hotel, a heavy south wind assailed me and pushed me north. I remembered being swept around the corner of Madison Avenue and Michigan on my way to ballet school at the age of eleven. I remembered being lifted up by the wind and flung against a building, and the power of that wind was familiar.

However, even in the hot humid air of a Chicago summer, I felt my arthritic hips complaining. Two blocks in humid, ninety-five-degree Chicago weather feels like ten blocks in Berkeley's temperate climate.

Staggering up the steps to the entrance of the Art Institute, past the beautiful recumbent bronze lions, I leaned against the door and asked the guard if there were any self-propelled wheelchairs available. She smiled at me, her braided, bead-entwined locks twirling around her face, and assured me that they were. In fact, she advised me to wait a minute, disappeared, and returned with a chair. She also announced with an air of triumph that today, Tuesday, was a free day, and that I could stay until seven forty-five if I wanted to.

I had never manipulated a wheelchair by myself before, and found that this mode of transportation had many advantages while viewing paintings. For one thing, it's possible to pause, sit comfortably, and drink in the magic of Renoir, Sisley, Monet, Manet, Picasso, Braque at one's leisure. I sat comfortably in front of any painting I wanted to contemplate while impatient gallery gawkers moved around me.

The collections at the Art Institute were even more awesome than I

remembered from my high school days, seventy years ago. I saw Picassos I had never seen in Spain, Chagalls that were not included in the San Francisco Museum of Art retrospective of his work, a Braque and a Picabia I did not remember. There was a group of Juan Gris paintings that were not included in his

Marshall High School

retrospective at the University of California Museum of Art. It was a thrilling way to spend an hour or two, and it was definitely easy on my aching hips.

Orchestra Hall is across the street from the Art Institute, and on impulse, I walked across the street and asked about tickets for that evening's concert. Orchestra Hall looked exactly as I had left it. I was so relieved that nobody had tried to spruce up its grimy exterior. Surprise, surprise! If I bought my ticket before five p.m., I could get a main floor seat for fifteen dollars, so I immediately bought a ticket and decided to attend a pre-concert lecture.

Since it was only four forty-five, I wandered around Orchestra Hall and discovered that it had expanded to include a Symphony Center, which boasted a gift shop, upscale restaurant, and wine bar. I followed directions down a red carpeted corridor, lined with portraits and testimonials from various members of the orchestra and their comments about performing with the Chicago Symphony over the years. Memories of attending concerts sitting in the gallery in 1934 and listening to Frederick Stock conduct the orchestra flooded happily over me.

I ended up at a wine bar called Rhapsody, which reminded me of Max's Opera Plaza on Van Ness Avenue in San Francisco, and one in Covent Garden in London. The décor was understated; the bar served an excellent Chardonnay from France, and smoked Norwegian salmon with a choice of rolls, all for eighteen dollars. The bar was full of young, upwardly mobile people in their thirties and forties, easy talk flowing between people of different sizes, colors, and shapes, all apparently in the same social and economic class.

In the audience on the main floor of Orchestra Hall at six fifteen, I noticed a mix of twenty-year-olds to eighty-year-olds, dressed variously in blue jeans with backpacks to elegant long dresses. There were a few people with walkers and canes. Men were in shirt sleeves and slacks; few with jackets, and most of the women wore sleeveless dresses or blouses with trousers. More dresses than pants for the women. When I sat in the gallery in 1934, people dressed casually, but not on the main floor. There, women were in long dresses and gloves; men in black tie or tuxedos.

I had a seat right in the middle, toward the back of the main floor. It was the first time in my life that I sat on the main floor of Orchestra Hall. Imagine! Me on the main floor of Orchestra Hall! I could hardly believe it. I wriggled with pleasure in my soft, velour padded seat.

Memories flooded over me. Between 1931 and 1934, my sister Fay and I sat in the upper, upper balcony for twenty-five cents a ticket. Those were formative years for me, between thirteen and sixteen. They were the years I spent as co-editor of our high school newspaper, the *Marshall News*, and was a participant in the Nathanson Group where we studied the writings of Goethe, Schiller, Heine, Nietzsche, and Spinoza. I was also a member of the Drama Club, and there I used all the various techniques I had learned in years of ballet school about the ways ballerinas walk and hold their heads. I reminded myself again that "no experience is wasted," realizing that the years spent learning to dance on point left a lasting impression on my body. I had joined the honorary dance society, Orchesis, when I first enrolled at Northwestern, and I made an easy transition from classical dance to modern. Dance has remained an important part of my life.

On Wednesday, early in the morning, I went to the Harold Washington Public Library on State Street, named for the only black mayor of Chicago. I walked under the familiar El structure, with El trains thundering overhead, and State Street seemed grubbier than I remembered, crowded with cheap fast-food places, papers swirling around in the warm hot wind. The public library was a building that looked familiar on the outside, but it had been gutted and remodeled on the inside. Nothing like the old library, the interior was spacious, well lit, with free computer access.

I saw a poster advertising Calvin Trillin, an author I respected, who was speaking that evening, so I decided to eat dinner in the hotel and go back to the library later. Eating alone in the deserted dining room, I found the attention from the many waiters just standing around rather amusing. I felt a bit like a friendly ghost, comparing images of what was then and what was now.

I was glad I had decided to make this a week for me — to connect again with the Chicago I grew up in and accept the Chicago it is today. I needed to remember the red brick apartment buildings jammed next to each other, the red brick sometimes interspersed with light colored granite, and I needed to find out how much things had changed.

Michigan Avenue seemed cleaner than I remembered. All the newly planted trees make a difference, as well as the potted plants and flowers lining the roads. When I drove down the Outer Drive to the University of Chicago with the car and driver I had hired, I noticed hundreds of trees with their roots still tied up in protective bags, waiting to be planted; green fuzz on the flat tops of warehouses; ivy crawling over the front of newly-constructed condominiums.

The journey I made through time was a successful one. My photos of the house on Millard where I spent my early years verified the memories that had visited me in my dreams.

Relationships

REMEMBERING THE MEN I MARRIED

I've often wondered about the three men I chose to marry, and about what there was about me that attracted them. Jim Pack was brilliant, poetic, vulnerable, and needy. Jim was a psychologist, and a poet. The next man I married was brilliant, poetic, vulnerable, and needy. Ric Skahen was an M.D., a pathologist. He never knew his father, who died before he was born. The third man I married was also brilliant, identified as one of Dr. Lewis Terman's genius children when he was growing up in California. Bob Holdeman was an artist, a recognized water-colorist, poetic, vulnerable, and needy.

All three of my husbands, Jim Pack, Ric Skahen, and Bob Holdeman, were genius intellects. They all had IQs well above one hundred and fifty; they were all articulate, interested in words and their origins, and they were well read. They had other things in common, too; they liked to drink, and they lacked what Daniel Goleman calls "emotional intelligence." I thought all three men were different, since they all had different professions and were very different physically. Yet I realized, very late in life, that they were the same men in different bodies. They were brilliant, but they all had similar problems. None of them got along with their mothers. They admired me, then challenged me, and ended up trying to control me.

What was there about me that attracted these men? I was a nurturer; I wanted to take care of people, men as well as women. I wanted to solve their problems, to help them realize their potential. Attracted to needy men because I needed to be needed, we balanced each other. It took me a long time to realize that I was stuck in what psychotherapists call a vicious triangle: Rescuer, Persecutor, and Victim. The individual stuck in this pattern may start out as the rescuer, and through interaction with the partner, gradually assumes the other roles as persecutor, then victim, and this cycle repeats and repeats. Breaking it is hard.

After years of psychotherapy, I was finally able to break that pattern, and didn't realize it was gone until I met Peter. Peter was eighty-five and I was seventy-two when we met, and he was the love of my life. Jim Pack was my first deep love at twenty-one, and I became his support and his nurturer. That pattern of nurturing which I followed through the other two marriages was not a healthy one. Peter wasn't needy, and therefore he was able to supply the love and support I needed, and that support enabled me to break the poisonous psychological pattern.

Peter had had a loving, warm, respectful relationship with his mother; had been married for thirty-six years to the same woman, who died of pancreatic cancer; and he was allergic to alcohol! He had all the other attributes I admired; he was brilliant, an accomplished painter in oils, acrylic, and watercolor; he loved words and was a great storyteller. Also, he was marvelously sensitive, gentle, and an accomplished lover. We had eight wonderful years together, until he died, at ninety-three, of a stroke.

Jim Pack

REMEMBERING JIM PACK

Who was James A. Pack III? When we met in 1939 at the University of California at Berkeley, I was twenty-one and Jim was twenty-two. We were both seniors. To me, Jim was a serious, courteous, intelligent psychology major who lived in a cooperative dormitory next to mine on Ridge Road in Berkeley. To his domineering father, he was the younger and less favored of two sons, the one who survived a boating accident on the Rogue River in Oregon. To his mother, he was an intellectual, a poet whom she didn't try to understand.

Jim was my first deep love; we married two months after we graduated, to the consternation of both his family and mine. His father cautioned him about marrying so early, and especially about marrying a Jew. My father wrote from Chicago to tell me that I was dead to him because I married a non-Jew. However, those rejections only brought us closer together. We both went on to graduate

90

school, intending to become academics in some small university town, and have a family of five children.

When Japan bombed Pearl Harbor in 1941, marking the entry of the United States into World War II, Jim and I had been married for a little more than one year. I was working as an elementary school teacher, and Jim was finishing his thesis for his master's degree in Applied Psychology. All our dreams of a secure, middle class academic life were blasted. Jim went into the Navy, and I went to Washington, D. C. to work as a journalist for the Office of War Information. I don't know what kind of parents we would have become, but I know that the war changed him — and me.

After our divorce was final, in 1952, something that was inhibiting me disappeared. I became an independent designer and manufacturer of leather clothing; I had my own business, and I became a different person. The child that I had borne Jim died after ten days; the scar remained, and I knew I would marry again. I still wanted to have a child.

I heard from friends in Marin that Jim had married again, this time to a lighting engineer, a talented, ambitious woman, and that he had fathered several sons. We both moved in different directions.

Ric Skahen

REMEMBERING RIC SKAHEN

Who was Ric Skahen? He was a small man, about five feet eight inches tall, with a thin, wiry body. He had intense gray-blue eyes, sandy hair, and he smoked nonstop. The year was 1953 when we met; I was thirty-five; he was forty. I was running my own successful boutique business on Grant Avenue, called Rhoda Pack Leathers. He was an M.D. working for the Veterans Administration while also studying for board certification as a pathologist. We married two years after our first date. He was my second husband.

Ric and I both connected in the early part of our marriage, but those connections disintegrated with his heavy drinking. Persistent, daily, habitual drinking changes a person, and Ric changed. I was intrigued by his wry sense of humor, and his Irish gift of storytelling. I was fascinated by him, and yet had a gnawing sense of unease. There was an aura of danger about him that was intriguing yet worrisome.

On our first date, we went to an elegant restaurant on Pacific Avenue in San Francisco, where the headwaiter greeted him by name. Walking to a secluded table, I noted the upholstered red plush walls, punctuated by gleaming mahogany panels, soft amber lights, and the general atmosphere of Victorian baroque. The place looked like a movie set, background for a posh brothel.

Ric ordered oysters and gin martinis, and then, with an upraised eyebrow, he asked me if he should order. Why not? I shrugged. After ordering the special, Ric and the wine steward huddled over the two-foot-high wine menu, selecting carefully the proper wine for our dinner. Ric settled back into the padded banquette, and fixing his intense eyes upon me, asked, "So what are your goals in life?" *What a gambit,* I thought.

"Ah, well," I responded, "I want to continue living creatively and intensely, and I want to marry and have five children. I'm sure I can do both. What are YOUR goals?"

At that point, the waiter arrived with the oysters and the martinis, and Ric never did answer my question. Instead, he began to talk about his tour of duty as a medical officer in postwar Germany, where he apparently spent most of his time wandering the countryside, sampling the local wine. I was happy to listen to his mesmerizing stories, enjoying the superb food and wine. I noticed that Ric just pushed his food around on his plate, but managed to polish off most of the wine.

During a whirlwind courtship, which involved Ric's moving into my apartment above the shop, Ric didn't tell me about his marriage to a professor at the University of Washington, with whom he had had two children. It was only after I agreed to marry him that he revealed that his divorce with the professor was not final. Of course I was furious, and demanded that he leave my apartment immediately, and not come back until the divorce was really final.

Ric went to Seattle and signed the final papers. We married in 1955 and went to Mexico for our honeymoon. On that trip, Ric told me that his mother, a Polish immigrant, had married his father, an Irish lawyer, when she was eighteen and his father was in his sixties. John Richard Skahen died two months after his son was born, and Marion's inheritance was stolen (according to Ric) by bankers who mismanaged the account set up by her husband. As a consequence, Marion was a single mother and almost penniless. She was young, desperate, and alone, and she sent Ric away to military school when he was five years old. Ric told me that he never went home for holidays, and he was one of the few boys at the school who were left behind. He was an unhappy child, and an unhappy adult.

When we lived together in the apartment above my shop on Grant Avenue, we had some grand parties. We started the Grant Avenue Street Fair, along with Peter Macchiarini and other artists on our block, and ended up having a kind of salon for a couple of years. Following are some stories about our life together before we married.

• Zoo Stories •

The following three stories are the true exploits of two friends, Ric Skahen and Stuart Lindsay, pathologists who became friends when they were both in medical school. Now in their forties, they had become connected with Carey Baldwin, head keeper of the San Francisco Zoo. Carey had been in charge of William Randolph Hearst's collection of animals at San Simeon, Hearst's castle. Hearst's will stipulated that the animals were to go to the Fleischacker Zoo (later to be called the San Francisco Zoo), and that Carey was to go with them as head keeper. Baldwin was not a veterinarian; he loved "his" animals and treated them with the same respect he gave his fellow humans.

Ric, a small, balding man, about five feet, eight inches tall, and Stu, six feet one, a well-built sportsman with a full head of hair, were passionately interested in animals — how they coped with disease, what kind of immune systems they developed, and whether or not viruses could migrate from species to species.

Carey and Ric and Stu were kindred spirits; they liked to drink good liquor, tell tall stories, and they were equally concerned with the welfare of caged wild animals. In the late 1950s, their interests converged with problems that came up with a lion, an elephant, and a hippopotamus.

I participated in some of the events, because Ric and I were living together. (We later married.) Stu and Ric removed a growth on a lion's paw, conducted an autopsy on an elephant, and tried to help a hippopotamus with a sore tooth.

— The Lion's Paw —

One night in June, 1956, all the animals were still on the outside of the Lion House of the San Francisco Zoo, except for one lion, large and handsome, who lay dopily in one cage near the west end of the building. There was an ugly growth on his right paw, above the claws, about where a human wrist would be. His paws were crossed in front of him, the right one on top, and his head was resting on them. From time to time he would raise his massive head, yawn, lick the sore paw, and lie down again.

Carey Baldwin, the head keeper, was keeping us entertained in his house on the grounds of the San Francisco Zoo, while we waited for the lion to fall asleep. Ric and Stu were getting ready to operate on the lion. We had invited several friends to come along and watch; Lucia, an internist, Belson, a dermatologist, and Weber, a cardiologist. No surgeons.

Time dragged on. Belson asked, "Will someone please tell us what's going on? All we know is that Ric invited us to watch an operation on a lion! Your liquor is excellent, Carey, but what's the drill?"

"Well," Carey said, "You know there's a problem with sedating a wild animal. It's very hard to know how much you need to knock an animal out and not kill him in order to operate. George is the most prized lion in our collection. He has a terrific personality; I would hate to lose him. I noticed the growth on his paw a few weeks ago; it looked cancerous, but I don't know much about those things, so I called Ric and asked him to come over and have a look. Ric said that we had to operate and remove that growth."

Ric took over the story at that point and told everybody that there wasn't much written about sedating and operating on wild animals, especially lions, including details about his call to the head keeper of the Berlin Zoo.

"Do you know what that German guy said when I asked him if he had any data on successful operations?" Ric laughed. "He said that the operations were successful, but the patients died. Then, getting serious, he asked me how much our lion weighed. I gave him my best guess, and he gave me his best guess as to how much sedative we would need. I asked him how long after putting the dope in his food it would take for the lion to fall asleep. He said about ten hours, but it was only a guess."

Carey looked at his watch. "It's been just about ten hours. I'll call the Lion House and ask Jack how he looks." He dialed, listened and then told us that George was sleepy but not out. "We'd better wait a while. Let's have another round."

At about ten p.m., the phone rang, and Carey stood up. "Okay. Let's try it. Jack says George is out. Do you have the thread and needle for the sutures, Rhoda?" I nodded. And to Ric and Stu, "Got your knives sharpened?" He laughed.

We all trooped down the path in the dark. We could hear the animals, locked out, banging on the outside doors of the cages, but we were not prepared for the effect of that banging on the inside of the Lion House.

We were in a state of anxious exhilaration as we walked into that dimly lit, cavernous space. The Lion House in the San Francisco Zoo is a huge, concrete structure about ninety-five feet long and three stories high. This formidable rectangle has steel doors at either end, small lights high in the cavernous ceiling, and is lined with cages on either side. The pounding of

96

the animals on the outside of the cages created a throbbing din around us. This rhythmic pounding went on the entire time we were there.

The lion was now staggering around his cage, occasionally falling down, getting clumsily up, rubbing his paw over his face, and crossing his eyes. All I could think of was Bert Lahr as the Cowardly Lion in the movie, *The Wizard of Oz*. Finally, George collapsed, rested his chin on his folded paws and closed his eyes. He sighed. We thought he was asleep, but every time we approached the cage, he would lift his massive head and stare at us blearily. Carey went into the cage and pushed and prodded George to put his paw through the feeding gate at the front of the cage. That accomplished, Carey went carefully out of the cage and back around in front.

We held our breath. Stu and Ric approached with their sharp surgical knives. Ric held the paw, and just as Stu raised his knife, the lion opened his mouth in an enormous yawn and emitted an ear-splitting, growly roar. Stu cut off the growth with one sharp stroke. There was remarkably little blood. I hovered nearby with the needle and thread. I was supposed to hand the threaded needle to Ric, who was holding a pad soaked with antiseptic to the wound. I was shaking so badly I couldn't get the thread through the eye of the needle, so I licked and bit the end of the thread to get it through. I nearly dropped everything as Ric yelled at me, "You idiot! It's supposed to be sterile!" Well, hell, this wasn't an operating room; nothing else seemed very sterile to me. I thrust the threaded needle at him and turned away. Ric managed to suture the wound, and pat it with more antiseptic just in time before the lion stirred. George withdrew his paw from the feeding opening, staggered over to a corner of his cage, and sank down sluggishly. He slept for three days.

As soon as George lay down, Carey pulled a switch and all the doors to the other lion cages swung open. All the noise stopped. The animals filed into their cages without a sound, prowled around a bit, and then settled down. *Why did they do that? Were they reassured about being allowed back into their cages? Did they know that something had happened to one of their caged friends and now it was over?* Of course, there was food in the cages, but even so, the quiet was deafening.

97

We all filed out slowly, subdued and silent, into the dark and fragrant night. We were as shaken by the reaction of the lions as by the operation itself. Ric and Stu were the heroes of the hour and became honorary members of the San Francisco Zoological Society. The rest of us were delighted to be mentioned in Herb Caen's column in the *San Francisco Chronicle*, especially after we learned that the lion recovered completely, no complications caused by nonsterile, licked thread.

— Why Did the Elephant Die? —

Whenever a prize animal died at the zoo, there was immediate concern, especially if the animal was young, and had not been obviously ill. Was it a virus? Was it contagious? Would it spread throughout the zoo? What was the cause? Everybody got into the act, from the president of the zoological society down to the keepers. As in any scientific endeavor, the process of identifying a cause resembled finding a killer in a murder. It required painstaking attention to detail; careful unraveling of hints as to what happened. Who was in contact with what or with whom, and when did the contact take place? What were the atmospheric conditions and even events that might affect the emotional condition of the animal? Most veterinarians do not have this training or attitude. But both Ric and Stu saw connections between ailments that affected animals and illnesses that afflicted humans.

One day in the fall of 1956, Ric got a call from Carey telling him that one of their elephants had died. Carey asked Ric, "Would you like to do an autopsy to determine the cause of death?" A grin spread over Ric's face; his eyes lit up, and he said he would call Stu and then call Carey back for details as to how they would do it. Carey didn't want to have to ask the Zoological Society people for permission; he was afraid they would say no, so the entire endeavor had to be done without telling anybody about it until it was over and they had the results. This was fine with both Ric and Stu, who seldom asked permission for things they really wanted to do.

There were a few problems. When did the elephant die? Where was he? Who would cut him open and how did Carey plan to get rid of the blood and other fluids? I'm not sure how all of this was settled; it's possible that Carey had a friend in the burial business who helped him out on siphoning off the fluids, but by the time Ric and Stu got to the animal, he was in an ice house, and fairly dry inside. I wanted to go along and photograph the proceedings, but was told politely that this was men's work, and women should stay outside, thank you. This is the story as told by Ric and Stu:

"We got to the ice house, and there was this huge carcass, almost filling the entire space. Even though it was very cold, the smell penetrated us. We were wearing coveralls, hiking boots, gloves, and masks, and we descended into the belly of the elephant by means of extension ladders slung over the side. We wished we had oxygen masks to protect us from the smell. We carried specimen boxes containing knives and slides and other equipment over our shoulders. Zookeepers, lying on their bellies, hanging over the side, lit our way with flashlights. We had fortified ourselves with strong drink before we went down, but it was still tough going."

Ric had asked Carey to make sure they had pieces of lung, liver, heart, stomach, and other organs to section, so that they could do as scientific an autopsy as possible. Taking sections was a problem.

"We kept slipping and sliding around on the bottom of the elephant's belly," Ric said. "It was hard to find a place to balance the specimen boxes, and it was also hard to keep from slicing off pieces of our own fingers in the process. Finally, we had sections of all the main organs, and we staggered over to the ladders." Ric and Stu had started at noon and finished at five thirty. By the time they got back to our apartment in North Beach they were wiped out. They stank, and I demanded that they undress on the back porch. The smell of rotting flesh was the kind that lodges in the back of your throat, staying with you through several glasses of wine. It's a smell you can taste, but wish you couldn't.

Autopsies are complicated affairs. Usually the pathologist conducts the autopsy in a sterile room with lots of air circulating around, and even then the smell is often overpowering. Many interns throw up or even faint. The pathologist examines the organs of the dead body and dictates his findings as he works. He weighs pieces of tissue, slices off others to be set aside to be frozen, then cuts them into sections for examination under a microscope. It's meticulous work. This autopsy on the elephant was not conducted in what you might call a controlled environment.

However, Ric and Stu were determined to make it as professional as they could. They parked the organs in my refrigerator/freezer compartment overnight and then took the pieces to the lab in the morning. There they subjected the organs to a deeper freeze, sectioned them off and began laboriously to look at the specimens under their microscopes. What was the elephant's illness? *Tuberculosis!* When Ric and Stu reported their diagnosis to Carey, he went into a panic. How was it transmitted? How likely was it that other animals would contract it? How did their elephant get it? Suddenly it was no longer a pathological problem but a social and political one. Carey wanted to know if it would be necessary to isolate the elephants. Isolate the elephants? How? How about testing the keepers? Could the infection be transmitted from a human to an animal? Those were the questions Carey put to Ric.

"I don't know," said Ric. "Try testing the keepers. We have to prevent an epidemic."

Carey tested all the keepers, and two of them tested positive. They were fired. No other animals contracted tuberculosis. There was a brief notice in the *San Francisco Chronicle*, to the effect that "one of the zoo's beloved elephants had died of unknown causes."

100

— The Hippo Has a Toothache —

We were sitting comfortably in my apartment above my shop in North Beach, San Francisco, on a foggy Sunday afternoon — Ric, Stu, and I — when the phone rang. It was Carey Baldwin from the San Francisco Zoo.

"Carey says that the hippo is wailing all the time," I said to Ric. "It seems he has a sore tooth. You'd better talk to him." I handed him the phone. Ric looked at Stu. "He wants us to come down and have a look."

Stu hesitated. "We don't know anything about teeth," he said. "Why doesn't he call a dentist?"

"You know that Carey always calls us first when he has any trouble with any of the animals at the zoo," said Ric. "I think we ought to go and look at the hippo. I know a dental surgeon we can call if we need to."

"Okay," said Stu. "Let's go."

I stood up with them, and although they weren't enthused about my coming along, they didn't say I couldn't. We could hear the hippo's roaring wails as we came onto the zoo grounds. The crowd was at a respectful distance from the edge of the hippo's pool; some of them standing with their hands over their ears. Gazing into the open mouth, we could see the inflamed area around the offending tooth and stood in awe, along with everyone else. Carey appeared, and the four of us gazed mournfully at the hippo thrashing around.

"Does he ever close his mouth?" Ric asked hopefully.

"Not for long," said Carey. "We're trying to figure out how to get some sort of tranquilizer down his throat. He won't eat or drink, just hollers and thrashes around."

We stood around a while, and then went back to Carey's house on the zoo grounds, to figure out a plan.

"We have to take photos of that mouth," said Ric. "Then I can show them to my friend, Doug Barber, and ask him for some ideas. Do you have a camera with a good close-up lens?"

"I think so," Carey replied. "But isn't there something we can do to get him to stop hollering? It's bad for business, and it upsets all the other animals. Even the monkeys on Monkey Island have their hands over their ears!"

"Let's try squirting some anesthetic down his throat," Stu suggested. "The stimulus will cause him to swallow, and he'll close his mouth simultaneously."

"Yes, but how much?" Carey moaned. "We have to know how much our hippo weighs. Remember the trouble we had with the lion? How are we going to figure it out?"

They talked over all sorts of ideas, some of them involving draining the pool, measuring how much they drained out, filling a pool the same size and measuring the difference. That idea, calculating the weight, figuring how much weight displaces that amount of water left all of us looking quizzically at each other. Carey shook his head vigorously, and nobody bothered to try computing the math. Then Carey suggested hoisting the hippo on a crane with a scale attached, as if they were weighing a sack of potatoes.

Everybody brightened up. Stu wondered if the crane could have a net attached, and Carey responded happily, draining his glass, "Yes! We can do it in the early evening. I don't want any publicity on this. We'll get a crane with a net we can drop over our hippo, pull it tight, yank him up, measure him, and then drop him gently down. Once we get his weight, we can call our contact at the Berlin Zoo and get some info on the amount and kind of anesthetic to use."

"Okay," said Ric. "But we haven't solved what we're going to do about the inflamed area around the tooth, and the tooth itself."

"Oh, we'll pull it out!" said Carey blithely. "Just use a pair of pliers and pull it out!"

"Wait a minute." Stu was pacing up and down. "Doug Barber lives in San Francisco. We need his advice. Will you call him, Ric?"

Doug was at home and answered the phone. "What? A hippo with a toothache? Good god! Where are you?"

Ric hung up the phone. "He said he'd be over in about an hour. Let's get something to eat."

Later that evening, after Doug had visited the hippo, we were back in Carey's living room. "Got any brandy?" Doug asked Carey.

"Yes, why?"

"We could get a long stick with brandy soaked in cotton on the end of it and swab the red inflamed area with the brandy. It ought to soothe him a little. Then, just for kicks, we could pour the brandy down the hippo's throat. I don't think it would hurt his digestive system. What do hippos eat, anyway?"

"They're vegetarians," said Carey. "They eat grass, weeds, and vegetables. We can use brandy. The idea sounds good to me."

We trotted down the path to the hippo's pool. One of the attendants propped the hippo's mouth open with two sticks, and Doug applied brandy liberally to the sore tooth and the area around it. Then, removing the sticks, the attendant poured a quart of brandy mixed with water down the hippo's throat. He closed his mouth, swallowed, and for the first time in two days, didn't open it immediately to howl.

We all looked at each other. "Maybe we don't have to call Berlin" was the thought that flashed through our minds. "Let's try another quart of brandy," said Ric, "and see what happens."

"I'd like to take a photo of that mouth," ventured Doug. "The inflamed area looks so far back on the lower right jaw, I want to see close up what's around it, and just how swollen it is. Wish I could squirt some novocaine into his jaw." He sighed.

Carey spoke to one of the attendants, who returned swiftly with a camera, tripod, and flash. Doug set up the camera, and the hippo obligingly opened his mouth, emitting another howling roar. After Doug took his photo, they poured another quart of brandy mixed with water down the hippo's throat. He sank into the water, just his nostrils showing, and we all went home for the night.

The next evening, we gathered at the hippo's pool again. He seemed subdued, not thrashing around so much, and the howling temporarily stilled.

"How much brandy has he had today?" asked Doug. "Enough to choke a horse," laughed Carey. "But not enough to satisfy a hippo. Let's call Berlin."

After a lengthy conversation with the Berlin zookeeper, Carey turned to the group somberly. "He wasn't much help. In fact, he advised us to drop the whole project. Said the hippo would get over it."

"But did he say anything about an anesthetic and how to administer it?" Doug asked anxiously.

"He did say pentobarbital would work, but he was dubious about how long we would be able to keep the jaw propped open if the hippo were sedated. He said the muscles in the jaw would relax, and the jaw would clamp down on any instrument still in the mouth. He said we wouldn't know how deeply the tooth was embedded, and how easily it would come out. He was afraid the hippo would clamp down on the tool we were using and even our hands if they were anywhere close. He was pretty dubious about the whole thing."

"I don't think he approves of our trying to treat animals as if they were humans," Rick offered.

Doug interrupted. "You know, I'd like to swab the area with novocaine. Let's get a long brush, soak it in novocaine, and spread it all over the inside of his mouth. I've been looking at the photos, and I suppose we could create a tool for the job. We'd have to get a pair of industrial pliers, bent like jeweler's pliers, wire them to two long handled steel tubes (he pulled out a drawing), rig the tool carefully to a pulley, and crank. Then we would lower the bent pliers to the tooth, clamp it tightly and crank the pulley with a lot of pressure." He threw a few pretzels into his mouth, and swallowed a bit of his drink. He went on. "We'd have to get the tooth out before the reflex action of the jaw clamped down. Even if the jaw clamped down on our tools, the hippo would spit them out."

There was silence in the room as Carey, Ric, and Stu considered Doug's idea.

Carey shook his head. "That's an inventive idea, Doug, but much too complicated. Let's try your idea about the novocaine. Maybe the combination of brandy and novocaine will quiet the hippo. The head of the zoo in Berlin advised us to leave him alone and he'd get over it."

The next evening we all gathered anxiously once more in Carey's living room. We walked down to the pool, and stood looking hopefully at our hippo. He was fairly quiet, but he was tossing his head from side to side. He yawned once, and the attendants quickly propped his mouth open with four steel poles. Doug picked up the brush soaked in novocaine and brushed it vigorously around the inside of the hippo's mouth. The hippo spit out the supporting poles, thrashed around a bit and slowly subsided.

We all looked at each other. Ric said, "Well, Carey, let's hope the novocaine works; if not, you can always give him more brandy!"

After the episode with the hippo, there were no more zoo adventures. Ric and I married in 1955, and we moved to Berkeley. Our son, Ricky, was born in 1957. Chingwah Lee, an elder of Chinatown, and Benny Bufano, a famous sculptor, were Ricky's godfathers. His godmother was Josephine Borson, our pediatrician. I closed Rhoda Pack Leathers in 1963.

Ric loved Ricky, but he didn't seem to know what to do around a small child. He continued to drink heavily, and he had difficulty holding on to jobs at different hospitals in the Bay Area. By 1967, Ric's drinking had become a really difficult situation — he refused to go to Alcoholics Anonymous, and I filed for divorce.

Ric was a fascinating man, but his inner demons destroyed him. He died in 1972.

Rhoda and Robert Holdeman

REMEMBERING ROBERT HOLDEMAN

Robert Holdeman was a very good painter; he used watercolor and acrylics with skill and finesse. He was also a good storyteller; he loved to sail and to fix things. He was brilliant, singled out when a child because of his extraordinary intelligence. He had a wide knowledge of art, aesthetics, history, and linguistics. Bob was one of the few men I have known whom I considered a true Renaissance man. We met when my marriage to Ric Skahen was tottering. He became a good friend and sensitive lover.

Bob loved my son, Ricky, who was ten when we met. He taught Ricky to sail, played baseball with him, and patiently helped with school projects. After my divorce from Ric, Bob moved into my new flat and became part of my household. As long as we weren't married, our life was harmonious, full of love, mutual trust, and shared experience. We went camping, fishing, swimming; Bob taught both Ricky and me a lot about how to learn from nature. He was an intellectual; he loved music, and he taught me to look at the world with a painter's eye.

When we finally decided to marry, in 1968, and to buy a house together, Bob changed. I don't know why marriage changes some men, but all of a sudden, Bob became very possessive, domineering, and behaved like the patriarch of the family. This surprised both Ricky and me, because I had always believed that a family should be a democratic establishment, with everyone having an equal say, and decisions made jointly, never singly. Bob morphed into his grandfather, who was an itinerant preacher, and apparently, a bullying man.

Bob had fought with his mother for control, and perhaps he felt he had to fight me too. Unfortunately, Bob was laid off, at sixty years old, from his job as an interior designer. Losing that job undid him. I tried to persuade him that we could live on my teaching salary, and he could devote more time to his painting. But there was something about not being the main contributor to the family that he couldn't deal with. He began to drink heavily, and he succumbed to his demons, which finally consumed him. We divorced in 1983. He died six years later, diabetic and suffering from liver failure.

I loved all three, Jim, Ric, and Bob, and they all contributed to my intellectual, spiritual, and sensual growth. We shared different lives, and each life was an enriching experience that included pain and joy.

Musings and Selected Stories

Musings

Rhoda and Ricky

ON BEING A MOTHER

When I was twenty-five, in 1943, my first child was born, and he lived for ten days. The United States was at war with Japan and Germany, and my husband was in the Navy. That birth and death, plus the physical circumstances of my life, blasted my hopes of a quiet life in an academic community, looking forward to a large family. I gave up on the idea of having a large family and never revisited that dream. Instead, I went to Washington, D.C., and became a writer for the Office of War Information.

I was finally able to try again, with my second husband, Ric Skahen, fourteen years later, when I was thirty-nine. This time my child lived, and I became a mother. This time I had my own business, Rhoda Pack Leathers, and was married to a pathologist. I had no idea what to do. I knew I wanted to nurse my son, and fought to do so, against the advice of my gynecologist. It wasn't fashionable, in those days, to nurse a baby, especially for older mothers, like me. But I prevailed for three months, after which I had to go back to San Francisco, to my shop.

110

Since my parents were dead, and my sisters and brother lived in the Chicago suburbs, I hired a grandmother to take care of Ricky. I wept all the way to the city, leaving him, and even tried to bring Ricky with me a few times. But it wasn't a good idea; I couldn't keep my mind on my work. So Nana Baird became part of my household.

On weekends, I was a full-time mother, and when I took my son to the park, other mothers thought I was the grandmother. That took a bit of getting used to. I don't know how it is for other working mothers, but for me, it was as if I was cut into several different pieces — I was a wife, a part-time mother, designer and manufacturer of my own business, and I felt fractured. I had no role models, but I felt guilty every day I left Ricky to go to San Francisco.

I started the procedure of closing my business in 1961 when my son was four years old and completed it in 1962, twelve years after my first jacket appeared on the inner front page of *Harper's Bazaar*. Several businessmen in San Francisco offered to buy me out for fifty-one percent of the business, giving me forty-nine percent, and a job as designer. I knew they would change the character of my business, which was aimed at a high-end clientele, and I refused. I wanted to spend more time with my son, and I didn't want to see my designs reconfigured to cater to a mass market. So I simply closed the business.

There was a fanciful picture in the back of my mind as to what a mother was supposed to be — nurturing, protective, pro-active in the school life of her child, and always available. I wanted to be in that picture. However, the economic realities of my life meant that I still had to have a paying job, so I applied to the Berkeley Adult School for part-time work, and was hired. That gave me time to volunteer in my son's second grade class, to teach clay sculpture, to join the P.T.A., and to run a fundraising event by creating a Frog Jumping Contest at the school. I had found out that there were frogs to be had from a laboratory in San Leandro that used them for pregnancy tests, and the lab was happy to give me frogs that they didn't need anymore. The contest was a great success; we sold the frogs for one dollar each, but some of the mothers complained because their children wanted to keep the frogs as indoor pets.

Being a working mother is not the same as being a mother supported by an economically solvent husband and/or partner. My husband became increasingly unstable, and when Ricky was ten years old,
I decided to separate and divorce. By this time, I felt totally involved in
the growth and development of my son, but I knew the environment,
living with Ric Skahen, was not a good one. I needed a job, and I took
classes in teaching English as a Second Language at UC Berkeley Extension. I moved into a different career.

By the time Ricky was twelve, I was living with the man who would
become my third husband, Bob Holdeman, a professional artist, landscape designer, lover of nature and the outdoors. He had been married,
but had no children. Ricky was in middle school at that time; it was the
late 1960s, early seventies, and Berkeley was in the middle of social and
political upheaval.

I was an active participant in the Telegraph Avenue protests, joining members of synagogues, temples, and churches in support of the
students who were protesting against the Vietnam War. Ronald Reagan, then governor of California, ordered the National Guard to occupy Berkeley, stationing the troops at the Marina, the foot of
University Avenue. He also ordered the dropping of tear gas on the
campus, but the gas spread all over Berkeley, and when Ricky came
home from school, his eyes were weeping and inflamed.

Reagan ordered a ten o'clock curfew, and young soldiers with fixed
bayonets rode up University Avenue to occupy Telegraph Avenue. Young
university women made "Mary Jane" chocolate chip cookies, laced with
marijuana, and they went up and down the avenue, poking flowers in the
barrels of the guns, and distributing the cookies to grateful soldiers. Soon
the soldiers were laughing and chatting with the striking students. The
next day the young soldiers were replaced with middle-aged men, hastily
deputized as volunteer soldiers. That was the end of cookies and flowers.

During that time, the Regents of the University of California extended their claim to land in Berkeley, razing neighborhood houses in
the vicinity with the excuse of needing land to build more housing for

Godparents
Benny Bufano (left)
Josephine Borson (center)
holding Ricky, and (right)
Chingwah Lee

Rhoda with Ricky in arms,
Benny Bufano and
Chingwah Lee at Johnny
Kan's restaurant

Rhoda and Ricky

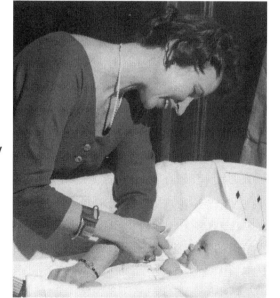

students. The land sat empty for more than a year, and students saw a chance to build a "People's Park." One weekend, a hastily mobilized crew cut through a chain-link fence erected around space on Haste Street, dug up the soil, trucked in tons of sod and planted trees. They worked mostly at night, but middle and high school students helped with the planting during the day. Ricky was one of the middle school students involved in that activity.

My son and I agreed on many things: freedom of expression, responsibility for one's actions, an equal voice in decisions. When I sep-

arated from his father, Dr. Richard Skahen, in 1965, I didn't tell Ricky all the reasons; I simply told him I couldn't live with Ric anymore. In 1967, Bob Holdeman and I became partners. We had known each other for several years — his wife had been my secretary during the Rhoda Pack Leathers years, and Bob had helped Ric and me remodel our house on Spruce Street. Bob and I decided to marry in 1968, and we bought a house together that year.

Bob was a different kind of father. He had a boat; he loved to go hiking

Ricky at 4, April, 1962

and camping; he was an accomplished painter and designer; and he was interested in language and aesthetics. He played catch with Ricky, taught him to sail, and I thought I had finally found a man who would be a positive influence in Ricky's life. I didn't pay attention to Bob's attitude toward decision-making in our family. Bob began to insist on the final word, no matter what the subject under discussion happened to be, and both Ricky and I chafed under that kind of control. I suppose I shouldn't have been surprised by what happened next.

In 1969, I was teaching at the Berkeley Adult School, and one day when I returned from teaching, I found a note from Ricky, age twelve, propped on the kitchen table: "Dear Mom: I have decided to run away.

Please meet me at the Runaway Center at six o'clock. Ricky"

I didn't know whether to laugh or cry. But I felt honored and validated. He was being responsible and thoughtful, and whatever happened, I had to respect his behavior. When I showed up at the Runaway Center, housed in the basement of a church in Berkeley, I met a young graduate student in psychology, and we had a long talk. This was 1969, two years after the Summer of Love, when teenage children flocked to San Francisco and the Bay Area, revolting against what they saw as restraints on their freedom. Joe told me that the Center was set up to handle many children, mainly boys, who were running away for one reason or another. The Berkeley City Council, in cooperation with the Psychology Department of the University of California, had created the Runaway Center in an attempt to help parents deal with the waves of rebellion raging in the area.

We had a long talk, and I wept. I was overcome with a sense of failure and of being completely inept as a mother. Joe said that he had had long talks with Ricky, and that he was a boy who would eventually become his own father. Joe encouraged me to join a

Ricky in the shop, Rhoda Pack Leathers

group called Parent Effectiveness Training, and of course I did.

Joe, Ricky, and I talked about his reasons for wanting to leave me and go to live with his dad. Joe had advised me to let Ricky go, saying, "He is going to live with his dad whether you like it or not, so I advise you to let him go." All Ricky would say was, "I think my dad needs me, and I want to live with him." I was terrified. Ric was an alcoholic; I didn't trust him, and I certainly didn't think of him as a positive role model. However, I knew that I trusted my son more than I trusted my ex-husband, and I had to settle for that reassurance. At least we lived in the same city, just a few blocks apart.

Ric arrived before I left, and I saw that he had already had a few drinks, but after a brief talk with Joe, he and Ricky left. Ric and I studiously avoided making eye contact.

At the next session of the Parent Effectiveness Training group, I told about the Runaway Center and my painful experience. I discovered that even married couples were having problems with their children. I was so full of guilt that I thought I had created a situation which my son couldn't tolerate, but I found out that married parents of teenagers were also tearing their hair out. It was a time when middle school and high school children were smoking marijuana and perhaps doing other drugs; when children were falling on the floor in their classrooms, so doped up they couldn't stay in their seats. My sense of guilt of not being a "good" mother wasn't alleviated by the horror tales I heard. I still had to deal with myself.

Bob and I had decided to go to Guatemala on a vacation, and we left the week after Ricky went to live with his father. We went to visit a former student of mine who was a registered nurse. My troubles paled compared to the difficulties of life in Guatemala, in the middle of a civil war. Plunging into a totally different way of living worked effectively to divert me temporarily from the Berkeley situation.

The day after we returned from Guatemala, I received a phone call from Ricky. It was three in the afternoon.

"Hi, Mom. I want to ask you something."

"Okay. What is it?"

"I want to come home."

"Okay. When do you want to come?"

"Now."

"Now?"

"Yes."

"Okay, I'll come and get you." My hand was trembling as I hung up, and I found it hard to breathe. I drove the few blocks to the house on Spruce Street and found Ricky waiting on the curb with his backpack.

He got into the car, and we didn't say anything until we got back to the house on Eunice. We walked silently into the house and sat down in the living room. I hugged him, and held his hands. He was withdrawn, and looked fixedly at his feet. I put my hands on his shoulders and turned him to face me.

"What happened?" After a long pause, he took a deep breath and said, "I can't save him." I held him close and we sat like that, silent, for a while. Finally, I got enough courage to say, "Can you tell me anything about it?" Ricky leaned back against the cushions, took another deep breath, and began to talk, the words rushing out.

"You know how he drinks. He has a drink for breakfast, and hardly eats anything for dinner. At school, we studied about what liquor does to the liver, and how it can kill you. I thought if I could get him to switch from alcohol to pot, it would save his liver and he would live longer. Marijuana doesn't mess up your system the way liquor does. But he was mad at me for smoking pot, and wouldn't let me smoke in the house. I used to climb out of my bedroom window and sit on the roof outside to smoke. He called it 'devil weed.' I don't know why he's so against it, but we had a lot of fights. I showed him some handouts from school about the dangers of drinking alcohol, and that's when he got really mad. He said I had no business trying to tell him how to live his life, that I was a punk pothead kid, and that's when I decided to leave."

"I'm glad you're home," I said. "We are all responsible for what we do, and we cannot live someone else's life. All we can do is live our own lives as well as we can. And you're doing it." I stood up. "Would you like something to eat? There's lots of stuff in the fridge. Why don't you take your backpack up to your room, and I'll fix something for the two of us. Bob is working late tonight."

He left, and I sat on the couch for awhile, my head in my hands, thinking about the intensity of his experience. I was stunned by the way my twelve-year-old son came to such a profound insight. At that moment, I knew that he would become his own father, as Joe had predicted, and that he had an inner strength that would stay with him during his entire life.

Ric and Remi's wedding, 1984

Rhoda, Ric, Remi, 2010

There is a saying that the job of being a mother is something that (a) you can never quit, and (b) a job from which you can never be fired. The leaders of the Parent Effectiveness Training group kept insisting that we trust our children, and they kept reminding us of the Catholic dictum: "Give us a child until he is seven," the implication being that whatever happens after that, the child will be imbued with the values of the family. They kept repeating that we needed to respect the ways in which our children were learning how to be adults, even though the rebellion was hard to take.

Ricky joined a rock band and dropped out of school. I had always told him that if he wanted to be a musician, he should become a good one, and he did. However, the connection with that particular rock band fell apart, and Ricky went into the Merchant Marine for two years. After that, he created his own group, and during that venture in the music world, he met a Yoruba priest from Nigeria, who was also a master of Yoruba drumming, and this man persuaded Ricky to go back to school. With that kind of encouragement, Ricky registered at the California State College at Hayward as a junior and graduated as a Certified Public Accountant.

While at Hayward, Ricky met his wife, Remi, a Ph.D. from the University of California at Los Angeles, who was also from Nigeria. Remi wrote her thesis on the music, art, and literature of West Africa. There was an immediate rapport between them. They have been married for twenty-five years, and they have two remarkable children, Adeyemi and Aba. Ricky, who likes to be called Ric, became a wonderfully loving adult and father.

The journey wasn't easy, for either of us, but I don't think a journey needs to be easy for it to be positive and enriching. I would have to say the same for being a mother. I learned to be accepting, to love and trust my son, and above all, to be flexible. I never completely recovered from feeling that Ricky was short-changed by my having to work while he was growing up. I don't claim any credit for his development into a remarkable human being; I'm just glad to be his mother.

THE "OTHER WOMAN": A Luminous Experience

After three marriages that ended in divorce, I decided that marriage was not a good idea for me. However, that didn't mean that I needed to give up the pleasure of male companionship. I remember a lovely summer in June, 1980, when I decided to see what it felt like to be the "other woman."

It was a warm evening and the full moon dominated the cloudless sky. Geoffrey Pembroke, my sixty-year-old British lover, and I, sixty-two, were driving south toward Rome after a marvelous five-course dinner in Venice. That dinner, served with five different wines, left me in a state of exuberance bordering on levitation. *How did I get here?* I asked myself.

It all began a year earlier when Geoff and I had met at a linguistic conference in San Francisco. We had been in touch by telephone ever since then; Geoff had called me every morning since we had a tearful farewell at the airport as he left for Cambridge. One morning in June, a year after we'd parted, Geoff called and came immediately to the point.

"How would you like to come to London for a few days and then drive to Rome with me via Venice? I have to be in Rome for an international conference. You have a school break about now, don't you? Just say yes, and I'll send you a ticket. When would you be able to leave?"

I hesitated for a few seconds. Geoff would be paying the bills; I would be following his lead — was I willing to let go of independence as I saw it? I decided, and said yes. After arriving in London, Geoff installed me in a basement flat in the East End, on loan from a friend who was vacationing in Morocco. I became the "other woman," being available to Geoff whenever he was free. He was married, the father of grown children, tied down by what he called his "obligations." It was an interesting experiment for me, since I had been making decisions for myself for three decades, through three marriages and four careers.

Shortly after I arrived, Geoff told me of his plan to drive through Europe to Venice, where another friend of his had loaned him his apartment on a canal for a week, and then we would drive to Rome. Geoff, an enthusiastic and persuasive lover, promised luxurious stays at historical inns, and it was easy for me to go along with the romantic prospects.

I managed to visit London's museums, attend a few concerts, and in general absorb London life on my own. Geoff's visits in the evenings began to seem like frosting on the cake. *Maybe life as "the other woman" wasn't so bad after all!* When we got to Venice, however, Geoff got an urgent call from New York, and he left the next day, promising to get back as soon as he could. I felt stranded and angry.

Once again, however, a lifelong habit of making independent choices provided an alternative to what seemed like abandonment. Before I left Berkeley, I had gotten in touch with a friend whose daughter was a cellist in the Venice Symphony Orchestra, and I had her name and phone number. As soon as Geoff left, feeling isolated in my little apartment on that noisy canal, I called my friend's daughter and discovered that Robin was delighted to make contact with a friend from home. (Barbara, Robin's mother, was afraid that her daughter might fall for an itinerant Italian looking for a way to get to the United States, and that was one reason she wanted me to contact Robin.)

Robin came over and told me that the commune, in which my rented apartment was located, was the center for local Communists and their families. They all gathered in the city square on Saturday nights, and she advised me to go if I wanted to sample Italian life at its most basic. Of course I went, and found a raised platform, about the size of a boxing ring, enclosed by ropes, where a small band was belting out the Beatles and other sixties songs. Young men and women were hopping around, with parents and elders sitting at tables on ground level around the ring, drinking beer, wine, and coffee. I had a good time, and restrained myself from mounting the steps to the platform and inviting one of the young men lounging around to dance with me.

Robin invited me to come to a rehearsal at the Venice Opera House the next day. She was the only woman member of the orchestra, and I was anxious to hear what this group would do with Mahler's Fourth Symphony. Robin said she regarded that choice as torture because it was summer, and most of the orchestra members wanted something less demanding as the last program of the season. She said that her boyfriend would join us for drinks after the rehearsal.

Barbara was right. The boyfriend was a gondolier, obviously not rich, and obviously devoted to Robin. I couldn't determine, from this first meeting, how Robin felt about him, although from the way they sat, with hands, arms, legs entwined, it was clear there was a strong connection between them. I invited Robin for lunch the next day. She immediately accused me of being a spy for her mother, and I readily accepted the accusation. So there we were. After clearing the air, Robin admitted that she was enchanted by Antonio. That was the word she used, "enchanted," so I asked her if she felt like a fairy princess. She was startled, and then she laughed and said, "If I'm a princess, does that make Tony a prince?"

I didn't say anything, and into the silence she sighed, saying, "Tell Mom I'll be coming home in September, but I won't be bringing Tony with me. He's married, anyway."

We both relaxed, and I told her a bit about my life, and how I was experimenting with the feeling of being the "other woman." I told her that I was sure by now that I didn't like it. Robin was sure she didn't like it either.

Geoff returned at the end of the week, and we resumed our journey to Rome. We left Venice and were traveling down the coast of the Adriatic, having booked a small hotel down the road.

"What a glorious night!" I said, stretching my arms over my head. I leaned out of the window, savoring the warm, liquid air. Geoff kept his eyes on the curving road in front of us. "Mmmm," he murmured.

Suddenly I said, "Pull over, Geoff. I want to walk on the beach."

Once out of the car, feeling the pull of the full moon, the small, sparkling waves, I felt drawn as a magnet drags a metal file. The beach was empty; we were totally alone. Geoff stood silently beside me as I knelt to test the water. "Here," I said, handing him my shoes. Then I quickly stripped off my pantyhose, skirt, blouse, brassiere, and thrust them at him. He stared at me, eyes wide, with a look of total surprise.

Not giving him a chance to say anything, I strode boldly into the sea. It was bathwater warm, and came up to slightly above my ankles. *Well! Might as well keep walking.* The air caressed my naked body. I flung out my arms and imagined myself climbing the moonbeam ladder right up to the moon itself. Splashing on, the water stayed below my knees. In love with the night, the moon, the air, I kept plunking my feet into the warm sand, on and on and on. Finally, the water at my knees, I stretched out in the salty, silky waves. My hands touched bottom. I kept my face and head above water.

Standing up, jolted to reality by the cool wind on my naked body, I looked toward shore. I felt like a fool. There was Geoff, fingering his pale tie, watching me. *What could he be thinking? Probably something like, "Good god! What is she doing? There's going to be sand all over the car!"*

I splashed hurriedly to the beach. Geoff stood silently as I approached. Without a word, he handed me my blouse and skirt, shoving my brassiere and pantyhose into his pocket. Then he took out his handkerchief, bent down, lifted one foot, brushed it off, and slipped on a shoe. Then he lifted my other foot, brushed it off, and slipped on the other shoe. With my hand on his shoulder for balance, a wave of love and gratitude swept over me. He was one unflappable Brit!

Geoff gave me his hand and helped me up the small embankment and into the car. We drove wordlessly to the hotel. I leaned my head back against the headrest, glorying in the silky feel the water left on my body, and ignored the stickiness of the salt. I tingled all over with the pleasure of that luminous moment, and looked at Geoff with deep appreciation. I touched his knee gently, and he grinned at me with amused acceptance.

In the morning, over breakfast, Geoff told me that he was meeting his wife in Rome and that after the conference, they would go off to their place in Cyprus. He said he had already booked a hotel for me. I gave him a stony look, and he said, "Look, I'm not abandoning you; I just have other obligations. I'll be with you tonight, but I'll have to leave early in the morning."

Then and there I decided my experiment was definitely over. I pushed back my chair and stood, looking at him. "Geoff, when we get to Rome, why don't you book a room for yourself, or join your wife at her hotel? You're right, you know. Obligations are always a first priority."

Geoff grinned, in that charming way he had, came close and embraced me. "You're a good sport," he said. "See you at the next conference in the States."

The following year, Geoff and I met in Florida, and we went to the Bahamas for a few days after the conference. Once we were settled in the hotel, Geoff said, "Rhoda, if I divorce my wife, will you marry me?"

I didn't hesitate a moment. "No," I said. "If the purpose of the divorce is to marry me, our relationship would be forever contaminated. If and when you decide to divorce your wife, for whatever reasons, let me know. If I am not committed to anyone else, I might consider your proposal. I really think, Geoff, you need to reorganize your priorities."

I knew then that I treasured my independence, and that I was not going to behave in an unethical manner by encouraging Geoff to divorce his wife.

ON ADDICTION

It is so easy to become addicted to anything. When I was working as the designer and owner of Rhoda Pack Leathers, I was under tremendous stress. I had a work space in a loft on Mission Street between Fourth and Fifth Streets in San Francisco. I had four sewers, a finisher, a pattern maker, a cutter, and a secretary. I was making jackets, coats, skirts to sell wholesale to Neiman Marcus, I. Magnin, Joseph Magnin, Roos Brothers, Bullock's Wilshire, Marshall Field, and Lord & Taylor. I created different lines for different stores, producing four collections a year — Spring, Fall, Winter, and Holiday.

I had moved my business from 1461 Grant Avenue to a loft on Mission Street, bending to pressure from the retail stores to which I sold my lines. The retail store managers didn't like the fact that I was engaged in what they called "cross-trading"— that is, selling both retail and wholesale at the same time. However, the retail trade provided a place to sell my samples and also a way to get rid of excess inventory. It took only three years after the move to go broke.

I was forty-three years old; I had a three-year-old son and a husband who was a pathologist and a compulsive drinker. Sometimes I felt I was multi-phrenic, not just schizophrenic. I got into the habit of having a martini as soon as I got home, and I found myself looking forward to that drink as I drove across the bridge to Berkeley. I could hardly wait to get home and taste that lovely dry martini. I didn't realize that anticipating the pleasure of the drink was the signal of the beginning of an addiction.

When does a habit become an addiction? I think it happens when the impulse to satisfy the habit becomes overwhelming; when the thought and the urge to perform whatever action the habit requires become irresistible. In that sense, my husband was addicted to both smoking and drinking. When I found myself looking forward to that first martini, I became frightened. A habit can quickly and easily become an addiction.

We have been told that some substances are more addictive than others. Tobacco, for instance, is a powerful addictive substance, and one of the most difficult to overcome; more difficult, apparently, than heroin or cocaine. For some people, alcohol, in any form, is also highly addictive. Perhaps addiction is connected to the comfort we feel when we create a regular routine, a habit we don't have to think about, like brushing our teeth before going to bed. Our lives are so full of the need to make choices about everything that a habit or routine is an easy pattern to fall into. The danger comes when a habit becomes an addiction.

It was hard to break that habit of a martini on arriving home. When I found myself mixing a second or third martini while I was making dinner, I decided I had to stop. I remembered that I had broken a smoking habit when I was twenty. I had started smoking when I was eighteen, and by the time I was twenty, I was smoking three packs a day and had a beautiful collection of cigarette holders. I would light a cigarette, place it in one of my elegant holders, and puff away as I typed papers for my various university classes. I developed stomach problems, however, and my doctor told me to stop smoking. I came home, threw out all the cigarettes and gave away the holders. If I was able to do that, I thought, I could give up martinis. And I did.

Seeking pleasure can also be addictive. Compulsive gamblers get a great deal of pleasure, even a thrill, from the danger and uncertainty connected with the turn of a wheel or the flip of a card. Women or men who are promiscuous lovers don't want a settled existence; they like the thrill of the chase, and the sense of control they have by seeming to choose between various attractive partners. They may feel choked or stifled by a committed relationship.

Habits and routine are soothing. I grew up with a pervading sense of obligation — obligation to finish any job I undertook, whether it was a book I started to read or a promise to clean my room. I developed a strong sense of guilt if I left a bed unmade or dishes in the sink after a party. Was that sense of obligation a habit or an addiction? I think it was a habit, because completing those chores did not provide pleasure or reassurance. The completion of those chores was just a nod to the guilt riding on my shoulders.

Why do I find addiction so repulsive? I think it's because there is an implied loss of control over one's emotions and actions through the pursuit of pleasure in spite of signals to the contrary.

During the years I lived with Jim Pack, Ric Skahen, and Bob Holdeman, we all drank and smoked. It was part of the culture we lived in. Except for Ric, I didn't regard drinking as an addiction, but just as a habit. It's only now, in the year 2010 that I realize what an addictive society we live in.

127

ON PERCEPTION OF IMPENDING DEATH

The year was 2000; I was eighty-two, and I had had a quadruple coronary bypass operation in 1997. Peter, the love of my life, died in 1998. I didn't realize that events like these could trigger such an intense physical and emotional reaction. After all, I had recovered well from the operation, and no one had told me that removing a vein from my left leg to use that tissue to repair the damaged arteries would cause continuing problems. Also, by the time Peter died, he had had two minor strokes and we were as prepared as one can be for an impending death. So I thought I would be all right, but I wasn't.

My body fell apart. I had no blood pressure in my left leg, very little energy, and I had the distinct feeling that I would die that year. One morning, as I deliberated whether or not to get up, I decided that I needed to write my obituary and to design the final party, even though I would not be there to enjoy it. That was enough incentive to get up and get dressed. After writing the obituary, I addressed a letter to my gardener, Jane, with instructions as to how to plan the final party. Jane and I had discussed the idea the year before, in a rather offhand manner, but I had asked Jane if she would be in charge of the party, and she said yes.

When Jane came to work in the garden, on her usual day, I read her the letter, saying that I wanted the party to be in the garden, with music and good food and wine, with singing and joy. I also told her that I wanted my ashes planted beneath my favorite rhododendron bush.

"You can't do that!" Jane exclaimed in horror.

"Why not?" I demanded.

"You'll kill the bush, that's why not! Human ashes are too acidic!"

I thought for a moment. "All right," I said. "Then you'll have to provide mulch and little buckets and spades for people; mix the ashes in with the mulch and just spread it around the garden. Will that work?"

"Yes," she said. "That will work. Then your ashes will be all over the garden."

"Ah," I said. "What a lovely idea! My spirit will always be in this garden."

Writing the letter to Jane, and planning the final party was a liberating experience. I decided to take a Qi Gong class with Vicki Dello Joio, who has a Qi Gong program called "The Way of Joy." Qi Gong is the ancient Chinese art of healing through movement. Working with Vicki helped restore both my physical and mental health. Within the year, I had created a new channel for the blood to flow in my left leg; the pressure was normal, and I knew death for me was no longer imminent.

Spurred by newly found strength, I went to a writing retreat created by Judith Barrington and her partner, Ruth Gundle, in Oregon. It was called "The Flight of the Mind" and there I learned that I could call myself a writer. Following that retreat, I joined a writing group directed by Monza Naff, and began to write my memoir, *Rhoda: Her First Ninety Years.* I finished it in 2007. I thought it would take at least a year to get it published, and that's why I chose that title. When I acquired enough rejects from publishers to cover a wall in my apartment, I published it with an on-demand company called Book Surge, now renamed Create Space.

I have been thinking about my decision to have that final party. Now, at ninety-two, I realize how satisfying that impulse was: to leave my ashes in my garden to fertilize it. Leaving a lasting impression on the earth fits with my belief that immortality depends on the actions an individual performs while alive. There is no afterlife. I have the firm belief that if I or anyone wanted to be immortal, and to be remembered with respect, we had better act in a positive manner when we are alive. Whatever impact we leave upon the earth, whether it's on a stone, on land or sea, on people, on institutions, on architecture, academia, whatever — to the extent that that impact lasts beyond the death — that's how we achieve immortality.

According to Jewish ritual, if someone, anyone, says your name at least once a year, as long as your name is spoken, you will be immortal. This ritual is called "Yahrzheit." It involves lighting a votive candle on the anniversary of the death of the deceased person, reciting a prayer and speaking the name of the person remembered.

Death does not frighten me, and I think I can manage the ordeal of dying without panic. Death is part of life, and dying is part of that process. We have no control over how long that process might take, so there is no point in trying to anticipate it. I am going to continue writing and living well for as long as possible; the process will take care of itself.

COMMUNISM, EDUCATION, AND THE CREATIVE PROCESS

My sister Jeanne and her husband, Arthur Quadow, returned to Chicago from Palestine in 1936, and I had a long talk with Arthur. I was awed by Arthur, who had persuaded my sister to take off for Palestine in 1932 to raise tomatoes on a kibbutz. When they returned, having failed in their endeavor, I cornered Arthur and asked him about the possibility of a Communist revolution in the United States. Arthur was a lawyer, with a Ph.D. in Economics from the University of Chicago. I was a freshman at Northwestern University at the time, and also the secretary of the League Against War and Fascism, which later was labeled a suspect organization by the McCarthy Investigation. I respected Arthur's mind and the clarity of his opinions.

In answer to my question, "Will the U.S. go Communist?" Arthur said, "No, the middle class is too strong in America. And, Rhoda, what you have to understand is that the tyranny of the middle class against their servants, including the black people of America, has never been the same kind of oppression that the serfs suffered under the Tsar of Russia."

I pressed Arthur, because I had had a professor of American history in high school who had pushed us to study the extent of African subjugation in the practice of slavery in the United States, and I was troubled by the difference between what I read in my history books and what I was reading on my own.

"Yes, you're right, Rhoda," said Arthur. "There is a history of brutality in our country; the treatment of slaves under the pretense of protection; the employment of workers with below-subsistence wages; the exploitation of the poor by the rich, but there is something else in the way this country works that I think would prevent the takeover of a totalitarian form of government — which, of course, Communism is. There is a special element in the collective psychology of this country which I don't think exists in many other places in the world."

Then Arthur launched into a long lecture about the lasting image of a frontier, available to persons willing to take a chance, to launch themselves into an unknown territory, fraught with dangers one could not even imagine. One thing he said that stuck in my memory: "There is no history in this country of unquestioning obedience to a higher power, never mind to a hierarchical status of society. The pilgrims fled a rigid Calvinist society that punished anyone who tried to live outside of those boundaries; by the 1900s the pattern of social life in the United States was determined by an atmosphere of freedom of thought as well as of action. Don't forget that."

"Oh," I said, "well then, what part does education play in this equation?"

Arthur responded, "A rigid, top-down, repressive educational system will help to produce an obedient citizenry, ready to follow orders. But, beginning in the 1900s, the educational system became based more on respect for individual expression. When you have teachers emphasizing the importance of individual thought and free expression of opinions, you produce students who are willing to question the status quo. That kind of educational system helps to provide a buffer for totalitarian thinking and practice."

"Ah," I said, remembering the reading I was doing for one of my classes, "when Dewey emerged as the new important guru in helping to determine how an educational system was going to be set up for the entire country, that signaled a change and teacher-training courses began to use Piaget's ideas about allowing children to exercise their creativity"— I was stuttering in my attempt to catch up with his ideas. I felt like I was in the middle of a whirlwind.

"I think you've brought up an important idea," Arthur said. "Humans, as well as other animals, are hard-wired for creativity, but only the human animal engages a process that creates a product."

I have never forgotten that conversation with Arthur, and it tied in with my thoughts about the nature of the creative process.

The creative process is so basic to all human endeavors that we have lost respect for its importance. We take it for granted; the way we take our sense of smell and taste, but it is just as basic. We are hard-wired for this process.

In terms of language acquisition, Noam Chomsky pointed out, in his first article in 1965, humans are hard-wired with a Language Acquisition Device, an "innate facility" for acquiring language. There are neurons and pathways in the brain that make this possible. Jerome Bruner, a cognitive scientist, and Jean Piaget, a cognitive psychologist, emphasize the importance of interaction between biological and social aspects of language acquisition. This means that human learning occurs with the interaction of both inherited traits (nature) and environmental influence (nurture). Caleb Gattegno, a mathematician and author of the theory called "The Silent Way," postulated that the process of language learning involves trying, testing, reflecting, trying again, until the desired result is achieved.

When teachers persist in using B.F. Skinner's theory of behavioral psychology, which involves imitation and repetition by rote in order to acquire results that can be measured and tested, the students don't use the creative ability with which they are born. When students are not encouraged to use their innate creative ability, they learn to become submissive, and to accept directions without question. While this may be a useful training device for preparing soldiers for war, it is not useful for preparing students for innovative, responsible, creative solutions to economic and political problems.

I believe that the creative process encompasses the common human impulse to explore, test, evaluate, and test again. I have observed children learning to walk, to use a pencil, pen, or drawing tool which reveals this process.

The child stands, tests out stability, takes a few tentative steps, sits down, stands up again, evaluates what happened, and tries again. This formula of try, test, evaluate, try again can be applied to other forms of human endeavor. A good cook puts ingredients together in a pot or bowl, adds some known (or unknown) spices, tastes the combination and either throws it out and starts over, or continues, depending on how it tastes. The part of this process that is most interesting to me is the evaluation.

The assessment determines the direction the creative process will take. That pause to reflect and evaluate is the crucial aspect. The child, the cook, the artist, all pause to assess the results of the previous action.

All learning processes are creative. The artist, creating a painting or sculpture or piece of ceramics, starts with an idea or a goal. Even random splashes of paint on a canvas, or the swath of black left by a sumi ink brush or a line of charcoal is the beginning of something. A child using finger paints will slap some paint on the paper, smush it around, and then experiment with it, looking at it quizzically and either leave it alone or mess around with it some more. That's a creative process.

The writer pens a line of poetry or puts a sentence on a piece of paper, looks at it, perhaps reads it aloud, makes a decision to leave it or erase it, and then continues exploring the idea that inspired the poetry or the prose.

We are continually evaluating and reevaluating our actions, our writing, our painting, our ideas and beliefs. It is the process of evaluation and decision that informs the way we live. We are all creative people, hard-wired for the process. Totalitarian and fundamentalist ways of thinking, learning, and living emphasize obedience to a higher power, reliance upon a hierarchical social structure, and deny the innate nature of the creative process.

Selected Stories

THE PITCH or WHO'S PITCHING WHOM?

His name was John. He drives the streets of San Francisco, Berkeley, Oakland, on the lookout for cars with dented fenders or scratched sides, and offers to fix the dents and scratches on the spot. As I was pulling up in front of my house in North Berkeley, on a clear afternoon in May, he pulled up alongside me and made his pitch.

"I can fix those dents and scratches for you right now," he said. "I have the tools in my car. I'll give you a good deal."

"No, thanks. My driveway is so narrow; I'll just scratch it up again. Look, I've even hung a red ball in the middle of the driveway to steer by when I back in. I've put silver duct tape on the right side of the driveway, and I still smash into the sides. Never mind."

"Look," he said, "I'll give you a real good deal," and went on with a long, involved story. I stopped listening and just looked at his scuffed shoes, his anxious eyes. He was clean-shaven, his narrow, brown face decorated with a small, carefully-trimmed mustache. I guessed him to be in his late forties or early fifties. His line was familiar, and I was amused by how rapidly his price dropped as I continued to shake my head. I reached into my battered car to get my groceries, which included a loaf of fresh French bread.

"That bread looks good," he said.

"Here, break off a hunk." I was hooked (if he was that hungry). As he munched on the bread, he kept reducing the price, and finally I succumbed.

"Okay. Do it," I said, and started to walk down the driveway to my apartment.

"Do you have any peanut butter or jam?" he asked.

"No peanut butter, but jam," I replied. "I'll be right back." I walked down the driveway, went into my small kitchen, cut off another big hunk of bread, spread it with my special health-food store margarine, homemade strawberry jam, took out an apple, and brought it up to him.

"I can't eat the apple," he said. "Poor teeth," he gestured toward his mouth, "but thanks for the bread."

I stood and watched him work for a bit, and then went inside. When I thought he would be finished, I went outside again, and once again he tried to talk me into more work on the car. I had already gone over the budget I had set for myself, and realized I was going to have to buy some touch-up paint anyway, since all he had done was to pull out the dents and work over the scratches with some regular scratch-remover stuff. Then I asked if I could write him a check.

"No, it has to be cash. It takes too long if I have to take it to my bank, and cash it, and..."

I cut him off. I didn't want to hear whatever made-up story would follow.

"All right. You'll have to follow me to Andronico's where there is an ATM."

"I can drive you there," he said. "Then I'll bring you back here."

Whoa! That would be pretty stupid, wouldn't it? "We could go in my car, and I could bring you back here. But what would be the point of that? Just follow me to Andronico's."

"Where's that?" He seemed stunned, and didn't seem to be able to understand my directions. I could hear the wheels clicking in his head. Finally he got it, and said he would follow me.

Before I got into my car, I asked him where he lived and if he had a business card. His eyes fluttered around, and evasively he said, "I'm living with a friend." I pressed him. "In Berkeley, or Oakland?"

137

"San Francisco." Then he said, "I don't write so good."

All my senses went on the alert. "You don't read either, do you?"

He shook his head, his eyes on the ground.

"Okay." I said. "I'll see you in the Andronico's parking lot, and we'll talk there."

As I drove, I kept looking in the rear-view mirror to see if he was following me, and when he peeled off to follow a different route, I knew he knew where he was going. When I got to the parking lot, he was already there. I went into the ATM, and came out with the exact amount he had asked for.

"Do you really want to be able to read and write?" I asked.

"Yeah, I'm ashamed. I can't even read a menu in a restaurant."

"I suppose you eat mostly in cafeterias, where you can just point to stuff."

"Yeah. How'd you know?"

No need to tell him that I had had years of teaching newly arrived immigrants how to speak, read, and write English. Neither did I have to tell him that years of teaching illiterate adults born in the U.S. to read and write had given me a diagnostic ability I wished I didn't have. A wave of sadness swept over me.

"I didn't. I just guessed. How far did you get in school?"

"Fifth grade. Then I left. Shined shoes. Didn't do no drugs though." He flashed a glance at me to see how I took that information. I kept my face still.

"Do you live in the Mission District?"

"Yeah." He looked at me oddly. "How'd you know?"

I shrugged. "You can go to the Mission Adult School in San Francisco and learn to read and write. It's free."

"Nah. They throw you out if you're late, or if you don't come to class. It's too hard. I have a couple of kids, they're growed now."

"How about your wife?"

He shook his head. "We was together; she got pregnant. Then she split."

Well! That was a condensed story of a life. "She stayed with you for quite a while, didn't she? She must have thought you were worth it. What happened? Did she get disgusted and leave after your kids grew up?"

"Yeah. That's what happened. You got nice hair, you know?"

"Yes, I know. Look, I can give you the names of some teachers at Mission Adult School who will pay special attention to you, but I'm not going to do it, unless you promise to check it out on your own. I won't give you my card, because you can't read it. You can still learn to read and write, and most of the students in that school feel just the same as you do. You can go to a few classes and drop out if you don't like it. It's open enrollment and open exit." Oops. I realized that the words "open enrollment" and "open exit" didn't mean anything to him. "You can just go and sit in on a class. If you like it, you can sign up. And you can leave any time you want to. No one will scold you."

He looked at me. "I wish you could be my teacher. I'm gonna get some business cards."

"I'm not the teacher you need. And if you do get some business cards, drop one off at my house. You know where I live. Just write three words on the back of the card, 'I did it.' Then I'll know that you did what you need to do, and I'll help you move on."

He nodded, but his head drooped. I reminded myself again that shame and longing are not enough to change a perceived sense of failure. Someone he trusted had taught him his sales pitch and his meager skills. Why did it matter to me? Was his pitch a well-rehearsed scam? Ah, well, if it was, I couldn't help falling for it. He was obviously getting by. Was I right? Was he really disappointed in himself? He knew how to hide his disability; he knew the ingenious ways an illiterate person gets by. I sighed, waved goodbye, and wrote down the license number of his van as he pulled away. His pitch was successful. He got his money. Was mine? I didn't think I would ever find out.

"FINDHORN," SCOTLAND, 1984

The film, *My Dinner With Andre,* made such an impression on me that I decided to go to Findhorn, located near Inverness, Scotland, to discover the huge cabbages and other delights Louis Malle talked about. In addition to cabbages, Malle had also talked about connecting with creatures from outer space, and dancing naked in the woods. He emphasized the other-worldliness of the experience. I liked the idea of dancing naked in the Scottish woods and decided to go. At sixty-six, I was ready for a new adventure. The brochure from Findhorn advertised workshop sessions of one- or two-week periods, and I opted for one week.

From London I traveled by train through the placid English, then Scottish countryside. Soothed by the rocking motion of the train and the steady click-clack of the wheels, I looked at the sheep, horses, and cows in the landscape sliding slowly by. Calmness enveloped me as I leaned back in the cushioned plush of my seat. I sank into reverie, dreaming of huge cabbages and romantic visions of the Scottish woods.

Arriving at Inverness at ten a.m. on a Sunday, the station was fastidiously clean and neat, with hanging baskets of flowers scattered throughout the waiting room. The bus to Findhorn was waiting outside the station, and I climbed in, along with several other participants. We eyed each other warily. "First time here?" "Yes. You?" "Yes." "Where are you from?" Confident answers tumbled out, each followed by smiling nods of acceptance. "Australia." "Canada." "Austria." "London." "New Zealand." "New York... and you?" "California." "Oh." Why such a silent staring? Immediately feeling like an outsider, or at the very least, an oddball, I stared back.

The bus wound slowly through the verdant countryside, brushing against trees bowing over the narrow road. We turned in at ornate gates and lumbered up to a rambling white nineteenth-century house, complete with porches, balconies, and outbuildings. There were a few people scattered about on the lawns — reading, talking, or leaning on a fence that separated the Findhorn property from a large, sprawling golf course.

Inside the house, cheerful staff armed with clipboards greeted us in the wood-paneled foyer. They handed us maps, room assignments, and other material. Each bedroom accommodated four people: bath, shower, and toilets down the hall. We walked through a complicated maze-like interior, found our rooms, looked at our programs, and saw that supper would be served in the dining room within an hour. There would be a bell. In our papers we found descriptions of the grounds and a statement of philosophy. No alcohol, no smoking in the building itself, lights out at ten thirty p.m., vegetarian food. An official welcome would follow supper, after which we would choose the program we wanted to follow. It all began to seem much more regimented than I had expected, but I was willing to go with the flow.

One of the three women assigned to my room was Anne, closer to my age than the other two, who were in their early twenties. I chose a bed next to one of the two windows; Anne chose the bed opposite me. I looked out the window, over the sloping slate roof at the golfers in their tartan-checked baggy pants and spiked golf shoes. They were plodding around, carrying their bags, deeply intent on their game. The midsummer amber light cast a warm glow over the deep green of the grass. Anne and I looked at each other, spontaneously holding out our hands.

"I'm from Victoria, Canada," Anne said. "I teach at a community college."

"I'm from Berkeley, California," I said. "I teach adults at the Berkeley Adult School how to survive in the English language." We established an immediate connection.

After supper we gathered around the fire, and went through a ceremony of welcome. The leader this evening, a tall, bulky woman in hand-woven tweeds addressed us solemnly. "Our ethic is liberation through group effort through work," she intoned. "We ask you to choose an area in which to work. According to the stated philosophy of the Findhorn Foundation, 'While we have no formal doctrine or creed, we honor and recognize all the major world religions, believing that there are many paths to God. Our focus is on learning to bring spiritual principles into our daily lives through our work, the way we relate to each other, and how we express our caring and concern for the Earth.'"

I knew I could live with that credo. A dedicated environmentalist, I also believed that work was vital for well-being. I liked the idea of working in a group, and decided to put aside the god business for the time being; I had found that when most people referred to God, they were talking about a Christian god. I didn't think it was an appropriate time to identify myself as a Jew. Having lived most of my life as a closet Jew in order to get and hold various jobs, I didn't think it an appropriate time to do any challenging.

As I walked into my evening classroom, I saw Anne and Jane, one of my other roommates, nodded to them, and chose a seat near Anne. The facilitator was a smiley man with a reddish beard from Edinburgh named Doug. He began by telling us that one of the important things we would learn was how to communicate with plants. He said that their welfare depended on how we talked to them.

I noticed a very droopy plant in the corner of the room and remarked that evidently no one had talked to it recently. Anne walked over and dug her fingers into the pot. "It's dry," she said. "It needs water." She went over to a water fountain, filled a paper cup, and poured the water into the plant.

No one spoke for a minute, and then Doug resumed his discourse about kinetic forces in the world around us. He beamed at us. "Do you know how Findhorn got started?" He didn't wait for a response. "It all began with a group of free spirits who camped out in a 'caravan park' on the sandy beach near the village of Findhorn. They were Eileen and

Peter Caddy, and Dorothy Maclean. They planted a garden, and the most enormous cabbages came up — to five feet across; firm and delicious. Other vegetables were equally astonishing. Representatives of British gardening groups came; examined the soil and the nutrients the campers used — mainly seaweed — and decided that some other spiritual factor must be working because just the seaweed and the nutrients in the soil wouldn't be enough to account for the phenomenal vegetables grown here. Support groups formed, and soon they had an organization with enough money to buy the clubhouse and a small part of land from the golf club association that owned it originally." He sat back and folded his hands over his stomach.

"Findhorn is organized on a democratic basis; please feel free to express yourselves on any subject. I ask you to search inwardly for questions to which you are seeking answers. Bring those questions to our group meeting tomorrow evening." Before I could ask him how big the cabbages grew these days, he reached out and grasped the hands of people sitting on either side of him; we all joined hands, some of us bowed our heads. Then we stood, said goodnight, and went off to our rooms.

The night was cool, and fog shrouded the golf course. As I climbed into bed that Sunday night, I told myself, "Relax, Rhoda, maybe you'll get to dance naked in the woods after all." But I doubted it.

Monday morning, the beginning of the work week at Findhorn, we gathered in the space outside the kitchen. There were ten of us in my garden group. Anne had settled for "repairs on outbuildings." We held hands and bowed our heads while the leader of our group, Joseph, tall, rangy, about thirty-five, intoned what sounded like a prayer. "Favor us, gods of the earth, for we seek to promote growth through pruning and weeding, planting and tilling. Give us the power to know how best to assist you." We squeezed the hand on our left after we received a squeeze on the right hand and then let go.

"We're going to weed the areas around the caravans," Joseph said. He looked at me. "A caravan is what you would call a 'mobile home' in America, I believe." I nodded. "We maintain these caravans for people who want to rent them during the summer months. People come from all over Europe, Asia and America too, to spend their vacations with us, and they rent the caravans. Sort of like a summer cottage, you might say." He handed out spades and trowels. "I presume you know the difference between a weed and a flower? If you are in any doubt whatsoever, please call me immediately. I'll be roaming around." He looked at us a bit anxiously, emphasizing the "whatsoever." We nodded obediently and trotted off to our designated caravans.

As I kneeled on the damp ground, I thought of my own garden in Berkeley, and hoped that someone was weeding it as I was weeding this one. The hours passed in a dreamy, repetitive way, and soon it was time for lunch.

"The space around the caravans seems rather bare. Will we be planting flowers later after the weeding is finished?" I asked Joseph as I gave him my trowel.

"I'm not sure. I'll have to check with the planning committee. Presumably they have a plan for the kind of flowers and range of color and so on." He seemed to be unwilling to go beyond his specific instructions for this particular day. We all joined hands again and this time Joseph said, "Thank you for a job well done." I felt like my grammar school teacher had just patted me on the head, yet I was reassured by the hand squeezes.

Upstairs, washing up, I asked Anne how her morning went.

"Oh, it was all right. I was rehanging doors. I had to take down doors that had warped after the spring rains, sand off the top according to instructions and then put them back. It was kind of fun. I have to do this sort of maintenance on my own place at home, so it's good practice. How did your gardening go?"

"All right. We were weeding the dirt around the caravans. Pretty boring. Actually, I hate weeding, and do as little as possible at home." I laughed. "Felt a bit like I was back in grade school, for some reason."

Anne gave me a sharp look. "That's interesting. I had the same feeling. Do you suppose that they get people who never get their fingernails dirty, or people who have never held a hammer?"

"That's it! They're not sure of us yet. Wonder what the afternoon program will be. Let's hope lunch is better than dinner was."

Anne was skeptical. "I wouldn't get my hopes up. After lunch, they'll announce options for afternoon activities following the rest period. Let's go."

I was glad to have a buddy with a similar "show me" attitude, and felt less guilty about my sense of holding back. As Anne predicted, lunch was a salad consisting of salad greens, a pink salad dressing, leftover boiled vegetables, sliced tofu imitation turkey, homemade doughy bread, and herb tea. After lunch, the activities offered were: meditation in the chapel (from one to two) and an excursion to Inverness Bay with the possibility of a swim, including a trip to a bamboo forest.

Upstairs in our room, Anne and I discussed the possibilities. "I have an unwelcome running bamboo forest in my back garden," I said. "I'm not interested in bamboo, except as a way of discouraging it from taking over! But a chance to swim in the North Sea sounds intriguing. Does the notice say not to bring a swimming suit?"

"Hmmm." Anne was taking a close look at the typewritten description of afternoon choices. "It doesn't say yes and it doesn't say no. I would say put your suit on under your overalls and take a towel. Then you'll be ready for anything. I would vote for Inverness Bay."

Anne was rising in my estimation every minute. "What a great idea! Are you up for swimming?"

"Are you joking? Not in that water! Do you know how cold it is?"

"No." I thought back to Lake Michigan. "Colder than 50 degrees? That's what Lake Michigan is, and I swam there most of my growing up time."

"I don't know the exact temperature." Anne was thoughtful. "But somehow I think the North Sea might be different from a freshwater lake."

"Oh, well. I like the idea. I'll put my bathing suit on under my overalls, as you suggest — it's a comfortable suit, and if I swim, okay, and if I don't, that's okay, too."

We relaxed on our beds until a bell rang at one fifty-five, then we got up and went downstairs to the lobby for our trip to Inverness Bay. We recognized the seventy-year-old couple from New Zealand, the Austrian transcendentalist, the German pacifist, the Swiss vegetarian. We didn't recognize the others. There was a tour guide on the bus who gave us more information about the area than we could possibly be interested in, but I told myself it was part of his job, and just let his voice wash over me. It was easy, because I was entranced by the lush Scottish countryside.

There was a dense bamboo forest on the edge of the sand leading down to the water, and we were encouraged to hug the trunks. As I did so, I voiced my own private prayer, like an injunction: "I love you where you are. Please stay here and don't feel inclined to send your seed across the water to Berkeley. Thank you."

We made our way to the sand and sat down, looking at the water across Inverness Bay. The sun was hot; it was midsummer in northern Scotland, and I felt the sun's proximity on my back and shoulders. I had brought a wide-brimmed cotton gardening hat, and I was grateful for its protection. Our guide told us about the formation of Inverness Bay.

"Movement of tectonic plates created this bay in. . ." I lost him at this point and fell into my own reverie, absorbing the beauty of the sharp blue unclouded sky and the smell of the seaweed-loaded salt water. Suddenly I got up, unhooked the straps of my overalls, stepped out of them and strode down to the water. Our guide gasped, "What are you doing?"

"I'm going for a swim. Okay?" I pulled on my swim cap and buckled the chin strap, snapping it into place. Plunging into the icy water, I struck out in a practiced overhand stroke, but suddenly lost momentum. My arms and legs lost feeling, and felt detached from my body. Floating, I realized I was losing conscious awareness, and something in my mind said, "Rhoda! Hypothermia! Go back!" I forced myself to swim side-stroke, an easy, comfortable stroke, and got close to shore. Struggling upright, I stumbled onto the sand, where helping hands enfolded me in my towel, and bundled me into the van. Then, as sensation slowly returned, I realized how cold I was and began to shake. The guide muttered, "Didn't she know the temperature of Inverness Bay never gets higher than 37 degrees Fahrenheit? Wasn't she listening?" Anne was rubbing my hands, someone else was rubbing my feet, the van was lurching from side to side in a hurried effort to get back to headquarters; I was in a state of semi-consciousness, none of it unpleasant.

Back at Findhorn, I overheard dimly a hurried, anxious discussion as to what should be done with me. At the word "hospital," I immediately sat upright. "Forget it! I'm fine! I just need a warm bath and rest in a warm bed and I'll be all right! After all, it was MY decision to swim!" With that pronouncement, I fell back into Anne's arms and whispered, "Get me out of here!"

I must have drifted off, because the next thing I remembered was being submerged in warm water, with Anne sitting on a stool beside the tub saying, "Well, now you know what swimming in the North Sea is like, eh?"

The rest of the week was unremarkable. We did plant flowers around the caravans, but the food didn't get any better. We were given one day off to go into Inverness for shopping or whatever. Anne and I joined the elderly couple from Australia, who said the first thing they were going to do was go to a pub and order shepherd's pie. They were starved for meat.

Anne and I went to a liquor store and bought some gin, limes, and tasty crackers. We decided we would have a cocktail before dinner, sitting on the sloping roof tiles, enjoying the sunset. We knew we were breaking the rules, but what would they do? Throw us out? Return our money? We felt it was worth the chance, and it would help soothe our palates.

The evening programs were fine; an Australian played the didgeridoo, someone else played the guitar, and there was a bit of group folk singing. One evening, we talked about thought transference, and I made a deal with the transcendalist from Austria. We chose a date and a time that would fit our different time zones, and agreed that we would send thought waves to each other and have a small conversation. Then we would write to each other, and see if we managed to communicate without written or verbal language. (We didn't.) Two visitors from Switzerland lectured us about super-terrestrial forces, but we never did dance naked in the woods.

My Dinner with Andre didn't really prepare me for Findhorn; there was nothing in my background that I could connect with that story. I went with an open heart and mind, really not knowing what the ten days would teach me, but I wanted to learn and/or experience something new and different.

Ade and Rhoda, 1989

■ STORIES FOR CHILDREN

— A Story for Ade —

Ade, my granddaughter, age three and a half, is sleeping in a small hammock, suspended between two poles in the family living room. She is taking her afternoon nap, and I push the hammock gently with my foot. The small apartment is overflowing with a Boston fern, begonias, a rubber plant, and ivy. Hanging from the corners of the room, they crowd in upon me as I watch Ade, sleeping peacefully on her side.

I pick up a small golden apple on the coffee table. It's gilded, heavy, a paperweight on a pile of papers her mother will correct when she returns from the class she is teaching at the local university.

I weigh the golden apple in my hand, thinking about the story of the three goddesses and the golden apple, often called the "Apple of Discord." I turn the apple over and over, letting my mind play with the sentences as they slowly form themselves. I struggle to remember the story. Ah, yes, one of them was the goddess of wisdom, Athena, one the goddess of beauty and love, Aphrodite, and one the goddess of the hunt, Hera, and I decide to tell Ade that story.

After Ade wakes up and she is cuddled on my lap, I begin the story.

"Once upon a time there were three little girls dancing around in a circle on a beautiful grassy hill." Ade fixes her black eyes upon me. "Where's the mommy?" she demands.

"She's at home, cooking dinner," I reply.

"Okay."

I put her down on the floor, take her hands and we start to dance. She stops.

"You said there were three."

"Oh, yes, well, let's pretend your doll is the third little girl." I pick up her brown rag doll and we each take one of the doll's hands. We continue to dance around the living room. I stop.

"All of a sudden a boy appears with a golden apple." I continue with the story. Picking up the gilded apple from the table, I throw it on the floor. "The apple rolls between the three little girls and they stop dancing. The boy says, 'This is a magic apple. Who wants it?' The girls look at each other and one of them says, 'What's magical about it?'"

I look at Ade. "I have to tell you about these little girls," I say. "They are very special, and they all have special talents. In fact, they are little goddesses. One of them is very smart. Her name is Athena; she is a goddess of wisdom. Another is very beautiful. Her name is Aphrodite; she is a goddess of beauty and love. The third girl is very athletic; she likes to shoot arrows; her name is Hera. Athena, the goddess of wisdom, is the one who asked what was so magical about the apple. The boy who threw the golden apple into the middle of their circle, spoiling their game, is named Paris, and he's mean."

"Why is he mean?" Ade wants to know.

"Well, there was a big wedding between the king of the gods and his new wife, but Paris was not invited. He was mad at Athena, Aphrodite, and Hera, because they *had* been invited, and he wanted to punish them."

"Tell more!" We are back on the couch and Ade is snuggled close against me.

"Paris pretended not to hear Athena's question and asked Aphrodite and Hera. 'Don't you want to be magical?' Hera said, 'If I have the golden apple, will I hit my target every time I aim at it?' Paris nodded his head. Aphrodite asked, 'If I have the golden apple, will everyone love me?' Paris said, 'Of course, Aphrodite! Of course, Hera! The apple will give you great power!' Athena looked at Paris and said, 'How can you prove that the apple will give them power? And what good will the apple do me? I have the power of my mind!'

"Paris knew that Athena was smart, and that he would have to be very clever to trick her into joining the plan. He said, 'If you have the golden apple, you will be able to see inside everyone else's mind, and then you will be the most powerful person of all! Now do you want to have a competition to see who is the best one to have the apple?'

"The little goddesses began to quarrel among themselves to prove to each other that each one deserved to have the apple more than the others. Paris smiled and slipped away, because he had done what he came to do. He had spoiled their game; he had made them into competitors and arguers, and he knew the argument would go on forever. No one can prove that being a better shooter of arrows is any better than being loved by everyone, nor that being loved by everyone is any better than being able to read someone else's mind."

"Is that the end of the story?" Ade looked dissatisfied. "Who *did* get the apple?"

"No one," I said. "That's why it was called 'The Apple of Discord,' meaning, 'The Apple of Disagreement.' Who do you think should have gotten the apple?"

"Oh, Aphrodite, of course. Being loved by everyone is the best of all."

— Seven at a Stroke —

Once upon a time, there lived a little tailor in a small town. All day long, he stitched and stitched. As he sat in his little house sewing and stitching, long stitches and short stitches, fine stitches and super-fine stitches, flies buzzed and buzzed around his head.

It was very hot in his town, and very hot in his little house, so he always left his door open. And the flies buzzed and hummed, hummed and buzzed. Those flies annoyed him, and he pleaded with them to go away. He chased them, but as fast as he chased them, they always came back.

One day, as he was sewing in front of his open door, he noticed seven flies in a small group right in front of him. He picked up a piece of heavy cloth and smashed them. WHACK! All in one stroke!

"Oh!" he shouted. "Seven at one stroke! Seven at a stroke! Seven at a stroke!" He was so pleased that he decided to make a special belt for himself. On this belt he stitched big letters: SEVEN AT A STROKE!

Now it happened many giants lived in the neighborhood of this town, and often they would come through the town, roaring and laughing. But there was one particularly mean and ugly giant, bigger than all the rest. Sometimes he would come down from the mountain, roaring and booming, demanding food and money and clothing. The townspeople were very afraid of him, more afraid of this big, ugly giant than of any of the others.

The little tailor, who had to make clothing for the giant, was afraid of him too, but he was also angry. He thought, "Why should we have to work for the giant all the time, when the giant never does anything for us?" But he couldn't figure out what to do, and the people of the town couldn't figure out what to do, either.

One day the tailor went out into the street, and walked down to the market, wearing his new belt. "Oh," said some of the people in the market. "Seven at a stroke! He must be very brave!" And the whispering grew and grew, and became a rumor. It became, "If he can kill seven giants at a stroke, maybe he can kill the super-giant too!" Nobody asked the little tailor what his belt meant, they just assumed that the "seven" stitched onto his belt meant "SEVEN (*GIANTS*)!" The people of the town gathered around the little tailor, praised him for his courage, invited him to their homes, and buzzed and hummed around him like anxious little flies.

Finally, the mayor, hearing all the rumors, came to see the little tailor. He brought with him ten of the important members of the town council. He said to the little tailor, "We have come to invite you to a special meeting at the town hall." Well! The little tailor was very surprised by this invitation, but he put on his new jacket and went with the mayor and the ten council members to the special meeting.

"Ahem!" said the mayor, in his best speaking voice, "We have a problem we wish to discuss with you. As you know, the Giant of the Mountain has been a terrible problem for many years. He demands food and money and clothing and free work on his house, and he shouts and hollers like thunder. We don't know what to do and we want you to help us."

"Oh, yes," said the little tailor. "I know all about the Giant of the Mountain. I have to sew clothes for him, and it takes a lot of cloth, and a lot of time. I often have to work day and night for him. Then I don't have time to do my other work. I don't like that giant either. What can I do to help you?"

"Well," said the mayor. "Since you have already killed seven giants at a stroke, we thought you could kill this one for us too."

"Seven . . .GIANTS? . . .Me?" stammered the little tailor. Then he looked down at his belt, and suddenly realized what the mayor and the town council members believed. "Oh, dear," he thought sadly. "Whatever can I do? If I tell them the seven means *flies*, they will laugh me out of town!" He swallowed hard and told the mayor and the council members that he would try his best to kill the giant for them, but he would have to think first the best way to do it. He said, "I will send you word when I am ready." He walked home very slowly.

On the way home, he thought and thought about the giant. He thought about the giant's feet. He remembered the soft leather shoes he had made for the giant, and the soft leather vest and the soft silk shirt and the soft velvet pants. He sighed and sighed.

Walking past the house of his friend, the "fix-it" man, he decided to stop in and talk to him. This man made things out of metal, and he fixed many different kinds of things. He sharpened knives and scissors and needles. Knocking on his friend's door, he thought to himself, "This man can help me."

After the door was opened, the little tailor went inside and closed the door tightly behind him. The little tailor and his friend, the fix-it man, closed all the windows, closed all the curtains, and worked quietly and carefully behind the curtains and the closed windows and the closed doors for several days.

At the end of three days, the little tailor came out of the fix-it man's house, went home and told his wife *(but no one else)* what he was going to do. Then he sent a messenger to the mayor to say that he was now ready to face the giant.

The mayor and people of the town were overjoyed. They immediately sent a messenger to the giant and told him that one of the people of their town — a little tailor — had killed Seven at a Stroke, and promised to do the same to him! The giant roared and hollered and stamped and bellowed. The ground shook, and the trees swayed, and the hills gave back the sound of the terrible noises the giant made. All the people hid in their houses. Then they heard the THUMP, THUMP, THUMP of the giant's great feet, and they looked out of their windows and peeked out of their doors to see what was happening.

They saw the giant come THUMPING, THUMPING, THUMPING down the mountainside to the little tailor's house, and they heard the thunder of his voice. "COME OUT! COME OUT! YOU MISERABLE LITTLE MAN! I DARE YOU TO COME OUT!"

The little tailor hopped out of his house, and stood in front of the giant, both hands behind his back. The giant reached down to grab him but the little tailor danced away. As many times as the giant reached for him, the little tailor danced away, leading the giant gradually to the open space in the middle of the town.

Standing directly in front of the giant, the little tailor tilted his head way back, looking up at him as if to say, "What do you want?" The giant lifted his foot as if to squash the little tailor. But the little tailor jumped aside and, quick as a flash, he brought out his right hand. What do you think he had in his hand? BIG, LONG, VERY, VERY SHARP PINS in a big pincushion! He quickly put the pincushion with its very sharp long pins right where the giant's foot came down.

"OW! OW! OW! OW! OW!" cried the giant, hopping on his one good foot. Quickly the little tailor brought his other hand out from behind his back. In it was another GREAT BIG PINCUSHION with more extra long, extra sharp PINS! Quickly he danced around the hopping giant, and carefully put the second pincushion where he thought the giant's other foot would come down. The giant came down hard on the second pincushion. "OWOOOOO! OWOOOOO!" cried the giant as he fell down.

The townspeople ran out of their houses, and surrounded the fallen giant. They brought many heavy ropes and quickly tied him up. Then they climbed onto his chest. The mayor walked up to the giant's chin, and his council members put up a ladder for him to stand on, so that he was even with the giant's eyes, and the giant could see him and hear him clearly.

"We have you now," said the mayor, "but we don't want to kill you."

"WHAT DO YOU WANT?" said the giant, in what was a small voice for him, but the mayor had to put his hands over his ears.

"You will have to speak more softly," he said. "Try to whisper. We want you to stop tormenting us. You can do many good things for us. You can help us plow our fields. You can help us build our homes. Then we can all live in peace."

"If I promise to do all those things," said the giant in a whisper, "will you take those needles out of my feet?"

"Yes," said the mayor, "but first you have to let us make a footprint with your blood."

"Yes, yes, yes," whispered the giant, "but be quick about it. My feet are killing me!"

So the little tailor cut off the giant's soft shoes with his special tailor's scissors, and took the needles out of the giant's feet. Then the mayor and ten of the council members took a huge piece of special paper and pushed it against the giant's feet. They climbed up on the giant's chest again and showed him the paper.

"Do you agree?" said the mayor.

"YES, YES, YES," said the giant. "Can you put some ointment on my feet?"

"Of course," said the little tailor, and he brought out the special oils his wife had made for him to heal his fingers whenever he stuck them with a pin or a needle. The giant gave a big, happy sigh; the townspeople untied the heavy ropes. The giant sat up and looked around. The townspeople ran away, because they were not sure the giant would keep his word.

The giant went down on his knees and touched his huge forehead to the ground three times and said, "I PROMISE NOT TO HURT YOU ANYMORE, AND I WILL TRY TO HELP YOU FROM NOW ON!"

■ STORIES ABOUT PETS

— The Case of the Stolen Duffel Bag —

On a hot Friday in late June, 2004, with a soft breeze stirring the new leaves on the locust trees, Melissa unlocked the door of the Harding's spacious apartment on Houston Street in Manhattan. Melissa Barton, twenty, and a senior in Drama at Columbia, was, as she advertised herself, a professional dog walker. She had come to New York from St. Louis on a partial scholarship, and had switched to Drama in her junior year. She walked dogs, typed term papers, and dreamed about acting. She was five feet five, with quizzical brown eyes, a pointy chin, and longish brown hair which kept falling over her face. She had a winsome, "trust me" look about her.

She loved Horace, one of her favorite charges, a big, hairy Briard who weighed almost as much as she did. As soon as she opened the door, Horace usually came bounding toward her, his body wagging all over. But this time there was no Horace. The apartment was ominously quiet. "Where's Horace? Things are too quiet," Melissa thought. She walked apprehensively through the empty rooms with their sheet-covered furniture into the kitchen, and there was Horace, her old, sweet compliant friend, spread-eagled on the Italian tile floor, very still.

Melissa tried to remember how to check on whether an animal or a person was alive. She touched his nose. It was hot. She tried to find his heart under his furry coat, and could find none. Ohhh nooo, it looked like Horace was really dead. She wet a paper towel, and wiped off the drool around his mouth. Squatting beside him, she stroked his silent head. Cindy and Dick Harding, her employers, had never paid much attention to Horace while he was alive. They treated him as if he were an aged relative. Cindy had inherited Horace after her mother moved to an assisted living facility on Long Island. Both Cindy and her husband were now both vacationing in the Hamptons.

Melissa picked up the phone and dialed their number with a shaking hand. "I'm so sorry," she began, "I think Horace is dead. I fed him after his walk yesterday and he seemed all right, but just now…" her voice trailed off. "I…I…I'm sure he's dead."

There was a pause on the other side of the line, and finally Cindy said, calmly, "That's all right. Horace was an old dog." And then, as an afterthought, "I'm just sorry we weren't there to say goodbye to him. I'm sure it wasn't your fault."

"He really seemed all right last night, but now…" Melissa caught her breath. "But what am I supposed to do with him? I can't just leave him here until you come back to New York."

"Oh, just call the vet," Cindy said blithely. "He'll tell you what to do. I think there's a place across town that takes care of dead dogs. Just do what the vet says. Don't worry, Melissa. You took good care of Horace. We'll be back in a couple of weeks, and we'll talk then. Take care. 'Bye."

Melissa looked at the silent phone in her hand, and dialed the vet, gazing mournfully down on the animal that had become her friend over the months she was his official walker. She brushed her hair back over her ears as she held the phone. When the vet came on the line, she identified herself and told him about Horace. Oh, yes, he knew Horace well, and gave her the address of the SPCA on the other side of Manhattan where she could take him.

Neither Cindy nor the vet had offered suggestions as to how Melissa was going to get the dog to the crematorium, much less get him out of the apartment, and she hadn't had a chance to ask. Both of them were so busy giving instructions, they didn't bother to ask Melissa if she had any questions. With no car, and not able to afford a taxi, Melissa realized she would have to take the subway. She sighed. Horace just lay there, a big, heavy lump. "How am I going to get him out of here?" She looked thoughtfully around the room, and her eyes lit on a duffel bag slouched lazily in a corner of the kitchen. Taking a towel from the rack, and dipping it into some hot water, she delicately wiped Horace's eyes and mouth again, and lifted his front paws. Could she stuff him into the bag?

She had a vague memory, summoned from a Biology class taken in her freshman year, that animals and humans got stiff after death, but Horace was still flexible. She drew herself up. This was a dramatic moment, she told herself. No matter what it took, she would take care of Horace as best she could.

Melissa brought the duffel bag close to the dog, and began to stuff him into it. Pushing, pulling, and tugging the limp lump that was Horace, she finally got him into the bag. Then she tied it and tried to lift it. Oufff. She managed to hoist the bag onto her shoulder and almost collapsed under the weight. She put the bag down and took a deep breath. Straightening her legs, then her back, she lifted Horace to her shoulder and staggered to the door in the foyer. Picking up her handbag, she maneuvered herself out of the door and dragged the duffel bag to the elevator. Down to the main floor, and then it was only one block to the subway, she assured herself.

At the lobby floor, Melissa looked around for the doorman, but he was nowhere around, so she pushed open the door to the street and stood under the awning for a moment, surveying the scene. The back of her shirt, covering her blue jeans, was already damp with sweat, and she brushed her hair back again over her ears. Stooping to pick up the duffel bag, she hoisted it to her shoulder and walked slowly to the subway station on the corner.

As Melissa rested the bag at the top of the moving stairway, a young guy who could have been a fellow student came up to her and offered to help carry her bag. He was tall and well built and Melissa happily relinquished her grip on the duffel bag. She and her helper stepped onto the stairway going down the platform.

"Where are you going?" he asked.

Melissa told him the number of the train she was going to take, and she asked him if he was going to take the same train. He replied rather vaguely that he could manage to take that train to his destination. Boarding the train, her new acquaintance asked what was in that bag; boy, it sure was heavy. Yeah, she thought, it was heavy all right, but how could she tell him it held a dead dog!

"Uh, well, I'm moving cross town and the van left today with most of my stuff," she said, suddenly inspired. "But there were a lot of precious things I didn't want to send with the van. I didn't want to leave my laptop, disks, and some precious books with the movers, so I stuffed everything into this duffel bag. I didn't realize it was going to be so heavy." She became a different person in the telling as she warmed to her new role, and she gazed earnestly at her companion.

The young man listened attentively. As the train slowed for the next station, he stood up, grabbed the bag and lunged for the door, jumping through just as it opened. Melissa stood up reflexively, hollering, "Wait, wait! That's my bag!" reaching out as if to stop him. Then, as the doors closed, and the train moved on, she looked through the glass door and saw him bounding up the steps, the bag bumping behind him. She let her arm fall and, looking around at the startled looks on the faces of passengers around her, shrugged and sat quietly down. An older woman, sitting across the aisle, reached over and put her hand protectively on Melissa's knee. "Don't worry, dear. Just get off at the next station and notify the police. They'll find him."

Melissa nodded; blinking back unbidden tears, and she got off at the next stop. She ran across the bridge to the other side of the tracks and waited for a train going home. She gazed across the tracks, feeling relieved that she had said goodbye to Horace in his own place. As it dawned on her that Horace was no longer her problem, she couldn't help smiling as she thought about the helpful thief, who was in for a surprise when he opened the stolen duffel bag.

— My Dog, Baba —

During the years I lived in San Francisco, between 1945 and 1957, in the area known as North Beach, I went through several life changes. In March, 1945, my first husband, Jim Pack, and I arrived on Grant Avenue from Washington, D.C., ready to start a new life. Jim had recently been discharged from the Navy; I was transferring from the Middle East branch of the Office of War Information to the O.W.I. Overseas. We had Jim's mustering-out pay of three hundred dollars as our capital.

We were determined not to go back to our academic life at the University of California at Berkeley. That had been interrupted by World War II. Instead, we started a business, creating handmade leather belts and bags. Between 1945 and 1950, our business expanded to include leather clothing for women, and we had an extensive clientele. Unfortunately, Jim succumbed to post-traumatic stress disorder, and after extensive psychiatric treatment, we decided to divorce. I assumed control of our business, changing the name from Jim Pack Leathers to Rhoda Pack Leathers.

The divorce was final in 1952; I had secured the apartment above the shop at 1461 Grant Avenue, and I had acquired a staff of five: three working on the sewing machines, a pattern maker, and a cutter. One Friday in May, one of my customers asked me casually if I knew anyone who might want a black standard poodle, free. Suddenly the idea of a dog was very attractive. I plied my customer with questions. How old was the dog? Was it housebroken? On and on. She held up her hand to stop me, gave me a name and a number, and left.

I rushed to the phone and talked to the owner of the dog, which was named "Baba." The owner's name was Emily, and the reason she wanted to give the dog away was that she had just gotten a new job in New York, where she was going to live in an apartment that absolutely would not tolerate pets of any kind. She had had Baba since he was a pup, and didn't want to sell him. She wanted to find the right owner and the right place for him. She was willing to come over and let Baba decide. She said Baba would have to decide whether or not I was the right person for him, since he had already turned down four other people. We made a date for five o'clock the following day.

Emily and Baba arrived promptly, and I felt as if I were being interviewed. Baba walked sedately into the shop, looked at me, circled around me, sniffed my legs and feet, then went back to his mistress and lay down. Baba was a big standard poodle with his black curly hair trimmed in what was called a puppy clip, but I preferred to think of it as the way poodles were trimmed when they were used as hunting dogs in France.

"Let's go for a walk," Emily said. "I'll give you the lead, and we'll see what happens." I locked the door of the shop and took the lead from Emily. Baba looked at me and I looked at him. I leaned down and scratched his ears. "Hello, Baba," I said. "We're going for a walk." He looked up at Emily, who was gazing into the distance. I thought she was going to cry. Then the three of us set off for Washington Park at the corner of Union and Stockton, a block and a half from my shop. Baba dutifully stopped at every corner, didn't strain at the leash, in fact, he acted as if he were leading me. When we got to the park, I asked Emily what she usually did when they went for a walk.

"I just take him off the leash and let him run and do his business," she said. "Try it, then call him and see if he comes back."

Before I took the leash off his collar, I leaned down and gave Baba a hug. "You'll come back when I call, won't you, Baba?" I whispered into his ear. Then I stood up. He gave himself a little shake and trotted off, turning to look at us from time to time. We sat on a bench watching him, and I asked Emily what kind of food he ate and where he slept. I also wanted to know if he was at all aggressive, and if he barked a lot. He seemed very polite, but I needed to know if this dog was neurotic in any way. He was, after all, about five years old.

Emily hesitated. "He's rather possessive," she said. "If he decides he likes you, he'll follow you around everywhere, and he will snap at anyone he thinks might hurt you."

I was worried about his behavior in the shop. "How does he behave around strangers? Is he likely to attack people who come into the shop? That wouldn't be good for business."

She said she took Baba to work with her, and he was perfectly behaved at her office. She worked in a travel agency, where there were people coming and going all day, and there had never been any trouble. "Except..." she said, and paused. I held my breath. "One day a street person came in and Baba leaped up, his ears laid back, and he uttered the most ferocious growl I'd ever heard. Then he sort of pointed, like a bird dog, but that street person backed out of the door so fast, he seemed to disappear." I laughed, relieved.

"Okay," Emily said, "try calling him." So I did. Baba stopped, looked around, looked at me, looked at Emily, and turned away. Emily then stood up too, and called, waving her arm. I decided to wave my arm too, and Baba came loping up to us.

"Here," Emily said, "give him this treat." She reached behind my back and slipped the treat into my pocket, as if trying to fool the dog. I held out my hand and Baba took the dog biscuit, giving my hand an extra lick.

We walked back to the shop, and Emily said she thought I'd passed, but maybe she'd better come back tomorrow, and just leave Baba for a few hours with me. "I think he likes you, but let's make sure. I'm not leaving until the end of next week."

Emily brought me Baba's eating dish and his drinking bowl, and we put them in the kitchen at the back of the shop. Baba checked them out and then made a careful inspection of the entire shop. He looked at Emily and he looked at me. When we walked into the front of the shop, he followed us to the door and stood waiting. Emily leaned down, scratched his ears and told him to sit, which he did, his whole body tense. She gave him a final pat and left. I kneeled beside Baba and we both watched Emily get into her car and leave. I gave Baba a treat and stood up. My arrangement with Emily was that she would leave Baba with me for a day and a night, and see how we got along. She would come back the next day and we would go for another walk. I felt as if I were on probation.

He watched me carefully as I opened a can of dog food and put it in his bowl, then I filled his water bowl and set it down. He finally condescended to eat, lapped up some water, and came over and lay down near where I was working on a new design. Resting his head on his paws, he watched me carefully.

I decided to take him for a walk to the park, but I would keep him on the leash. If I let him off the leash in the park, would he run off and try to find his way back to Emily? I couldn't take a chance. As soon as I picked up the leash, Baba was up and at the door before I could get my coat on. We walked sedately down to the park, and then on to the grass. Baba seemed to know he wasn't going to get off the leash, so he sniffed around a few trees, left his mark, and finally squatted. I gave him a treat, and we walked companionably back to the apartment. Upstairs, he sniffed the entire apartment very carefully, checking each room, especially the bedroom, where he located his special blanket at the foot of my bed. He reassured himself that it was really his by scuffing it with his paws, circling it a few times, and then lying down with a small sigh. Baba was obviously not a barker, but when neighbors who lived upstairs came clumping up the stairs, he raised his head and gave a low growl. I liked that evidence of awareness. He finally stretched himself out and went sound asleep. I was reassured, but I knew that the real test of his acceptance would be if he came back when I called.

Emily called early the next morning, wanting to know how it went. I told her that everything seemed fine, and that Baba was adjusting. She came over at five thirty; Baba was happy to see her, but he seemed a bit reserved. Emily noticed this too, and told me she felt relieved.

"I'd like to try something," I said. "When we go to the park, I'd like to take him off the leash, and you hide somewhere, maybe behind a car or something. Then I'll call him, and if he comes back to me, we'll know he has made the connection, and he won't run off. But if he doesn't come back, you'll have to call him, and we'll know he's decided I'm not the right owner for him."

Emily put her hand on my arm. "I can see you really want to have my dog, and that makes me feel good. But you're right, if he's going to run off, it won't work. We'll just have to try it."

Off we went, the three of us. I walked ahead, holding the leash, and Emily sometimes walked behind us or in front of us. When we got to the park, I took Baba off the leash, and Emily turned around and walked away. He bounded off and I held my breath, watching him carefully. After he had performed his nightly ritual and was just snooping around, I called and waved my arms. He looked up, looked around, and came loping toward me. I threw my arms around him, hugged him, and scratched his ears, feeling silly and happy at the same time. Emily came out from behind the parked car where she'd been hiding, patted Baba, and we both grinned at each other. That lovely poodle with a mind of his own had decided for us.

Now that my dog had decided he was going to live at 1461 Grant Avenue, he became part of the family. Gradually, he took it upon himself to check out every person who came or went into the shop. He found himself a spot in the showroom, lifted his head as the staff came into work, and checked them out. However, if a stranger came in, he was up instantly, sniffing politely, and if he felt the customer was okay, he would go back to his place and lie down, his head on his paws, his eyes following every move. I found his presence reassuring and comforting.

Baba also made himself at home in the neighborhood. I decided to let him out every morning to roam the streets around the shop. I knew he would come back and lie down in the sun in front of the shop or scratch on the door window if he wanted to come in. I found out from Bruno, the butcher, that Baba made the rounds of every delicatessen in the surrounding two blocks. His first stop was Bruno's. He would pause in front of the door of the butcher shop, sit expectantly and happily take his daily handout of a bit of meat or a bone. Then he would go across the street to the delicatessen, where he would get a bit of prosciutto or salami. If he was satisfied, he would come back to the shop. If not, he would trot down to Green Street and check out the shops there. He strode his territory as if he owned it, and since there were no other dogs around, he really did.

164

Sometimes Baba would decide to squat in the middle of Grant Avenue to do his business, often around five or five thirty in the afternoon, when the street was full of cars going home. He paid no attention to the honking, calmly looking over his shoulder and giving a little shake when he finished, walking leisurely back to the shop.

He showed off his possessiveness, too, when Ric Skahen was courting me, in 1954. Ric had come over for dinner, and we were sitting on the couch in the apartment above the shop, having an after-dinner drink. Suddenly Ric jumped up and said, "Let's dance. That's a great tune on the radio." No sooner were we up and dancing that Baba also jumped up and inserted himself between us, pushing Ric so hard that he almost fell down. Ric lifted his foot to kick Baba away, and I stopped him just in time. "No!" I said. "Pat him instead! If you kick him or hurt him, he will never forgive you." Ric stopped and glared at Baba. Baba stood stiffly, looking fixedly at Ric. If dogs can be said to glare, Baba returned glare for glare. I finally told Baba to sit, which he did, reluctantly, never taking his eyes off Ric. I handed Ric a small dish full of Baba treats and told him to pat Baba and give him a treat.

Baba lived until he was twelve years old; he adjusted smoothly to life in Berkeley with Ric, who became my second husband, and to our son Ricky from the day Ricky was born, in 1957. He never wavered in his complete devotion to us, taking the changes in our lifestyle in stride.

Fashion Show at Napa, CA

THE FASHION GROUP
AND THE FASHION COURSE

(Names of women used in this story are fictitious, but the story is true)

By 1952, the year Baba came into my life, I was the sole owner of Rhoda Pack Leathers and had acquired a reputation for high fashion leather clothing for women. Most of the top models in San Francisco wore my clothes and carried my handbags. I had won prizes for original design at state fairs, and I was designing collections for top retail stores all over the United States. Despite this kind of recognition, I did not consider myself a professional designer because I hadn't gone to design school, nor had I served as an apprentice under a master designer. When I was invited to become a member of the Fashion Group and to help plan the annual fund-raising show, I was happily stunned.

The Fashion Group was conceived in 1928, in New York, when Edna Woolman Chase, Editor-in-Chief of *Vogue*, invited seventeen women for lunch. Those women had several things in common: they had a job of consequence in the business of fashion, and they held a belief that fashion needed a forum, a stage, or a force to express and enhance a widening awareness of the American fashion business and of women's roles in that business. The San Francisco branch came together twenty years later.

According to the statement of the Fashion Group Foundation, their mission was to promote educational programs devoted to fashion and to the study of fashion related businesses through the creation and awarding of scholarships, to establish internship programs, and to provide career counseling services. Another part of the mission was to sponsor public service activities in which the fashion industry could serve relevant community needs and concerns. It was that part of the mission statement that concerned the San Francisco Fashion Group members in 1952.

The purpose of the meeting was to plan the annual fund-raising fashion show, but another purpose was on Janet Wallace's mind. Her advertising office was decorated in classical modern, with black leather upholstered chairs, a glass topped table designed by Isamu Noguchi, and original modern paintings on the walls. Janet was talking as I came in.

She was a trim, slim woman in her thirties, dressed impeccably in a black tailored suit with a ruffled white silk blouse. She was standing at her full five-foot-two height declaring, "We should do something to benefit women in general, not just raise money for scholarships." Janet paced around her office, her small, elegant hands beating the air, saying, "I recently visited my cousin Ruth in a mental hospital in L.A., and it was awful. She's not very sick, but still… they took away everything connected to her identity, even her make-up, and gave her this awful gray gown to wear. She seemed to shrink before my eyes … they robbed her of her dignity. We ought to be able to do something!" She sat down and leaned forward earnestly. "Those women need to have a sense of self restored to them. I feel so helpless."

She continued, "What do you think about doing a course in fashion for women in a mental hospital? My idea is to create a six-week course, in which the patients will be encouraged to make their own dresses and be models in their own fashion show. Well?"

Here we were: Janet, head of her own advertising agency; Elena, an outstanding custom designer of original clothes; Martha, owner/director of the best model agency in San Francisco; and me, a fledgling designer and manufacturer. Coming from different backgrounds, with different skills, we sat silently, mulling over the possibilities from our own points of view. Elena kept bringing up the ethical question of how women who were confined and restricted would react to contact with the outside world. Martha was concerned with the effect on her models by contact with women in mental institutions, and I was preoccupied with how we would make everything work. I was convinced that any contact with the outside world was a positive. I had a gut feeling about the awful impact of prison in any form, and here was a way to help alleviate the effect of being institutionalized. After three hours, we hammered out a plan.

We agreed to get the cooperation of designers, manufacturers, cosmeticians, models, and anybody else connected with the fashion business to help us out. We wrote out a proposal, and asked Janet to make an appointment with supervisors at Napa State Hospital. We went to the hospital the following Tuesday, where we presented our plan. In the 1940s and 1950s, we never questioned our assumptions that clothes and make-up were important to all women and neither did anybody else we knew. All of my friends were expert at using make-up; in fact, Janet's son had told her he liked her better in the morning "with her face on," a remark she repeated more than once. Since I was allergic to most cosmetics, I had the upper part of my glasses tinted blue to simulate eye shadow, and that was how I was able to get the "right look."

In The Fashion Group and in our own businesses, we knew how important fashion was, but we also wanted to make a difference in the lives of women confined to a mental hospital. We arrived at Napa Psychiatric Hospital hopeful but apprehensive. We needn't have worried.

The nursing and support staff were wildly enthusiastic. The supervisor said they would select twenty women who were the least sick, and ask them if they would like to attend a course in fashion. During the conference, we saw that the nursing staff and supervisors were sensitive people, who said they hoped that most of the women would be able to sew their own dresses, but that some of the support staff would sew outfits for patients who might not be up to the task.

Traveling in a caravan, we went to Napa to put on a fashion show. There were six models in a van with clothes donated by stores like I.Magnin, Joseph Magnin, Roos Brothers, and the City of Paris. Martha, the model agency owner, and Elena were in one car; Janet and I in my car were part of the caravan.

The façade of Napa State Hospital looks like a California adaptation of a Southern colonial mansion with a bit of Italian villa décor thrown in. The hospital staff people were waiting for us in front

Model and patient

when we arrived, and we must have been quite a sight, pouring out of our cars, with our glamorous models, our garment bags full of beautiful clothes, piles of fashion magazines, and the four of us, dressed to the nines with hats and gloves, ready to perform.

Once we entered those portals, however, we felt as if we were in a prison. We paraded down a narrow, dimly lit corridor, through steel gates which locked shut behind us, into another corridor. Our high heels clacking on a brown linoleum floor, we passed walls hung with static photographs of famous people. We finally came to an auditorium and scurried backstage, where we bustled around while patients and their nurses filed into the main area.

I peeked through a hole in the blue faux velvet curtain to get a look at the people in the audience, and noticed that some of the women were wearing regular clothes, not hospital gowns, so I figured they were going to be our students. When I took a good look at the women in the first row, I nearly fell over. "Janet, Elena, come quick! Look through here!" They came over and put their eyes to the peephole.

"Oh!" gasped Elena. "That's Helen M., who used to be the buyer of Third Floor Better Dresses at I. Magnin!" Elena shuddered and made the Russian sign of the cross. We all knew how tough the fashion business was, yet here we were…and there was Helen.

Elena straightened up and said, quietly, "All right. Let's get back to

the business of setting up the show." We all took deep breaths, turned around and got back to work.

The curtains opened, the music started, Janet stepped to the microphone, and out came our model bride. (We had designed the show to run backwards, with the bridal costume first and swimming suits last.) Janet said, "Here is Hazel Andrews, wearing a creamy white lace dress by Dior as her bridal gown." In-

The Show

stant applause and cries of delight. As Hazel walked slowly across the stage in her model's walk — pelvis forward — one foot directly in front of the other so that the hips swiveled from side to side, Janet said, "Notice how Hazel releases the skirt from the waist of the dress." Hazel paused and undid the skirt, swinging it around her shoulders. Janet said, "Now the skirt becomes a cape!" We heard a collective "ooohhh" from the audience. "Now our bride has a lovely dinner and dancing dress to wear after the ceremony." I was so happy that Janet had not dumbed down her spiel for this audience. She acted as if she were doing the show for sophisticated San Francisco women.

I knew we were selling dreams and fantasy. Our audience consisted of members of the staff, women and men, and our patients. It didn't matter that the women in our audience may never have had a formal wedding or even attended a wedding where any of them would be concerned about a wedding dress that could double as an evening dress. But the patients and staff at Napa State Hospital saw movies, and movies sold dreams and fantasy. Dreams and fantasy were part of the world we lived in.

After the last model in a smashing bathing suit walked off, swooshing a big towel disguised as a beach dress, the audience wanted us to do the whole thing over again! But we persuaded them that we had different things planned. Everyone except our patients left.

Our models came out then, as planned, in their street clothes and circulated among our twenty women. They sat with different groups of women, looked over the fashion magazines, and talked. Many of the women touched our models' hair, felt the fabric of their clothes. I saw Hazel take off her shoes and put them on the feet of an older woman in her group. She helped this woman stand up and walk a few wobbly steps. They all giggled, and I wondered if Hazel would get her shoes back. But the woman smiled at Hazel, sat down, and took the shoes off.

Through the interaction between the patients and the models, we saw that our goal of humanizing both the models and the patients was working. The models had a chance to get to know the patients as real people, and the patients saw that the glamorous people on the runway were also real. The designers had a chance to sketch some ideas for the patients they talked to, ideas that would later be used to match with available patterns.

Pretty soon it was time for the women to go back to their usual routine, and we all waved affectionate goodbyes. Then we had a conference with the supervisor and the other nurses. They were very happy with the whole scene, and we talked about the next part of the plan.

"What we thought we would do," said Janet, "was to come back in two weeks with hair stylists and make-up people, wash hair and teach your women how to use foundation cream, eyebrow pencil, eye shadow, rouge, and lipstick. We can give out samples, too, if you think it's all right."

"With the carefully selected group we have chosen, we think it's all right," the supervisor offered. "The women who just left are the ones who said they wanted to be in the course."

"Is one of them the quiet woman who sat in the front row near the end?" I asked.

"Yes, that's Helen M., she's been here almost a year, and has never spoken a word since she came. She sits in the psychiatrist's office every week, and never says anything. But when we asked who wanted to be in the program, she was the first one to raise her hand. Nobody ever comes to see her. She understands everything, she just doesn't talk."

At our next meeting in Martha's office, we talked about Phase Two of the Course. We all had different things on our minds. I started the meeting. "We talked about hairdressers and cosmeticians," I said. "Where are the sinks? Who's going to do the actual hair-washing — the professional hairdressers? The staff? What about towels and hair dryers?"

Elena chimed in, thoughtfully, "We have twenty women," she said. "So if we have ten women getting made up and ten watching," she said, "the watchers can wander around or sit and watch. We're going to need at least five hairdresser/stylists, and at least five cosmeticians. How do we get them?"

Martha said she had friends at the Elizabeth Arden salon who owed her a favor, and that she might be able to get some of Arden's trainees. Then Janet mentioned that the beauty salon at Macy's had opened a new department, and that she had just finished writing the copy for the opening. She said she thought she could get samples from them.

I brought up the practical idea of the sinks, etc., and suggested that I go up to Napa to discuss the situation. I felt it was important to find out where they washed their hair now and other logistics. They all thought it was a good idea, and we decided to meet again the following Friday.

Model in Patient's Garment

My special trip to the hospital was a very good idea. None of us realized what an impact our fashion show had had on everybody. I sensed an animation I hadn't noticed on our first visit. Miss Johanson, the supervisor, greeted me warmly.

"Sit down! Sit down!" she said, excitedly. "I have something wonderful to tell you! Remember Helen? The woman I told you about? The one who has been here for a year and never said a word? Well! Last week, she spoke! She told her psychiatrist that she wanted to make a black dress!" Miss Johanson's cheeks were pink with excitement, and her eyes shone. "Right after you left the first time, and after she said she wanted to make a black dress, she began to talk nonstop. We all thought it was simply wonderful. I think this program is the best thing that's ever happened here!"

Of course I agreed, and we got down to the practicalities of the hairwashing. We found six sinks with reclining chairs, similar to the chairs you can find in every hair salon. Miss Johanson called her handyman, Frank, and we talked about what we needed. Frank said he would take care of everything. He was delighted to be part of the project.

When we arrived the following week with a different caravan, the patients and the staff were again eagerly waiting for us at the entrance to the hospital. The hairstylists and the cosmeticians were very nervous. On the way up, they quizzed us. They wanted to know what kind of sinks they would have; the beauticians wanted to know what kind of light they would have, and whether or not there would be mirrors.

I laughed. "You'll have regular beauty salon chairs, and they'll be sitting down," I said. "Don't worry; the women you'll be working with will remind you of your own regular customers. You'll see. They will love you. Whatever you do will be fantastic."

All of them were apprehensive about whether or not they would be able to function in an unknown environment, but I knew that once they got inside, and saw the way Frank had fixed up the "salon," they would feel relieved. And I was right. Frank had somehow gotten hold of professional mirrored tables and lighting, and had created a wonderful workspace. As the stylists and the cosmeticians bustled around, the women waiting their turn watched with quiet fascination as their friends were transformed. We distributed lipstick, rouge, and eyebrow pencils to all of the women when we left. We found out later that they refused to wash their faces for twenty-four hours, and wouldn't comb out their hairdos for at least a week.

The third week was the session when we chose the patterns that came closest to the drawings our designers had created for the patients during our first visit. Choosing the proper fabric for the patterns, we needed to lay out the fabric, cut it, and check to make sure there were enough sewing machines to make the clothes. We also had to make sure that we could rely on the volunteers and staff who had said they were willing to help our patients stitch their dresses.

As we spread out the patterns and the fabric in a large room adjoining the auditorium, I noticed that Helen M. was fingering a beautiful piece of black crepe. I asked Miss Johanson how she was doing. "Look at her; she's more animated than she's been in months." She clasped her hands and beamed at me.

I looked over at Helen. She was totally absorbed in the fabric and its possibilities. She didn't pay any attention to the models or to any of us. Turning away, I looked more closely at the women in our group of twenty. Yes, they definitely looked better than they did the first day we saw them.

Three weeks later, we got a call from Miss Johanson that the clothes were finished, and that we could come on a Friday afternoon to put on the final fashion show. It turned out that ten women were able to sew their dresses with help, and they were the ones who participated in the final fashion show. The other ten women didn't seem to mind; they felt they were part of the project anyway.

Janet had gotten donations of perfume, and I had printed up the fashion course certificates. The certificates congratulated the recipients for having completed a six-week course in "Fashion Appreciation." We brought all the models who had been with us on the first day, and several of the hairstylists and cosmeticians. Of course the hairstylists and cosmeticians did the patients' make-up and hair. We were all in a state of high excitement.

We spent about an hour before the show demonstrating how to walk and pivot. We decided to have a model escort the patient out to the center of the stage and stand with her as she received her certificate. Our models were ready to walk out with them, holding their hands, if necessary. We told the ones who weren't modeling that we would include them in the next show. We didn't know if there would be a next show, but hope is never a mistake.

Helen M. was our lead model, wearing the elegant black crepe dress she had made herself. She went on alone, without a model accompanying her. She wore pearls and high heeled shoes, provided by Janet, and her walk was proudly assured. Tears almost obscured my vision.

In the audience were other patients — both men and women — relatives and friends, doctors, nurses. The show was a huge success, and the word spread like wildfire around the hospital. They asked us to do another program in the fall. We did those programs for three years. After that, it got too hard to get donations of shampoo, lipstick, and foundation creams from cosmetic distributors; donations of cloth from fabric houses; and donations of time from models and designers. The program at Napa petered out, but we continued to do a smaller program for women patients in a special ward at San Francisco General Hospital.

Womens Wear Daily, the trade paper for the fashion business, wrote up the story and called the program "Fashion Therapy," a catchy title in the sixties. Fashion Group people in France and Italy wrote, asking us to send our plan, which we did, of course. We ended up persuading hospital authorities at Napa and other hospitals in California to give new patients a choice of pastel colors in hospital gowns. We hoped we had made a lasting difference in the way women patients were treated at Napa. We felt good about ourselves — all of us, the models, the hairdressers, designers and we, the organizers. And, we were always glad we could leave.

All of us were deeply affected by our experience with the Fashion Course, where we learned the importance of hope and trust. We learned that while the product was important — the final fashion show — the process was even more important. We never could have foreseen the positive unintended consequences that occurred for both the patients and for us. We all learned that even though the idea of a fashionable appearance may be hyped for monetary gain, it is connected to our own self-images, and the whole experience reaffirmed the value of our profession.

Teaching and Travel in Other Countries

When I was teaching at the Berkeley Adult School in the years from 1965 to 1980, I managed to travel during the summers that I wasn't working. I worked year 'round, saved my money, and every other year, drew it all out and traveled for sixty or seventy days, depending on when I left. I managed to go to Mexico, Guatemala, England, Scotland, Denmark, Norway, Sweden, Finland, France, Italy, Spain, and in each country I was able to stay with students I had taught in my classes at Berkeley. I also had a research project for all the trips, and kept copious notes in various journals.

My encounter with Japanese cultural norms began in 1965 at the Berkeley Adult School. My students included elderly Chinese and Japanese women, as well as young Mexican illegal immigrants. The class was supposed to prepare students for citizenship, but my students wanted to learn how to fill out an application for a driver's license, how to respond to letters from their children's teachers, and how to communicate more efficiently with the people they met every day.

My Japanese students had experienced the humiliation of being forced out of their homes and into camps set up in 1942, as a reaction to the Japanese bombing of Pearl Harbor in December, 1941. The camps have been called by various names: relocation camps, resettlement camps, concentration camps. They were not exactly "concentration camps" in the way that term has been used with reference to the German extermination camps in the 1930s and 1940s. The United States government allowed the Japanese internees to create their own schools, their own vegetable gardens, and their own self-governing system. They were not required to do forced labor, but the conditions under which they were housed, in poorly heated barracks, situated in barren parts of the country, did not resemble anything like the comfortable, middle-class homes from which they had been ousted.

My Japanese students refused to talk about their camp experiences. One of my students said, when pressed, "If the Americans had bombed Japan, and there were Americans living in Japan, they would have been rounded up and killed. At least, we were allowed to live." They were deliberate about their intention to incorporate their experiences into the present reality, and I honored their choice. We established an easy camaraderie, and we focused on everyday problems in the class. We visited Small Claims Court, so they could get a glimpse of how the legal system worked; we took trips to Sacramento, General Vallejo's ranch, and the State Fair. Our classes became a kind of introduction to Bay Area life, since many of my students had never ventured far from the few blocks that constituted their familiar environment.

In addition to my elderly ladies from Asia, and my young Mexican workers, I also taught visiting professors from Japan at UC Berkeley and their wives, who wanted to improve their conversational skills. The visiting professors and young graduate students were different kinds of students. They were educated, proud of their language, and resistant to different styles of learning. One of the professors, who became a close friend, explained to me that Japanese learners had highly developed left brains, which made it difficult to learn languages with different syllabic structures and syntax. He implied that Japanese brains were superior to Western brains.

In the 1970s I was also teaching special three-week summer courses at San Francisco State University for foreign teachers who wanted an excuse to come to San Francisco. I taught Italian teachers who hated the summer fog that gave them colds, and who felt betrayed by their expectations of sunny California. Teachers from Central and South America were enthusiastic and left with crates of teaching material.

In 1977, I taught an intensive English course to Japanese teachers of

English and I realized that there was, indeed, a cultural attitude toward learning English that was inhibiting. English in Japan was taught the way Latin was taught in the United States — by translation. Therefore, after ten years of studying English, Japanese students were not able to speak English with clarity, comprehend what they read, nor were they able to write coherent sentences. They could read tests given in English, because they had memorized the grammar, but they really did not read any literature with understanding, nor could they write original sentences. When languages are taught by translation, the effect is to strengthen and refine the native language. That's what happened to me when I studied Latin in high school, and that's what happens to Japanese students of English.

The dedicated Japanese teachers in my class at San Francisco State were eager to learn new methodology, and hoped that we could give them the magic wand that would open the gates leading to the mysterious world of the English language. However, at the end of the intensive three-week course, I asked them if they would be able to use any of the methodology they had learned. The answer was a resounding "no."

The reasons had a pragmatic and cultural basis. All the tests for entry into college were based on rote-learned grammatical rules and formulaic memorized phrases. All teachers taught to the test, and innovative methodology was viewed with suspicion. Those were the pragmatic reasons. Culturally, tenured teachers set the rules, and anything not initiated by those at the top of the pyramid was suspect.

The head of the department at SFSU wanted to build up his foreign teacher-training program, and asked me to go to Japan to recruit teachers for the program. San Francisco State would pay for my ticket, but that was it; I would pay for my own expenses in Japan. I wanted an excuse to go to Japan; I was attracted by the intelligence and dedication of my Japanese students at the Berkeley Adult School, and I wanted to get to know them better. I immediately contacted some of my students from the Berkeley Adult School; arranged with friends from International House to stay in Tokyo, for at least a few days, and then travel around the country.

Rhoda in Kimono, Nara, Japan

JAPAN

As soon as I arrived in Tokyo in June, 1977, I called my contacts, Shunichi Kagami, Akira Tago, Fusako Koyama, and Masa Kubooka. Professor Tago was at Chiba University; Kagami worked for Chiyoda Chemical Company; Koyama worked for a travel agency; and Masa was in the insurance business at that time. I told them all that I was there to make contact with possible students for intensive programs at San Francisco State University, and they all understood immediately what kind of contacts I needed. They assured me they would work on it, and they created a program for the three weeks I planned to be in Japan.

All four of my contacts had been students in my classes at the Berkeley Adult School in 1972, '73, and '74. We had stayed in touch by mail and telephone. Professor Tago was the eldest, and the most sophisticated. Shunichi Kagami, Fusako Koyama, and Masa Kubooka were all in their early twenties.

I remembered when Masa and his wife Chieko first arrived in my class in Berkeley. We were out for a walk on one of the frequent excursions I organized, and I noticed that Chieko walked five paces behind Masa. I stopped and insisted that Chieko walk beside Masa and me. Later, when I asked them about the pattern of their walking, they shrugged, and Chieko said she had never thought about it at all. Full of a strong insistence on feminine equality, I said that since they were in the United States, they should follow U.S. customs and walk side by side! They thought that was pretty funny.

When I connected with them again in 1977, it was my turn to learn proper Japanese customs of behavior, and what happened was the most extraordinarily warm and cushioned experience I have ever had, at home or abroad. Masa and Chieko insisted that I regard their home in Nishinomiya (near Kobe) as my home. That meant I could take off for various places, do teacher-training seminars, and come back "home" to unwind. One of the first experiences I had reminded me of that walk Masa, Chieko, and I had taken in Berkeley.

I was on my way to a university town north of Tokyo, which required a layover at a small town on the way. July in Japan is very hot and humid, and when I got off the train, the heat hit me like a hammer. I had about three hours to wait for the next train, and I decided to try to get to a public bath. Using my dictionary and many gestures, I conveyed my need to the agent in the train station. Soon a small man appeared, ready to guide me to a public bath. I managed to persuade the agent to allow me to leave my baggage behind his counter, and we took off.

My guide started off at a brisk pace, and, following my cultural experience as an American, I tried to keep up with him, planning to walk beside him. Oh, no, that was not the Japanese way. As fast as I ran, he ran faster, and finally I stopped running. I looked at him, and he had stopped, also, exactly five paces ahead of me. Suddenly I remembered Chieko walking five paces behind Masa, shook myself and proceeded at a leisurely pace. I realized that although it seemed as if my male guide was setting the pace, actually it was the woman following, who was in power. His pattern was in maintaining the distance between us, but I set the speed at which we walked. When we arrived at the street of the public bath, my guide pointed to it and left.

I noticed two entrances, one for women and one for men, walked up to the women's window and opened my small purse. Pouring the change into my hand, I offered it; she took the amount she needed, and I was handed a ticket and a small towel. She acted with great restraint, doing her best not to look as if she had seen an alien. After undressing, I made my way into a large tiled room with a bath the size of a swimming pool from which steam rose enticingly. There were small wooden stools scattered around the pool, and three women in the process of washing themselves. I watched. They soaped themselves thoroughly, scooped up buckets of water and sloshed themselves, rinsing thoroughly, and then stepped into the bath. They looked at me with great curiosity. I smiled and sat down on one of the stools.

One of the older women came over to me, and tentatively offered to scrub my back. I nodded enthusiastically, and pretty soon I was being scrubbed, massaged, and fussed over. They looked at the two Caesarian scars on my belly, and I pointed to one of them, then passed my hand across my throat and pantomimed death. They cluck-clucked. Then I pointed to the other scar, smiled, held my thumbs up and they nodded happily. We communicated enthusiastically across language and culture; we exchanged information about our children, and our satisfaction with their development. It was a marvelous cross-linguistic and cross-cultural connection.

After the bath, I stepped outside and realized I still had two hours before the train was due, so I walked into what I thought was a small restaurant. It was a bar, and there were two men seated at the counter. Of course I didn't know that it was not proper for an unaccompanied woman to go into a bar, even in the late afternoon, but they greeted me with interest and courtesy. I sat down at the counter, ordered cold sake, and asked if they served food. The woman behind the counter looked at her daughter; they nodded, and the daughter asked me in halting English what I would like. I replied, "Sashimi or sushi, preferably sashimi (raw fish). Do you have it?" They looked at me with astonishment, since most Japanese believe foreigners, especially Americans, will not eat raw fish. The daughter disappeared. I was offered edamame (boiled soybean pods) and more sake, until the young woman returned with sashimi. Later, describing the scene to Masa, I realized that the daughter had run to the local fish market and bought sashimi especially for me.

By the time the food arrived, my male companions and I were buddies, singing songs, buoyed by many cups of sake. They sang in Japanese, I hummed along; then I sang in English, and they hummed along. It was fun. After eating my fill, I stood up, pointed to my watch and pantomimed a train, writing down the time. The men immediately stood and signaled to me that they would escort me to the train. We made our way to the train station and I reclaimed my luggage. Bowing deeply, we said goodbye and I walked up to the platform. I was the only one there. Promptly at eight p.m., the train arrived, I boarded and immediately the train took off. I entered a dark, curtained section of the train (it was a sleeper) and made my way to my upper bunk. I wondered if there was a club car, because I was not in the least bit sleepy, but decided not to try to find out. Instead, I scrunched down in the small space allotted to me and turned on the feeble night light. At least I could read myself to sleep.

Arriving at my destination at eight a.m., I was met by a delegation from the local university and escorted to what I assumed was a professors' lounge. I was offered a breakfast consisting of tea and hot rice with dried fish. This breakfast did not surprise me, because I had already encountered it at Masa and Chieko's house. Then I was ushered into a large classroom filled with eager graduate students anxious to get the magic words about teaching English.

I was totally unprepared for this kind of encounter. I thought I was going to meet with five or ten professors, and we would talk about teaching English in Japan in a very general way. This was definitely a

**Professor Akira Tago
and wife, Suma**

**Path to
Tago-San's Villa**

**Hideaki Kubooka and wife
with Rhoda, 2010**

new challenge. I looked over at the Japanese professor who had arranged this "seminar," and he smiled, bowed, and waved me to a microphone. I assumed he would translate, and he did.

My memory of that morning is a blur, but I remembered some of the outstanding remarks of the Japanese teachers who had attended classes at San Francisco State, and I repeated them, hoping it would resonate. I noticed several of the older teachers present nodding their heads, so I assumed that they understood what I was saying about the difficulty of presenting new ideas, when the national tests for university admittance were mired in nineteenth-century ideas of how to teach English.

When I returned to the Kubooka residence, I was exhausted, and they welcomed me as if I were a member of their family. After an exquisite soak in a hot bath, Chieko prepared a fantastic meal, and Masa provided delicious sake. Hideaki and Yuko, their children, looked at me solemnly, and I often wondered what they thought about their parents' foreign friend, a special sort of "Gaijin" (translated as stranger, or sometimes as barbarian).

(Flash forward) I needn't have worried, because, twelve years later, in 1989, my son, Ric, his wife, Remi, and their two children, Adeyemi and Aba, went to Japan for a three-year stay. Remi was a visiting professor from UC Berkeley, teaching at the Osaka University of Foreign Studies, and Ric was an accountant with an international firm which had a branch in Japan. Masa and Chieko immediately absorbed them into their family, and Hideaki and Yuko became a surrogate older brother and sister.

After my stay with the Kubookas, I connected with Professor Tago, and he invited me to his villa where I had my own tatami-mat room overlooking his formal garden, and my own private soaking tub, which also overlooked the garden. Tago-san also created an atmosphere for me that was both welcoming and accepting.

He arranged a gathering in his garden for advanced students and me, where they asked questions about the United States and about San Francisco State University in particular. The session turned into a mini-teaching seminar, where I was completely comfortable. Later, we all went out to an elegant restaurant, and the talk continued. Professor Tago arranged an elaborate meal — rare dishes seldom offered to Americans, including elaborate dishes of raw fish and plenty of sake. Since I was a professor, plus being an older woman with gray hair, my ability to drink a lot of sake and stay sober was a plus. That meal turned into a more intimate teaching seminar, in which I felt that I was listened to with great respect. I never knew how much they understood, but I talked as if they understood everything.

My next contact was Fusako Koyama, a young woman I had sponsored in Berkeley. Fusako's student visa had expired, and I offered to sponsor her, which meant presenting my income tax return and current bank balance in order to prove that I was a bona fide sponsor. That small act had reverberations I never expected. Her mother considered herself forever indebted, something I found out about later.

Fusako was now working for a travel agent in Osaka, but she lived in Nara, so I went to Nara for a few days. It was July, and July and August in Japan are hotter and more humid than either Chicago or Washington, D.C. Fusako, her sister, and mother lived in a two-story house with a small garden. I had a large room on the second floor overlooking the garden. It was Fusako's mother's room, which she had given up for me. I felt guilty about pushing Mrs. Koyama out of her room, but I realized this was part of the pattern of Japanese hospitality.

Fusako's father had been a renowned chef at a prestigious hotel in Nara, and the family had a special status in the town. Nara had been an important administrative and cultural center, and it was still the center for regional festivals.

I discovered the importance of Japanese daily customs while living with Fusako and her family. They insisted that I use their house as a base, and when I traveled, I would always come back to Nara as a home away from home. One of the daily customs was the ritual soaking bath at night. The bath is filled with clean, hot water, and the guest (or the husband) takes a bath first, then the eldest child (if one of the children is male, he goes next, even if he's not the eldest) bathes, and finally the mother, and then the female children. Before you get into the hot soaking tub, you sit on a small wooden stool next to the tub, wash yourself off with soap, and slosh water over yourself from the tub. The water is kept hot by a connection to a thermostatically controlled heater. (The ritual is the same as the public bath.) Only then do you get into the soaking tub.

One evening, I got home from a trip so tired that I decided to go straight to bed, and when I said I wasn't going to take a bath that night, I got such unbelieving looks from Fusako's mother, that I realized I had made a terrible gaffe. But it was too late. It's not polite to turn down a hot bath, especially if you are a guest.

On one of my trips away from Nara, I took the Shinkansen (the high speed train in Japan) to a small town where I was scheduled to conduct a special seminar. It was hot, hot, hot when I boarded the air-cooled train, and I sank down thankfully next to a pleasant-looking Japanese woman. She seemed to be my age. I had no Japanese, she had no English, but we smiled at each other, and, as I wiped the sweat off my face, she handed me a cold tangerine. I smiled in deep gratitude, ate the tangerine, and leaned my head back.

After I sat up, and glanced out the window to her left, she intercepted my glance and tried to engage me in conversation. We conversed in pantomime. I held out my ticket; she nodded, and held out hers. All railroad stops on the Shinkansen have stop signs written in Japanese and in Romaji (Japanese words transliterated into a Roman alphabet). I noticed that the stop she indicated was a town renowned for its Taiko Drum celebrations, and I did an imitation of a drummer on my knees. She grinned and nodded. Then she looked at my ticket again; it was for the port city that was also what I called the Taiko Drum town. I intended to take a ferry from there, across the Japan Sea, to my destination. After further rapid consultations of dictionaries — hers Japanese-English and mine English-Japanese — we decided that I would leave the train with her, spend the night in her town, and take the ferry the following morning.

I checked into the travelers' hotel near the port, and surveyed the

Mrs. Koyama, Rhoda, Kumiko, and Fusako in front of their house in Nara

Koyama Family; Fusako, sisters, Mrs. Koyama

Kubooka Family; Masa, Toshiko, Hideaki, Chieko, Chieko's mother

189

tiny room I was in. I filled the deep tub with hot water, had a reinvigorating bath and was settled into bed with a novel I had brought with me, when the telephone rang. It was midnight. My train mate, whose name I had written down was Hiroko, was calling me. I heard "Hiroko said I call you," in accented English, and then the voice said, "I am daughter, and I teach English at high school. We like to take you out to see our city. We come in a few minutes." I sprang out of bed and barely had time to get dressed when I heard a knock at my door. There stood Hiroko, another woman about her age, and two young people, a young woman and a young man. The young woman was her daughter, Hitomi, the teacher, and the young man was her husband. They both spoke understandable English, and it turned out that both of them had been to the United States for graduate studies. The older woman was Hiroko's sister. They apologized for coming so late, but Hiroko's sister had just gotten off from work.

We went down to the lobby and out into the street. For the next four hours we walked through the lively life of this port city. There were food stands lining the edges of the streets, and we stopped at one after another of the favorite ones. All the food stands were full of people. Many cries of "Oh, we must go over to that one, it's my special favorite!" Hitomi and her husband went home around two a.m., but my two escorts showed no sign of tiring. We had many cups of sake at various stands, and wound up walking down the middle of a quiet street on our way back to my hotel, arm in arm, singing whatever song we could harmonize on.

I have no recollection of what we were singing, but I have a deep, happy memory of the three of us weaving our drunken way down that dark street.

They dropped me at my door, assuring me that they would be back at eleven to make sure I made the one o'clock ferry. I set my alarm, and I was ready when they knocked. There was a bit of a hassle at the dock, as Hiroko and her entourage argued with the dispatcher at the port over the question of my ticket. They argued, successfully, that since the train was late the previous night (they made this up), and I missed the last ferry, the company should honor my ticket. The agent finally reluctantly agreed. Hitomi and I exchanged addresses and promised to write to each other. I sent a letter to Hiroko, care of Hitomi, thanking them all for a memorable visit, and we wrote back and forth for a bit. I often wonder if they regarded my visit as remarkable as I did!

When I returned from this teaching trip, I brought a beautiful piece of hand-woven fabric for Mrs. Koyama. I had bought it in a town known for its weavers. We were sitting in her formal living room, furnished with a plush sofa, Western chairs and footstools, all this heavy furniture stuffed into a very small room, when I handed her my package. She flushed crimson, and rushed from the room. I looked at Fusako, bewildered.

"What did I do?" I was shocked.

"Don't worry," Fusako assured me. "She'll be back."

Mrs. Koyama came back into the room with a carefully wrapped package and handed it to me with a bow. I opened it and there was an exquisite piece of antique brocade, which she had retrieved from her treasure house in their garden. I realized at that moment that I was never going to be able to thank Mrs. Koyama for her kindness and her hospitality. For every gift from me, she would consider it obligatory to reciprocate.

The weather was hot and muggy, and I needed some lighter clothing. There was a sewing machine in my room, and I decided to make a loose blouse from two silk scarves, one for myself and one for each of Mrs. Koyama's two daughters. I joined the two pieces of fabric at the top, and stitched up the sides, creating an opening for the neck and the arms. I sewed the shoulder seams on a curve and shaped the sides slightly as well. The blouses were easy to wear and quite beautiful. That would be the kind of thank-you gift that would satisfy me, and which might not demand a reciprocal gift. I presented them to Mrs. Koyama the day I left as a going-away present that I thought would not require a return present, but Mrs. Koyama was not going to be outdone. She made an excuse to disappear for a moment, and returned with two beautiful silk scarves as a present for me.

I had one other remarkable experience, which was an afternoon performance of Kabuki theater in Osaka. It began at noon, and the theater was filled with Japanese non-working women, leaning across each other, talking animatedly, eating their lunches from bento boxes. As the performance began, they continued their conversations. The seating was arranged in a semi-circle around a raised stage.

Two musicians were seated on one end of the stage (to the right, as I faced the stage), and at the sound of a gong, one actor appeared on the right side of the stage and another on the left. There were a series of unlighted, tented spaces on the back of the stage. The actor on the right side of the stage carried a large spool of thread, and the actor on the left had an empty spool. As the actor on the right progressed across the stage, the different sets lit up, and it soon became obvious that each tented space was a period in the life of a person. And as the actor progressed, the spool became thinner, while the spool in the hand of the actor on the left became thicker. When the actor reached the opposite side of the stage, her spool was empty, and she collapsed. The spool in the hand of the actor on the left was full.

I was astonished. This was an acting out of a story my father had told me when I was a child. He had told me that we are all born with a full spool of thread, and as we go through life, the spool unwinds. When it is empty, we die. So our lives are a gradual unwinding of that spool of energy, of life force, of whatever we want to call it. Here was a tale told by my father, a Jewish immigrant from Romania, acted out on a stage in Osaka, Japan, obviously a deeply familiar tale to the Japanese. I was also stunned by a sense of déjà vu.

Everywhere I went, people made sure I got on the right train, was met by someone, and taken care of as if I were a precious piece of porcelain. I felt as if I were wrapped in cotton wool. Everyone made me feel as if I belonged, a most extraordinary feeling in a strange environment. Japanese are extraordinary people, with a deep sense of courtesy and kindness. They know their boundaries; they know their roles; and their depth of understanding is remarkable.

I knew my boundaries as well, and as long as I stayed within my role as teacher (sensei), I was able to be myself. I left Japan at the end of three weeks, knowing I would return. I didn't get any firm commitments from students who wanted to study in San Francisco, but this visit prepared the way for future visits, and eventually we recruited more teachers for our teacher-training program at San Francisco State University. That was 1977; I went back in 1978 and 1979.

My connection with the Kubookas is still strong. Masa's son married recently, and he and his wife came to visit their "American Family." There was a grand reunion at my son's house, and it was affirmation of a deeply satisfying thirty-seven-year friendship, across culture and language.

I had a strange déjà vu feeling in Japan, almost as if I had been there before. I found the Japanese kimono easy to wear, and I don't know why. Perhaps I like ritual and formality, which appeals to my sense of drama. I don't have much ritual or formality in my American life, but I do have some. My Japanese friends are sensitive and gently polite; they know how to create calm oases in the middle of noisy environments, and they know how to create personal space in a crowded land. They have an inherent sense of beauty in flower arrangement, in the everyday pottery they use, and they understand the beauty of simplicity of interior and exterior design.

My life was permanently and positively changed by my experiences in Japan.

Rhoda with Buddhist Monk, Monastery

KOREA

After my return from Japan, I knew that I needed more training in teaching English, so I enrolled at San Francisco State University in the fall of 1978, and graduated with a master's degree in TESOL (Teaching English to Speakers of Other Languages) in May, 1979. I had been offered a teaching position at St. Mary's College in Moraga, California, provided I had a master's degree. When I offered to get my master's degree within a year, the priest who hired me agreed. I was sixty years old. I taught at St. Mary's in the morning and commuted to San Francisco for late afternoon and evening classes. That was a long, intense nine months!

I had taken an unpaid leave of absence from the Berkeley school district, but I wasn't quite ready to retire. In 1980 I created a course called "Introduction to the Process" for the University of California, Berkeley Extension, which was based on my master's thesis, and seventy-five students showed up. The Certificate in TESOL, a graduate course, was born. I taught the course on weekends, and continued to teach at the

Berkeley Adult School.

In 1981, Professor Norbert Tracy of the University of San Francisco invited me to come to Sogang University in South Korea. The Korean Department of Education in Korea had authorized a program to improve the teaching of English by one hundred selected teachers of English, from high school teachers to university professors and had contacted the Fulbright commission in Washington, D.C. to assist in carrying out this program. USF had bid for, and gotten, approval for co-sponsoring the teacher-training.

The University of San Francisco was directly affiliated with Sogang; both universities were founded by Jesuits, and Father Tracy was the senior professor at Sogang. I was not enthusiastic about going to Korea, but I was intrigued by the challenge. Father Tracy persuaded me to take a job as one of the three administrators of the two-year program. He explained that we would be a triumvirate: Tracy at the head of the pyramid; John Harvey, a former soldier who had been in Korea for twenty years; and me, a specialist in TESOL, as the other two arms of the triangle. Father Tracy said that, following Jesuitical theory, we three would function as one. My position was funded by a Fulbright Fellowship, and the idea appealed to me. I was firmly convinced that I would be able to work with two males on an equal basis.

However, once I arrived in Korea with the ten instructors I had assembled for our program, I realized that theory doesn't often translate into action. Tracy and Harvey made most of the administrative decisions, and I was assigned the task of making those decisions work. We were supposed to create an outreach program for business executives, in addition to the program for teachers, but I had to fight to be included in the business arrangements. All the business executives were men, and whenever I managed to be included in the planning, there were uncomfortable silences during the introductions.

Korean society is structured vertically, and the language reflects this structure. There are more than twelve different ways to say hello, depending on age, status, and gender. I had more status than other women instructors in our program, since I was sixty-three years old and had gray hair, but there was no precedent for women administrators of any kind of program in 1981.

Women were expected to be homemakers, responsible for the education and discipline of children, and to obey their husbands. As a Fulbright fellow, I joined the University Women's Organization and conducted seminars at various women's universities. I was surprised by the way these educated women had internalized their secondary status without question. When I asked about equality of chores in the home, and whether or not their husbands or sons helped with washing dishes or taking out the garbage, they laughed. They said their husbands barbecued meat on weekends, but that was the extent of their cooking and/or cleaning up. I had seen how the role of married men in the United States had changed during my lifetime, and encouraged them to be part of such a change in Korea. I knew that this change was partly due to economics, since more married women have become part of the work force in America. I pointed out that such a change might happen in Korea as well.

Age is important in Korean society, especially for women. When Korean citizens reach the age of sixty, they are considered wise, and there is a special celebration, similar to the coming-of-age ceremonies like Bar Mitzvahs and Confirmations. Women at sixty often went into business for themselves, opening jewelry stalls in the market, becoming pharmacists, and in general declaring their independence. I observed over-sixty women's groups on vacation trips, some of them wearing baseball caps and a club uniform, smoking, drinking, laughing, singing, obviously having a wonderful time.

A young woman, Seong-Ja Kim, lived with me and was my informal assistant and interpreter. She was a painter and fabric designer, using batik on silk for her designs, and she was a student at the Buddhist University. Her mother was a shaman, and in the spring of 1982, she invited me to a New Year ritual.

Seong-Ja told me what I needed to do to attend the ritual. "Choose a piece of underwear," she said, "a bra, or slip, or panties; something you've been wearing all year, but something you won't miss. Just bring it with you. Oh, and bring a warm coat. We will be down at the river in the evening, and sometimes it gets cold."

On the appointed day, we took a bus to her mother's house on the outskirts of Seoul, and joined about twenty other women. They all looked at me curiously, but Seong-Ja explained who I was, and her explanation was obviously satisfactory. We then left in two vans, and headed to the river. Three women unloaded the van. I noticed a bundle of wood, a bag of rice, some blankets, and several jugs of Soju (a fermented Korean barley wine).

The women quickly built a roaring fire; Seong-Ja's mother gathered all of us around the fire, chanted what seemed like a blessing to me, and then we all threw our underwear into the fire. I didn't know what they were chanting, but I hummed along. Then they opened the bag of rice; we grabbed handfuls of it and threw it into the river with more chanting. After that, we took 100-won notes,

Rhoda with Buddhist monk, Rhoda's painting in background

threaded a small stick through them, and sent them sailing down the river.

By this time, it was rather cool, and they built up the fire. We all stood around, drank several cups of Soju; there was more singing, and then we piled into the vans to go back home. Seong-Ja got the driver to let us off at the corner of our apartment building, and she explained what the entire ritual meant.

"We are getting rid of all the bad things that happened to us last year," she said, "and we said prayers for good things to happen in the next year. We throw rice into the river to feed the river god, and we send money down river for anyone who needs it." It all felt rather familiar.

When I came to Korea, I was determined to experience as much as I could of the Korean culture, just as I had tried to do in Japan. I discovered that there was a Korean-American Hiking Club, and I decided to join it, despite Father Tracy's warning. He said, "Rhoda, this is not the kind of hiking you might be thinking of. Korea is mountainous. This is not so much a hiking club as it is mountain climbing. It's mostly for young people."

I heard his admonition, but signed up anyway. As soon as I appeared at the appointed spot for the bus, and the leader of the group noticed my gray hair, he beckoned to two young people, who immediately became my companions, sticking close beside me. Tracy was right. When we arrived at the starting point of the hike, I looked up at the narrow path up the mountain, but adjusted my small backpack, and off we went. My two young Korean friends positioned themselves behind and beside me, ready to push and pull if I faltered.

We reached the first level of the hike, and spread out around the open area. Drinks and snacks appeared, and then the singing began. As the eldest in the group, I was supposed to lead. Singing is not my strong point, so I quickly decided on a group song. I chose "She'll Be Coming Round the Mountain When She Comes" and it was a wild success. After that breather, we continued the hike, which turned out to be a four-thousand-foot climb. At the top of the mountain, we spread out in various positions of rest, while the food crew prepared a marvelous lunch. Then came the Korean entertainment. They were wonderful singers and actors, and I was captivated by their beautiful voices and musical skill. They had brought guitars, drums, and other percussion instruments strapped to their backs; it was an impromptu concert.

The descent down the mountain was tricky, and my companions positioned themselves carefully; one behind me and one in front. As in Japan, they were most considerate of me as an elder American, and as a teacher/administrator. The word had gotten around of my position at Sogang, and I was treated accordingly. I never felt at a loss because I couldn't speak Korean. I was surrounded by Koreans who were quite

Seong-Ja's aunt, cousin, Rhoda, Seong-Ja's mother

**Seong-Ja's mother,
The Shaman**

fluent in English.

I also managed to join some of the underground artists' groups. Chung Doo Hwan was not quite the benevolent dictator Father Tracy had described to me, and there was strict political and military control of student groups. I found out about another group that sounded interesting: a Korean-American Cultural Society. I discovered that this group went on organized tours of museums, temples, and ruins. One of the tours was scheduled for JeJuDo, an island off the southern part of Korea. This was a favorite vacation spot, famous for its pearl divers, all of whom were women.

We set off one Saturday morning from Seoul, and traveled to Pusan, a southern port, where we would take a ferry to the island. There were several University professors, members of the various diplomatic and trade departments of the U.S. embassy, teachers from Sogang, and a large contingent of Koreans, who wanted to make sure our ten-day excursion would be rewarding. It took a day's travel by train to get to the ferry at Pusan, so we had about eight days on the island.

The rooms in the tourist hotel that welcomed us resembled a youth hostel more than it did the kind of hotel many of the Americans expected. We roomed two to three in a room, and one of my roommates was an elementary school teacher who was close to my age. Day One was fine; we went on a water excursion to several beautiful caves, and got to swim in the clear, warm water.

Day Two was a bit overcast and windy, Day Three was windier and the sea was very rough. By Day Four we were in the middle of a typhoon. The rain poured and poured and poured; the winds roared; the humidity was stifling, and restless pessimism infected all of us. Rosemary Crawford, the elementary school teacher, and I looked at each other, and almost simultaneously said, "Time for RAINY DAY games!"

We decided to write a musical, with parts for everyone, including the children on the tour, and we would require everyone to create a costume. We decided to frame it as a prayer ritual to the Rain Gods, but we would use familiar musical comedy tunes for the words. When we suggested this idea at dinner that night, it was received enthusiastically by

Steps leading to mother's house

Woman in Seoul market

everyone, including the Korean staff.

The Korean leader of the program had thoughtfully brought along a hefty supply of local Korean wine, stronger than sake, the kind of beverage that tastes benign, but sneaks up to crack you on the head before you know it. He also had visited the island beforehand and had laid in a supply of fresh fish, noodles, and vegetables, so he kept all of us well fed.

The rain continued for two more days, which gave everyone plenty of time to make their costumes and learn their parts. Rosemary and I commandeered the adolescents aboard our floating hotel to copy out the parts as fast as we wrote them. It was fun. We included a chant to the Rain Gods which required everyone to line up, stomp around in a circle, and then one by one sing a special prayer, somehow connected to the costume the singer was wearing.

By this time, we were not only well fed; most of us had imbibed freely of that potent Korean beverage, including me. One of the Koreans had brought along a portable record player and a few records, which included some jazz, and I let go with a bump and grind number that had everyone rolling with laughter. Fortunately, there were no movie cameras onboard.

It's hard to believe, but the rain let up on Day Six, and Day Seven was hot and steamy. We had two more days to explore the caves along the shore, watch the pearl divers take off from cliffs high above the water, and swim a bit in the sea. We all declared the excursion a huge success, in spite of the typhoon.

MORE STORIES FROM KOREA

— The House —

When I arrived in Seoul, South Korea, in September, 1981, I found the weather cold, damp; the skies gray, the air smelling of smoke, reminding me of Chicago in the winter. I did not feel prepared (does one ever?) for my new adventure.

I had agreed to go to Korea for two years as a Fulbright Fellow to assist in setting up an Institute for English as an International Language at Sogang University. The contracts I wrote for the ten instructors I had recruited provided for shared housing, plus seven weeks of paid vacation (three weeks in one chunk, and four weeks scattered throughout the year). There were six women and four men, all holders of master's degrees in TESOL (Teachers of English to Speakers of Other Languages) in the program.

The business manager of the enterprise, Mr. Hagen, had decided to put the six women together in a beautiful old house in upscale Seoul, since he was having difficulty finding three suitable separate apartments. Of the six, one was a Canadian in her fifties; a woman from Utah in her forties, with her ten-year-old daughter; an East Indian woman from Fiji in her thirties; a woman from Ohio in her late twenties; a bilingual Korean woman from San Francisco; and me, a Berkeley, California woman in her sixties.

Mildred and her daughter Shirley had a room to themselves, and I, as senior teacher and administrator, had a room to myself. The other four shared the remaining bedrooms. It was a beautiful house, with inlaid parquet floors, tastefully furnished. The first thing I did was to bring everyone together to decide how we would handle kitchen privileges, space in the refrigerator, plans for eating together or not. As with any attempt to achieve consensus on anything in a group of individualists, my planned fifteen-minute meeting went on for sixty-five minutes, and ended up with a formation of two committees. We agreed to meet again in the evening, but we did manage to divide up the shelves in the refrigerator, and posted our names on our sections. Mildred insisted that Shirley have a voice in the discussion, and she rose to the occasion.

The evening meeting went a little more smoothly. We agreed to share one evening meal per week, rotating the shopping, cooking, and cleaning up details. Cathy Kim, our bilingual Korean member, would be a permanent member of the shopping committee. That would be a conference kind of meal, with an opportunity to air complaints and grievances before they escalated. Cathy had relatives in Seoul, and she wanted to be free to spend time with them. We were on our own on weekends. We agreed to clean up after ourselves whenever we used the kitchen.

The weather turned cold in October, and life in the house was fairly smooth, but I did have a problem with laundry. I decided it was time I used the small washing machine in the laundry room on the lower floor of the house, instead of sending all my laundry out. I went shopping in a local grocery store for some laundry soap — I should have taken Cathy with me, but I was overconfident about my ability to read Korean. There was a box on the laundry supply shelf that looked exactly like Tide, well-known laundry soap in California, and I decided to buy it. I used the Korean word for soap, which I found in my dictionary, pantomimed washing clothes, and the clerk nodded. I felt encouraged.

The water that ran in the washing machine was not very hot, but I tried it anyway. When it came time to hang up the laundry on the outdoor patio (there was no electric dryer in the house), the sheets seemed very gray, but I attributed that to the lukewarm water. It was cold on the patio, but the sun was shining, and there was a brisk wind. I got everything on the line, and went into the house feeling satisfied that I had accomplished a small domestic detail all by myself. However, when I went to check on the laundry later in the day, I found that the sheets were all frozen stiff, and they certainly didn't look clean. I rushed back into the house, knocked on Cathy's door, and asked her about the washing machine and the laundry routine. She asked, "What kind of soap did you use?" I showed her the box, and she sagged against her door, laughing so hard she nearly fell down. "You bought starch!" she gasped between bouts of laughter. "No wonder the sheets are all stiff! Come on, I'll help you take everything down and we'll take it to the local cleaners. Most people in this neighborhood never do their own laundry anyway." We folded the board-like sheets into a box, and she took it to the cleaners.

— The Fire —

One snowy afternoon I was in my room upstairs in our comfortable Korean house when I heard screaming coming from the kitchen downstairs. Running down the curving staircase, I found Mildred and Shirley in the boiler room adjoining the kitchen, screaming and pointing to an oil fire on the floor. Grabbing a package of flour, I threw it on the fire, and followed up with a package of sugar. Not sure if that would be enough, I rushed to the phone and dialed 119, the Korean number for emergency. Looking quickly through my small, pocket-sized English-Korean dictionary, I said, "Topda!" and then the word for "Fire!" The person on the other end of the line hung up. I tried again, and the same thing happened. This time I called Mr. Hagen, our business manager, and he said, "Okay, I live right across the street from the fire department. I'll go over there and tell them about your problem. A fire in the boiler room, you said?" I told him we had thrown flour and sugar on the fire and the room was pretty smoky. I wasn't sure the fire was really out, and that's why I tried to call the fire department.

I went out onto the patio, which gave a good view of the hill leading to our house, and watched for the fire department truck. Suddenly I didn't want the crew with its fire hoses traipsing through the living room of this elegant house, so when I saw them at the bottom of the hill, I waved madly, directing them to the back of the house.

A crew of about six men arrived, quickly ascertained that the fire was out, and doused the smoky remains. Since the boiler provided heat for the entire house, I asked them to relight it, and to make sure that it worked. The lead fireman spoke pretty good English, so I asked him why nobody in the fire department understood me when I telephoned. I told him what I had said on the phone, and showed him my dictionary. He turned bright red, stifled a laugh, and ran out of the house. We cleaned up the boiler room, and the household settled down.

The next day, when I went into our offices at Sogang University, I went to see John Harvey, the third member of our administrative troika. Father Tracy was at the head of the pyramid, and John Harvey and I were the other two parts of the triangle. John had spent twenty years in Korea, staying on after the end of the Korean War. He was married to a Korean woman, and I figured he would be able to unravel the mystery of what I said.

"John, we had a fire in the boiler room of the house, and I tried to call the fire department, but nobody understood what I said. Can you help me?"

"What did you say?" he wanted to know.

When I told him, "Topda!" and then the word the dictionary gave me for "fire," he fell off his chair laughing. When he recovered, he said, "What you said was 'I'm hot, and I'm burning up!' That's a polite translation of what you said."

"My god. Well, how do you say, 'Help!' in Korean?"

"In the first place, 'Topda' doesn't translate into anything, and you have to be specific, like 'fire burning,' or 'thief running,' or 'ship sinking.' Where did you get that stupid dictionary anyway? I'd throw it out if I were you. Get yourself a good one."

When I left, he was still chuckling.

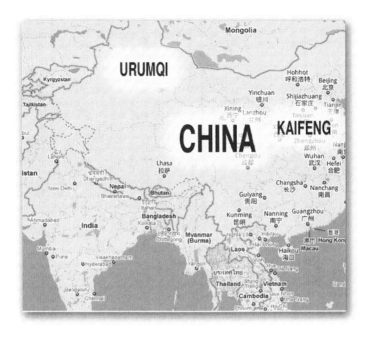

INTRODUCTION TO TRAVELS IN CHINA

I have written extensively elsewhere, in my first book, about my experiences in China, in different cities and in different places, but there were a lot of stories I left out. In trying to recapture some of those stories, I found myself reaching back and back and back into my memories. I knew I had kept journals and copies of letters I had written twenty-four and more years ago. But where were they? Certainly they were nowhere in my computer. Ah! I went into the back room of my small garden apartment in Berkeley, and there, in an old metal file cabinet, were three plump files, labeled "China." The material was handwritten, or copies of typewritten letters and essays.

I found that most of the entries contained small details about each place I had been, and I identified those places by the degree of heat in the room and the availability of hot water. Details about temples, statues, and gardens came in a different section, almost as a dutiful afterthought. My notes on Xi'an tell about how cold it was and about the stupidity of the

Trip down the Yangtse River, 1985, before the Three Rivers Dam was built

Countryside which was flooded when the Three Rivers Dam was built

Sign on Lanzhao campus

Rhoda and students at Lanzhou U.

Children from school opposite living quarters. Children would greet us with a chorus of "Hello how are you I'm fine." Giggle, giggle, giggle.

Foreign Affairs Officer in arranging my railroad ticket. Extensive notes on Kaifeng mention the warmth of my greeting there by former students, the two hot water bottles and four quilts on my bed, and how I slept with my hat and gloves on. Notes on Luoyang mention how grateful I was that the room was warm, the bathroom was heated, and I was able to wash my underwear and socks because there was hot water day and night.

— URUMQI —
Xinjiang Province, Fall, 1985

Three of my colleagues at Lanzhou University in Gansu Province and I took advantage of a weekend holiday to take a train to Urumqi. Samia, Bob, Jennifer, and I, fortified with hard boiled eggs, rice, and boiled water, carrying sleeping bags, and wearing our identity pins, left in high spirits for a city we had heard about in hushed tones. Our identity pins showed that we were instructors at Lanzhou University. Our students, Han Chinese, had told us conflicting stories about the "strange people" who lived in Xinjiang Province, on the edge of Tibet. The chair of the Department of English at Lanzhou had told us that we were not allowed to travel to Tibet, but we wanted to get as close as we could. We had seen Tibetans in the shops of Lanzhou, wearing their coats with one shoulder bared, accompanied by barefoot, hungry looking children, and our students had referred to them with a scornful twist to their mouths.

We were met in Urumqi by a representative from the university, who was waiting for us with a van and driver. On the way to the university, the driver pointed to his nose and said, "People here not Chinese." We knew that the area had been "liberated" in 1949, but we had also read reports about Xinjiang being an "autonomous province." We had also been told that the inhabitants of this province were Muslims and that there would be mummies in the Urumqi museum, plus some interesting caves and ruins to explore.

Samia, one of the youngest instructors, was fluent in Arabic, and she was excited to see signs in Arabic along the road, usually in front of food stalls. She kept pointing this out to us as we went up the mountain to the university. We had also noticed signs in Arabic in the marketplace next to the railway station. Our driver dropped us off in front of what looked like a hotel, but which turned out to be a dormitory for students, who were off on a semester break. There was no one around, not even a concierge to show us which rooms we could occupy. Two backpacking Americans showed up in the afternoon, and advised us to just make ourselves at home. "No one's around," they said, "it's sort of like a hostel. We'll show you the kitchen; you can choose any room you like. No one has said anything, but we assume that hostel rules apply — keep the place as clean as you found it."

We chose the best rooms we could find; Jennifer, Samia, and I found a room with mattresses on the steel cots, and Bob found a room with a mattress also. We were sitting around the covered patio, eating our rice and boiled eggs, when two boys showed up, eager to help us. They spoke their version of Chinese-English and offered to be our guides, for a price, of course. Jennifer bargained with them, in her version of English-Chinese, and we set off for the university on foot.

Apparently, the day we arrived was some sort of holiday; there were very few students around and only a few instructors. Once we established our presence with the Foreign Exchange Office, and told them where we were staying, we felt we had followed the rules as we understood them. The clerk at the office advised us to come back the next day, and we would be assigned an official guide to the ruins, the museum, and other recommended sites. We said we especially wanted to go to Turpan (pronounced Tulufan by the Chinese), and she said that could be arranged. Apparently someone in the Lanzhou office had notified the person in charge of foreign experts at Urumqi, so they knew we were coming, or we wouldn't have been met by the van, but no further information was offered. We shrugged and set off for the market.

The Urumqi market was full of vegetables, large crates of live chickens, goats, ovens for the baking of flat bread. The ovens intrigued me; these were vertical, round, iron structures, about a foot across and three-feet-high, suspended over a hot fire. Bakers rolled out flat pieces of dough, about the size of large tortillas, and slapped them on the inside of these ovens, reaching in with long paddles to turn them over. They tasted like pita bread. You bought your bread at the ovens, then went to the next stall for grilled goat meat and spices, to the next stall for tomatoes, and then to benches and tables set up for diners. There was hot tea from a kind of samovar available, beer, and yak butter tea. The bread was an edible plate.

We sat in a large, dirt-floored space, like a giant open tent, with the fabric overhead supported by large poles. All around us were chattering men, women, and children who looked more like Middle-Easterners than Chinese. We noticed red-bearded, hawk-nosed men with blue eyes, women with curly hair, children whose dark skin and faces didn't look at all Chinese. Soldiers, however, who paraded around the perimeter of the marketplace, casually cradling their weapons, were all Chinese.

Walking toward minarets near the marketplace, we watched women and men moving toward huge prayer wheels set up around them. They moved at a slow pace, prostrating themselves in the dust. They would get up, throw themselves down full length, get up, take another step and repeat the process. When they arrived at the prayer wheels, they would spin them, one at a time, going around the tower a set number of times, ending at the temple doors. Before going in, they prostrated themselves again, and this time kissed the stone before getting up. We looked into the open door and saw young boys with shaved heads sitting in a circle around their priest, all of them in dark red robes. The air was full of melodic Buddhist chanting.

I was deeply moved by this display of intense religious ritual, acknowledging to myself that I was incapable of following any part of such ritualistic practice. I remembered seeing devout Catholics in a Mexican village at Christmas walking on their bloodied knees toward a cathedral. Family members threw down pieces of cloth before them as they walked, the cloth becoming bloodier and bloodier by the time they reached the cathedral, many blocks away from where they started. At least the Tibetan ritual did not require painful laceration of flesh.

Arriving back at our hostel, we discovered a Chinese caretaker busily

Truck in which we traveled to Urumqi and Turpan from bus station

Uighur farmers traveling to market

Outside of Urumqi Market

Inside of Urumqi Market

Rhoda with tea vendor in Urumqi market

sweeping the dirt in the courtyard. She collected the required amount of renminbi, showing us the showers and places to do laundry. She spoke minimal English, and Jennifer's command of minimal Chinese came in handy. We asked about a trip to Tulufan, the ruins and caves we had heard about, and she told us that a van would come to collect us the next morning at nine a.m. We pointed to our watches, she pointed to hers, and we corroborated the information by holding up nine fingers and saying the word for tomorrow. We didn't want to take any chances with miscommunication.

Rhoda at ruins of Jiahe

Tulufan (Turpan in Turkish) is a three-hour journey southeast of Urumqi, in the basin of the Tian Chan Mountains, and is the lowest place in the world, at minus ninety-eight feet below sea level. Tulufan was the center of a fertile oasis and an important trade center; it had been an important stop along the Silk Road's northern route. All of us were fascinated by the route of the Silk Road, especially since Lanzhou and Gansu Province were also important places along the route.

The history of Tulufan is one of back and forth fighting between various tribes and the Chinese. In the museum we learned that it had been part of one kingdom called Gushi (Kushih), but Gushi was subdivided after being conquered by a Chinese tribe in 107 BCE. Trying to make sense of the historical plaques, we learned that Tulufan became an independent kingdom ruled by a Turkish tribe from 487 AD to 541. Jumping ahead to 856, the Uighurs established a sub-kingdom in that year. Then the Kyrgyz Turks took over. They called themselves "Saint Spiritual Rulers" (Idikuts).

As far as we could figure out, the last Idikut left the Tulufan area in 1284 for Gansu Province, seeking the protection of the Yuan Dynasty. Ah, we thought, another connection to Lanzhou! Local Buddhist rulers

214

Road outside of Urumqi,
showing effect of irrigation

Mosque near Market (Urumqi
is main town of Xinjiang
Province which is homeland
of Muslim Uighurs)

Uighur boys

Yurt and modern building in
Urumqi side by side

Uighur girls

hung on until Moghul Hizir Khoja invaded in 1389. One small plaque told us that the local Buddhist population converted to Islam in the last half of the fifteenth century. It didn't say anything about how that conversion was accomplished.

My observation of the Uighur population and their Buddhist customs did not reinforce any kind of conversion, either to Confucianism or Islam. The written language used Arabic script and the verbal language was a mix of Chinese melodic pronunciation overlaid with guttural, glottal throat sounds.

I was totally fascinated by the water system. The Tulufan Water Museum showed how water is collected from mountain streams and channeled underground to agricultural fields. We certainly could learn a lot from this system! Since the climate boasts very hot summers, very cold winters, and minimal rain, it meant that the heat and dryness of the summer, combined with the advanced irrigation system, produced wonderful fruit, melons, and grapes. The area also produced wheat, cotton, and poppies. Some streets in Tulufan were shaded by grapevine trellises, giving us a sense of peace and abundance as we strolled along. At the local market, we gorged on watermelon, and peaches, stocking up on grapes to take back with us.

On the way back to Urumqi, we stopped briefly at Jiahe to get a quick look at the caves and ruins, dating back to 108 BCE, when Jiahe was the capital of the Anterior Gushi Kingdom. There were ruins of Buddhist temples, stupas, and burial caves. Wandering among these ruins in the silence and heat of the desert filled me with the same sort of awe I felt when I visited the Dunhuang caves near Lanzhou. Once again I felt both important as an inheritor of a long line of ancestors I never knew, and insignificant as merely one more cog in a large cosmic wheel.

We were quiet on the trip back to Lanzhou, happily sated with the fresh fruit, and silently musing over the history to which we had been exposed. I mused sadly over the ways in which American arrogance stands in the way of learning from other cultures.

— KAIFENG —
Spring, 1986

My classes at Lanzhou University were over at the beginning of the Chinese New Year in February, 1986, and I embarked on a final journey to places I wanted to visit again, and new places on my must visit list. My graduate students, working on their master's degrees in TESOL (Teachers of English to Speakers of Other Languages), came from all over China, and they created an itinerary for me once they found out where I wanted to go.

I wanted to go back to Xi'an, to have a closer look at the full-sized clay figures of armies, which included soldiers and horses, and to roam a bit more around the town. My next stop would be Luoyang, where there were some caves with historic sculptures, and from there to Kaifeng. The rail journey from Lanzhou, in Gansu Province, to Xi'an in Shaanxi Province, was about seven or eight hours — the actual distance didn't matter to me — I measured my trips in terms of time, not distance. Theoretically, the trip from Xi'an to Luoyang in Henan Province was supposed to be shorter, and from Luoyang to Kaifeng shorter still.

Expectations are seldom fulfilled.

Traveling in China, alone and separate from a group, was difficult, but possible. I managed to get a "soft seat" — that is, a compartment with four bunks. I was ushered into a compartment on this train, only one compartment away from the toilet — a good sign. The server indicated that the upper berth was for me, and I wanted a lower berth. I argued with her in my limited Chinese, and she said she would see.

Shortly after leaving, at five forty in the afternoon, the server came by and indicated that yes, I could have the lower berth. The ticket was collected and put into a large book. I expected to receive a little metal tab as a receipt, but didn't get one this time. Only one person arrived to share the compartment, a Chinese man who tried earnestly to engage me in conversation. He saw by my identity tag that I was a "foreign professor" at Lanzhou, and he identified himself as a professor at Luoyang. He tried very hard, but I couldn't keep up with him. I couldn't help thinking of immigrants and refugees in the United States who can barely understand English and can't even read the written language. What an awful feeling. I mimed sleepiness and curled up on my bunk. My companion sighed and the compartment became an oasis of silence.

A word here about traveling in "soft seat" trains, which usually meant a compartment shared with two to three companions. Once the seats were transformed into a berth, that's the way they stayed. They did not become seats by day and beds at night. The food in the dining cars was wholesome and cheap, plain and often greasy. The sheets were clean; a towel was provided, as was hot water in a thermos for tea. There was practiced good humor and no drinking. Since I had cultivated a modicum of equanimity and persistence, traveling alone in China was mind and soul expanding. Men and women shared compartments as a matter of course.

Rhoda's colleague, Rhoda, and peasant women outside of Kaifeng

We arrived in Xi'an at nine a.m. and I managed to get a room in the Friendship Hotel. Blissfully warm. I contacted the Foreign Affairs Officer and told him I wanted to travel to Luoyang, and then to Kaifeng, and that I wanted him to book soft seats for me for both journeys. Ah, how naïve it was of me to assume that travel plans would work the same wherever I went. The Foreign Affairs Officer in Xi'an was either new to the job or naturally inefficient, but he messed up all the connections between Xi'an, Luoyang, and Kaifeng. Happily I didn't know that at the time I gave him the money and the necessary travel documents.

I took the tour, and this time I noticed how the faces looked like the Chinese I saw around me. In the museum next to the full-size clay figures, I discovered that the sculptors who created the figures changed the

218

Rhoda and peasant women in front of bus, in Kaifeng area

Street scene in the Kaifeng area

Building in the Kaifeng area

heads according to prominent Chinese men who paid to have their own heads placed on the bodies of the commanders. Going along to other sites in Xi'an, I met a Japanese man from Osaka, who was in China to buy silk, and it was fun to be able to talk in English about how the government was carefully preserving sites of ancient China.

I left the next day for Luoyang — only a three-hour trip — and checked into the Friendship Hotel there. There was a tour to the caves that afternoon, and I signed up immediately. They were called the Long Men Caves, meaning the Dragon Gate Caves. The caves were sad, so sad; so many statues destroyed; faces smashed, headless, so many empty caves, plundered by foreigners seeking treasure. Yet I had to remind myself that the men who took the statues did so with the approval and connivance of the monks (just as in the plunder of temples in Korea) whom they paid — or bribed.

The Foreign Affairs Officer in Luoyang handed me my train ticket for Train Number 140, but the ticket didn't show the departure time, and when I asked him, "When does the train for Kaifeng leave?" he shrugged. Finally, during dinner at a local restaurant, I decided to leave at seven thirty. As I was walking out, I checked a timetable lying on a counter in the restaurant, and I found that Train Number 140 left at seven thirty! The only thing I could do was go to the station and exchange the ticket for the next train — number 54, but all I could get was an entry into a hard seat car. All the seats were occupied, so I ended up in the dining car, a brightly lit, unheated space, inhabited by cigarette-smoking, loud-talking men. I put my head down on a table, pulled a scarf over my eyes, and tried to sleep.

When I staggered off the train, at nine thirty a.m. the next day, I was met by three students, Tang Bao Ming, Dai Ping, and Zhang Ruo Fei. They had a car, and their welcome was so warm, I thawed immediately. We went to Tang Bao Ming's home, a compound with four small, unheated rooms around a courtyard hung with laundry, and a pen for chickens. Walking into the main room, I noticed a beautiful, massive three-hundred-year-old rosewood table taking up most of the room. There were two carved armchairs, some straight chairs, and a long rosewood sideboard against a far wall. A round stove with a vent, burning polluting pieces of soft coal, kept the room warm.

Bao Ming's family had prepared a bed for me, and quickly placed two hot water bottles in it. My sleeping room adjoined the common room and was unheated. I went to bed, fully clothed, and slept until noon. When I awakened, the table was set for a sumptuous lunch of soup, boiled eggs, rice, and vegetables. After lunch, we went sightseeing, and then I went back to bed.

The next day, Day Two in Kaifeng, turned out to be a combination teaching seminar and more sightseeing. After breakfast, my three students showed up with seven friends, all teachers in local schools. We had an informal teaching seminar, consisting of their questions and my in-depth answers. All of them wanted to know what they could do to inspire and keep the attention of their students. They felt inhibited by the rigid, standardized texts they were supposed to use, and they felt pushed by their post-Cultural-Revolution students. My own post-graduate students had not been subjected to rote-type learning designed to prepare students for standardized exams. They had grown up during the Cultural Revolution, not attending regular high school classes, roaming the country, empowered by Mao and his Little Red Book. These were the kind of questions I met everywhere. "How do we teach students who are interested only in passing the exams?" They all wanted a magic answer to that question.

Radio and television programs featuring active English were now being broadcast throughout China, and the material taught in school was far less interesting than the TV programs, especially the BBC series, *Follow Me.* It was gratifying and fun for me to show them how to utilize the TV and radio programs. I gave them connections to the BBC consulate office in Beijing, and also to the "Voice of America" programs at the American Embassy. They didn't know that free materials were available, and they gobbled up the information. They made lists of the kind of materials they could use, and immediately began to set up a committee to travel to Beijing with their lists.

After the seminar, we wandered around Kaifeng. We went to the mosque, and I was invited into the women's prayer hall. They sat on mats, chanting and swaying, reminding me of the way Jews pray; it's called "davening." We went to the Catholic Church, which was recently reopened. There was no trace of a synagogue. Even the hospital, which was built on the site of the former synagogue, was gone.

I did see three stelae in the courtyard, which contained inscriptions of the history of the area. One of them was dated 1489, and Shih translated it for me. That stone commemorated the rebuilding of the synagogue, destroyed by the Yellow River flood of 1461. Another stone contained the names of those involved in the rebuilding of the synagogue. That one was dated 1663. The third stele, dated 1679, dealt with the accomplishments of the Zhao clan, which must have been an important Jewish family.

The Chinese called the Jews Muslims with blue caps. Since culture is defined primarily by food, prayer, and marriage customs, the Han Chinese could see no difference between Muslims and Jews. Both groups wore little hats; neither group ate pork; both had Sabbaths that began on Friday night, and men and women prayed separately. As far as the Chinese were concerned, the external similarities defined the groups — never mind fine points of doctrine.

We went back to Bao Ming's house, where we had another banquet, and after dinner, the mahjongg set came out and I watched while they played with beautiful tiles. Before going to bed, I went to the outside toilet, down a packed hard dirt path past their pig pen, and I was glad this was not my first visit to toilet facilities in a Chinese town, because otherwise I might have been traumatized by the cold and the smell.

During my final day in Kaifeng, I discovered that the government planned to transform the main street into a recreation of how the town looked in the days of the Song Dynasty as a tourist attraction. Workers were already tearing down the old buildings, and when it's all reconstructed, the plans were to have people dressed in the clothes of the Song Dynasty wandering around the streets. The government had given the town of Kaifeng a great deal of money for reconstruction and repair of all the important sites. No one knew whether or not the synagogue would be rebuilt.

Some of the buildings looked exactly like buildings in Oakland's Chinatown before those buildings were torn down by developers. Everywhere the real present was being destroyed in order to build up the unreal past.

From Kaifeng I traveled to Luoyang to explore more caves, then back to Lanzhou. Before I left China in March, 1986, I had a final meeting with some of my students. They were extremely angry, because the Beijing government had reneged on a promise to grant them their master's degrees in teaching English. They were supposed to get their degrees after the New Year celebrations. Without any warning, my students were told that they were to return to their work units without the promised degree. No explanations were given, and there was a lot of heated discussion about what they could do about it. When I returned to Berkeley, I expected to hear about a student revolution some time that year, but it didn't happen until June of 1989.

What did I learn from my teaching and living in China? My Chinese students were much more flexible and confident than my Korean and Japanese students when it came to learning language. The Chinese calligraphic symbol for China means "The Center of the Universe," and the people I met reflected this self-esteem, even when the conditions under which they lived might encourage despair. When the Russians invaded China and demanded that Chinese learn Russian, they shrugged. It didn't make any difference; the Chinese knew who they were. When the French came and took over the transportation and shipping lanes (postal cards and all post office and shipping notices were written in French and Chinese), the Chinese shrugged. They knew what renminbi would buy, and they issued Foreign Exchange Certificates for the inevitable black market in money. When the British and the Americans came, with their emphasis on the use of English, the Chinese shrugged again. They would use English to carry on their traditions and their culture; they would bend, like bamboo, and never break.

RUSSIA, 1993

During the summer quarter of 1992, I was teaching the Practicum in the TESOL Certificate Program at University of California Berkeley Extension, and one of my students came to me in tears. "My husband has been transferred to Moscow, and I'm afraid I won't be able to finish the program. I need this certificate. Is there anything I can do?"

I thought quickly. I was seventy-four years old, and was deeply involved with a wonderful man, Peter Meilleur, who was eighty-seven. "Tell you what," I said. "Once you get established in Moscow, try to get a teaching situation anywhere, in an international school or a Russian school teaching English as a foreign language. You already have an elementary teaching credential, but a TESOL certificate will give you more opportunities. I'll find out if I can come to Moscow and observe your teaching, then send the approval back to UC, and you'll be able to get your certificate. In addition, you can send us your lesson plans and comments; we'll discuss them in class, and send you our ideas. It will add an international dimension to the curriculum. Maybe Peter and I will be able to come in August of 1993."

When Peter, eighty-five, and I, seventy-two, first met in 1990, I had planned to visit Russia as part of an academic group from UC Berkeley. But Peter had encouraged me to buy a beautiful handmade walnut rocker instead, saying: "You can always go to Russia, and I'll go with you." Here was my chance to go, and take the trip off my income tax!

Janet thought that was a marvelous idea. "Once we get settled in Moscow, I'm sure we can make room for you and Peter in our apartment. What a lovely idea! We have to leave in a couple of weeks, but I'll contact you as soon as we get there."

I contacted my department head, and she also thought it was a splendid idea. She liked my plan to have my student mail us her lesson plans, which we would then discuss in class. By June of 1993 Janet had two part-time teaching jobs, one in an international school for expatriate English speakers, mostly connected with the Embassy, and one in a Russian foreign language school, specializing in English. They had a beautiful apartment, and had set aside a room for us with an adjoining bathroom. Peter and I arrived in Russia on September 3, 1993.

Janet and Fred's apartment was situated right across the street from the American Embassy, and the Russian Parliament Building, known as the White House, was visible from our bedroom window. Janet and her husband had five children and a nanny, and the apartment, with its high ceilings and parquet floors, was spacious enough for all of us. Janet and her nanny, Olga, shared the shopping and cooking; their driver, a young Russian friend of Olga's, was also part of the ménage. Both Olga and Andrei (nicknamed Andy) spoke very good English, and Andrei especially was an excellent interpreter.

I had studied Russian before we left Berkeley, and had taught Peter to decipher Russian road signs and subway station letters. I could understand some Russian, especially when spoken by English speakers, but was looked upon with amusement when I tried to speak it. Once again, being able to read a little of the native language and write some of it, just as I did in Japan, proved to be strong survival tactics.

One of the things I didn't do, which I regretted later, was to research the political and economic climate of Russia. It was impossible not to be involved while I was in Korea. After all, there I was on an assignment for the Department of Education of the Korean government, and my students let me know immediately that there would be spies in my classes. My situation in Russia was different. I was there as a visiting professor and consultant, and expected to be in an expatriate bubble. We didn't know that in three weeks we would be in the middle of a governmental uprising.

Peter and I loved to walk around any foreign city we were in, so we wandered. Walking down the main shopping street in Moscow was to run a gauntlet of people selling all sorts of things: doorknobs, lightbulbs, shoes, scarves, single cups and saucers, teapots.

Peter wanted to buy a shopping bag, so we went into a large department store, ducking the money-changers on the street, calling "shange, shange, shange" and waving bundles of rubles in their hands. They were offering more rubles in exchange for American dollars than the banks; it was a common form of black market business. In the store we wandered around looking for shopping bags. We asked a Russian shopper, pointing to her bag, using our dictionaries. She laughed and pointed to the umbrella counter. Well, what the heck, we bought an umbrella, which taught us the drill: you choose what you want, make a note of the number and the price, go to the cashier, stand in line, present the piece of paper given you by the stall keeper, pay for the item, get your piece of paper stamped, and go back to the stall, hoping your selection is still there. The umbrella seller pointed to the shopping bag stall which proved to be nearby, so we managed to get a striped plastic shopping bag after all.

By this time we were hungry, and I noticed a small hole-in-the-wall café on our way back to the apartment. Luckily there were photographs of the dishes available from an open window in the back of the café. Stepping up to the aperture, we could see a large stove presided over by an amply proportioned chef behind the cashier, and using the word for "soup," which we had memorized, we pointed to the picture and pulled out rubles and kopecks. She nodded, turned and shouted her order to the cook, took our money, and pointed to a samovar standing on a table beside us, saying, "Te, take." We were the only non-Russians in the café, who all seemed to be workers. They simply nodded to us and went on eating quietly. There was no buzz of conversation. The soup, which was cabbage, potatoes, and carrots, was delicious, and it came with a huge slice of black bread.

After lunch, we continued on to the apartment, passing vegetable and fruit sellers, and were often stopped by Russians, asking directions from Peter. With his French beret, his green coveralls with many pockets, usually containing sketch books, pens and pencils, his striped plastic shopping bag, he looked like a Muscovite. They all looked disappointed when he shrugged and said, "Inglesi."

On another day we were walking through a dismal apartment complex which had an open space with a few pieces of playground equipment sadly in need of repair. We had just settled ourselves on a bench, and Peter had begun sketching, when an outraged woman came over to us. She gestured wildly, shaking her head, hollering "Nyet, nyet!" pointing to the playground and the concrete apartments surrounding it, and ordered us to leave. We didn't have to understand Russian to understand her gestures. We asked Andrei about this later, and he explained that she was probably the commissar in charge of the apartment complex and that she was afraid we were spies for the government.

Thanks to Janet, I was invited to do three teacher-training seminars for teachers of English at Moscow State University, one of the prestigious universities in Russia, where each department has its own English section. Engineering had one, Biology had one, Mathematics and Psychology each had their own English sections, believing that English for Special Purposes was the only way for their students to connect with the kind of English they needed to do their research. Rote learning was the pattern, grammar translation was the method, and anything else was a waste of time. That was the background of the teachers of Engineering who attended my seminars. I knew that a gray-haired naïve American would be regarded with skepticism, but I decided to go ahead anyway with my plan for demonstrating the advantages of group learning and verbal communication.

Twenty teachers attended the first seminar, and I organized them into groups, as I usually do, and assigned an exercise I had created: "Learner Generated Questions as Class Content." Students have to create their own questions regarding any aspect of learning English, prioritize their questions, dictate their number one question to a recorder, then discuss the questions and try to come up with their own answers. They then select the most important question of the lists they have created, and try to answer that. The second part of the exercise is led by the instructor, who solicits questions and answers from the groups of students. At that time, the instructor has an opportunity to add her own answers to their questions and answers.

The teachers in the seminar were in groups of five, and they all settled down to the task. That is, all but one, Katrina, a large woman in a beautiful hand-knit purple sweater. She sat in her group with her arms folded, a defiant look on her face. I asked her whether she had any questions at all about learning English, and she replied, "I have been teaching English for twenty-two years, and I know what I am doing."

"Yes," I replied, "and have you no questions about how well your students have been learning?" She looked at me, and her bright blue eyes widened. It was as if that question had never occurred to her. She didn't begin to write anything, but she did engage in the discussion that followed.

I pointed out that when instructors allow students to think about problems connected with learning English (or anything else), their attention is already engaged, and the instructor's words are more likely to be heard. I also pointed out that teaching agendas and curriculum would probably provide answers to the questions the students had in their heads, but that students feel they are more engaged in the process when they are included.

At the end of the second seminar, which included different exercises, one of the teachers asked if I would teach a demonstration class, while they observed. I readily agreed, thinking that it would take place on another day, and I would have time to do some preparation. "No," she said. "Let's have a demonstration class right now." Well! I was stuck, so I nodded; the door opened and twenty students marched in. Apparently, everything had been planned ahead of time.

I used my group set-up again, this time creating five groups of four students. I asked them to write something about themselves: their major, the reasons for studying English, and their future goals. After I called time, I asked them to rotate what they had written, so that each person had someone else's profile. Then I chose one person at random from each group, asking that person to introduce his neighbor. (All the students were male.) This exercise relaxed them, and then we went on to another exercise, which I also knew was foolproof.

After the demonstration, I was invited to have tea in a small teachers' room near the seminar classroom. Katrina came late, bursting in with a triumphant cry, "I'm trying the method!" She gestured toward her classroom. "They are there, working, and I am here, having tea!" She certainly got the point that when a teacher creates a student-oriented classroom, and puts the burden of learning on the student, rather than on the teacher, the teacher can relax.

Andrei drove Peter and me to the university for the first seminar, and then took Peter to the Pushkin Museum so that he could do some more sketching. He was creating a Russian Sketchbook. On the days I observed Janet teaching at her part-time teaching jobs, Peter took photographs of the class and the schools, always with permission. We managed to get the photographs printed before we left Moscow, and when we returned from St. Petersburg, we found them prominently displayed on the walls of the schools.

We left for St. Petersburg on September 15, intending to stay ten days, during which time we would visit the Hermitage Museum and two English teachers who were friends of a friend in Palo Alto. We had the use of an empty apartment belonging to the daughter of another friend. As soon as we announced our plan to travel to St. Petersburg by train, well-wishers barraged us with warnings: "Be careful of gypsies; they will surround you and pick your pockets!" "When you get into your compartment, be sure to lock your door and stuff towels underneath to make sure there are no openings for gas to get through." When our friends saw the unbelieving expressions on our faces, they began to regale us with horror stories.

"Haven't you read the papers? Thieves will spray sleeping gas into your train car, and then they will pry open your compartment door and rob you while you sleep."

I thought all these warnings were ridiculous, but Peter took them seriously, and before we retired for the night, he dutifully stuffed towels underneath the door. When a knock came on the door in the morning, and we opened it to find the car attendant standing there with two glasses of hot tea, I felt pretty silly about all the precautions we had taken. However, there was a headline in the English-Russian newspaper staring at us as we debarked, detailing a robbery which had occurred on the train preceding ours, in exactly the way we had been warned about. Thieves had saturated a train car containing many foreigners with sleeping gas, broken into several compartments and made off with a substantial haul, jumping off the train several stops before St. Petersburg. We shrugged; this was Russia, so what? Thieves and scoundrels are everywhere.

Wandering around the neighborhood, we saw playground areas with broken-down equipment in shabby center courts surrounded by highrise concrete apartments similar to the one we were living in. However, we came across a large building which had a sign in English, "Tribune," and Peter was sure that it meant it housed a periodical of some sort. I wasn't so sure. The door was open and we walked in. There was a reception desk in a small office, and in my halting Russian, I asked the receptionist if she spoke English. She gave me a terrified look and immediately plugged in her switchboard, speaking urgently to someone. Then she waved us to some chairs and we waited.

A tall, handsome woman came over to us and greeted us in flawless English. She laughed when she discovered our interpretation of the sign outside. We had walked into a factory that put together underwear for a company called "Sara Lee." The cut pieces arrived by plane from Lithuania or Poland or places in Scandinavia, were assembled, stitched, and shipped from St. Petersburg to New York, London, and other places.

Our interlocutor's job was to check the invoices and make sure that the subcontractors weren't cheating by short-changing the shipment.

I was intrigued by her appearance and her ease in English. It turned out that Nadya was a cardiologist and daughter of a Russian diplomat, who had spent her youth in Washington, D.C. She said that the practice of medicine was at such a low level in St. Petersburg that she found herself unable to do more than simply hold her patients' hands, and she couldn't bear it. The factory owners were friends who needed someone fluent in English with a sharp mind and eye. Her husband was a violinist with the St. Petersburg Orchestra. She was as interested in us as we were in her, and we agreed to meet at the best hotel in St. Petersburg the following day.

During dinner, Nadya explained why there were no teahouses or cafes where one could sit down, have a coffee, and chat. All the places we saw for a casual drink demanded that the customer stand at a round counter while drinking tea or coffee or having a Russian-type sandwich. Nadya said that during Stalin's time even small public gatherings were discouraged. The repressive administration didn't want small groups of people gathering to talk about anything.

We talked about the symphony, and she arranged for us to have box seats at that evening's performance. She said the symphony was about to leave for an extended tour of North America, including Victoria, and Montreal, Canada, New York, Chicago, Washington, and Miami. Then the players would go south to Cuba, Venezuela, and Brazil. She would catch up with them somewhere along the tour. Our encounter with Nadya gave us a glimpse of St. Petersburg we would never have had otherwise.

We hired a student to take us around to interesting places in St. Petersburg. Ivan was a scholarly looking young man wearing horn-rimmed glasses and a serious expression. He said he would meet us at our apartment and then go for a walk around the Neva River. He added (with a raised eyebrow) that he had a special surprise for us.

Ivan showed up promptly, and we took a bus to the banks of the Neva in an area that seemed rather rundown. Then he announced that we would walk a few blocks to the place where Raskolnikov and Alyona Ivanovna, the Pawnbroker, had lived. Peter and I exchanged quizzical looks. We both knew that Raskolnikov was Dostoevsky's main character in *Crime and Punishment* and we were surprised to hear him referred to as if he were a real human being. We soon arrived at the courtyard of a bleak concrete apartment building, and Ivan gestured toward a fifth-floor apartment.

"That's where Raskolnikov lived," he said proudly. And then he gestured to an apartment on the other side of the courtyard. "And there's where Alyona Ivanovna lived!"

"Excuse me," I said, "but aren't Raskolnikov and Alyona Ivanovna fictional characters in a novel by Dmitri Dostoevsky?"

"Oh, yes," he replied, "but they are more real than real."

That summed up for me the attitude of many Russians toward their literature: it is more real than real.

Walking along the Neva, I realized how important the river was to the vitality and economy of St. Petersburg. The Neva was meant to be the "main street of the city," and throughout most of the eighteenth century, people were ferried from one bank to the other, the way Peter the Great intended when he founded his "Venice of the North" and what he called "Paradise."

We returned to Moscow on September 25, to find that we had missed an attempted coup which started on September 21. Andrei picked us up at the railway station in the Volvo van with bullet holes in the windshield. He said we would hear all about the excitement once we got "home."

Yeltsin had dissolved parliament on September 21, and there was an armed conflict that would last for ten days. There were snipers on all the rooftops of the buildings across from the American Embassy; defenders and attackers of the Moscow White House, which was located directly behind the Embassy. Janet's seventeen-year-old son had gone up to the roof to "watch the action" — as he said later — along with a young woman typist from his dad's office. Unfortunately, she was caught in the crossfire. John picked up her unconscious, bleeding body, wrapped

View of our apartment
building in Moscow,
1993. Janet's teen-age
son climbed down
from roof with girl shot
by snipers wrapped
around him

Moscow, Bread Line in 1993

233

her legs around him, and climbed down from the roof on a steep iron ladder. It was impossible to get an ambulance to the apartment complex, so the family improvised a stretcher made of a piece of wood, and rushed her to the American hospital. Her liver was punctured, but the doctors were able to repair most of the damage, and they put her on a plane for home in Ireland the next morning.

I found Janet and Walter torn between admiration for John's quick thinking and wanting to reprimand him for being on the roof in the first place.

Walter explained that the armed conflict was started by conservative deputies who wanted to oust Boris Yeltsin and destroy his reform policies. These conservatives gathered their armed supporters and stormed the parliament building, the White House. We could see the building burning from the window of our room. By October 4, Yeltsin's government shelled the building and arrested as many of the coup members as they could find.

We watched looters running out of the parliament building with typewriters, telephones, chairs, tables, almost anything they could carry; there were tanks in the streets, and constant gunfire. We were glued to the television set, and tried not to feel as though we were under siege. By October 5, the streets were quiet, and we were free to leave the apartment. Janet and I went off to her school for a final demonstration teaching lesson, and Peter went off to add to his Moscow Sketchbook.

Peter and I left Moscow on October 6 for Budapest. I was scheduled to give a presentation at the IATEFL Conference (International Association of Teachers of English as a Foreign Language) and at that point I was happy to leave Russia.

The musical, artistic, and literary life of Moscow and St. Petersburg was thrilling and enriching, but I was saddened by the bleakness of Russian ordinary, everyday life. The long lines for bread, the scrounging for ordinary things of life like doorknobs or light bulbs; the potholes and the broken-down equipment in playgrounds — all of those things made me sad.

TRAVELS IN HUNGARY

We flew to Budapest from Moscow with the Russian airline Aeroflot, in a small, well-equipped plane. Taking a taxi from the airport to Budapest, we drove through a pleasant countryside, so different from the glimpses we had had of the Russian countryside.

We were met by one of the organizers of the IATEFL Conference and he insisted that we stay in his apartment in an outlying section of Budapest rather than in a downtown hotel. The conference was going to be held in a different part of Hungary, and I wanted to repack, taking a small amount of baggage with us and leaving the rest in a hotel baggage room. But Henry, wanting to be hospitable, insisted on hosting us.

Here we were, Peter at eighty-eight, me at seventy-five, being hosted by a vigorous thirty-five-year-old eager expatriate from San Francisco. He treated us as if we were peers, flattering but exhausting. We carried our luggage up four flights of stairs and collapsed on couches in his small living room. Henry had planned a small party for us, to introduce us to his colleagues at a local university, and we managed a short nap before the party.

Henry was an architect and was part of a special group I had trained in San Francisco before we left for Moscow. That training was a seminar, sponsored and paid for by the LEED Foundation (Language for Eastern Europe Development) to train twelve specialists in various fields of business and academia to teach English for Special Purposes in Hungary. The Foundation was underwritten by George Soros with the encouragement of Tom Lantos, a Congressional representative from Los Altos, California. One of the main reasons I had decided to come to Hungary was that I wanted to visit the people I had trained, to see how they were getting along. Henry was teaching at one of the universities with which LEED had established a contract, and he had become an active member of IATEFL. The party would give me a chance to assess Henry's success in an informal manner.

Eight people, plus Henry, Peter, and I, assembled in Henry's small living room that evening, and Henry provided Hungarian take-out: goulash from a local restaurant, plus vegetables, cakes, wine, and beer. The eight colleagues were all Hungarian teachers of architecture, who were eager to participate in international conventions. Henry was their linguistic bridge.

I tried to steer the conversation to the kinds of English they wanted to learn, but they were much more interested in my relationship to Peter. "Were we married?" "No."

"Did we plan to marry?"

"No."

"Why not?"

At that point, I wondered how to convey my reasons in a cross-linguistic fashion that would fit their academic ability in English. I decided it was too difficult and simply said, "We decided we didn't want to," and left it at that. After that exchange, the young students decided they really wanted to have a good time, which meant drinking lots of beer, singing American pop songs, and speaking their own Hungarian version of English. I understood only part of it.

The next day, over breakfast, I asked Henry what he was teaching. He said he was teaching his students to write abstracts for presentations to international conferences on architecture. The abstract had to be in English, and they had a choice to present in English or Hungarian. Most of his colleagues were willing to write in English, but not speak in English. They said that their presentations would be translated simultaneously into different European languages, as well as English, so why should they bother trying to speak English?

Henry admitted they had a point, and so did I. We both found Hungarian difficult to read and write, as well as speak. As long as Henry taught his students to write academic English for Special Purposes, they accepted him and worked with him. As soon as he tried to teach idiomatic or spoken English, they turned him off.

After breakfast, I warned Henry that we would have to leave very soon to catch the express train to Veszprem, the location of the IATEFL conference. "No problem," he said. "We'll just catch a cab outside."

Unfortunately, it was rush hour, and there were no cabs to be had. Henry tried to call a taxi, but they were all booked. We took a tram to the railway station and arrived just as the express train pulled out. Henry had to leave for class, so Peter and I hung around the train station for three hours until a local train arrived that would take us to Veszprem.

There is a large inland sea in Hungary, with small towns located all around the edge. Our train stopped at every one. A trip that should have taken two-and-a-half hours took eight. We traveled in a Toonerville trolley that went "Toot, toot, toot," chugging alongside Hungary's inland sea. Peter and I had gotten a Hungarian hamburger in the Budapest station and luckily had also bought a substantial snack package, including water. Bouncing around on the rattan seats, I still felt very bored, and decided to read the Raymond Chandler mystery novel I'd brought with me. Peter said, "Hey, read aloud, will you? This train bounces so much, the words blur." So all the way to Veszprem, I read Chandler aloud under the tiny lights of our railroad car. We were its only occupants by ten o'clock.

A plump female ticket-taker came by at one point, looked quizzically at us, and shook her head sadly when she saw our destination.

She patted Peter's shoulder and shook her head again when she left the train at the next station.

We arrived at Veszprem at eleven p.m., and the station was empty except for a lone taxi driver. I showed him the piece of paper on which I had written the name of the hotel where the conference organizers had put us. He nodded, said something like "organizatione, ya," and we took off.

It turned out he was German, not Hungarian, and had picked up some Italian somewhere along the line. He had no French, and no English. He proceeded to teach us German phrases that would be useful in Hungary! When we arrived at the hotel specified on our reservation paper, we were told that we were too late; all the rooms were occupied, and that we should try somewhere else. The story was the same at the next hotel, so this time Peter and I went with our taxi driver to the front desk. There we finally reached someone at Conference Headquarters, who told us to go to the "Castle Gasthaus." We got back into the taxi and made our way to the castle. Yes, we were on the list of registered guests.

After unloading our luggage, our driver looked at his meter and told us what we needed to pay him. It was such a small amount that Peter tried to give him extra money for all his trouble. After all, it was midnight by this time. "No, no, no," he protested. It was his pleasure, he said, "And besides, I taught you some German!"

The castle had probably been a bishopric, judging from the way it was laid out. It overlooked a valley and an old Roman ruin on top of limestone cliffs. Dates inscribed on the buildings near the castle were 1640–1670, but the sign over the gate leading into the courtyard stating that it was a Gasthaus seemed recent.

Inside the castle, we walked up a broad, red carpeted stairway with curving polished wood banisters to the second floor, and then along a hallway to a corner room with a view of the valley. There were three narrow cots in this large room, so Peter and I immediately moved two of them close together, quickly undressed and fell fast asleep.

I woke early, and remembered vaguely a posting to the left of the stairway about times for breakfast, lunch, and dinner. I didn't want to miss breakfast, so I threw on my robe and went downstairs. It was then six a.m. The sign on the board said, "Breakfast, 6:30 a.m. to 8:30 a.m." Making my way to the kitchen, I procured a cup of coffee in a take-out container, and started back to our room. However, I had remembered going up two flights of stairs, not one, and I found myself in a corridor where all the doors were painted green. That didn't seem right; I remembered the doors on our floor painted brown. What to do?

Walking along the quiet corridor, I noticed a partly open door and peered in. A lovely young woman, sitting in bed reading, waved at me. I said, "I'm lost. I'm trying to find my way back to my room, but I seem to be on the wrong corridor." She laughed, put on a dressing gown, and joined me in the hall. "You're on the third floor," she said, "and you need to be on the second floor." She introduced herself as "Agnes" from Budapest, took hold of my arm and steered me down to the second floor. I described our corner room, in a kind of alcove, and we wandered around for a bit. Then Agnes saw one of the cleaning women at the end of the corridor, and we hurried over. After talking to Agnes, she shrugged and pointed to a passageway we hadn't even noticed. "See you at breakfast!" Agnes waved and disappeared.

I came into our room, uncovered the coffee container, and let the perfume waft across Peter's nose. His eyes flew open. "How did you manage that?" I shrugged and said, "It's a long story. We'd better get dressed and go down for breakfast. They stop serving at 8:30. I don't even know when I'm supposed to do my presentation." I never did get the advance literature I was supposed to get before we left for Moscow, and none of my attempts to call Budapest from Moscow worked.

Agnes waved to us when we came into the dining room, and indicated two seats next to her. We were seated on long benches, and breakfast was delivered to us by silent female servers. There was a large pitcher of orange juice and another of coffee on the table, plus piles of cold toast. Scrambled eggs arrived shortly.

"Do you have a program for the conference?" I asked Agnes. "I don't know the schedule for my presentation. I didn't receive any confirmations before we left for Europe, and I wasn't able to contact conference headquarters by phone. We had a devil of a time finding accommodations. But we're here, and that's all that matters."

Agnes handed me the program, and I noticed with horror that I was scheduled for ten a.m. that morning. We looked at the map printed in the program, and the building in which we were to assemble at nine a.m. was in what looked like downtown Veszprem. "Not to worry," said Agnes. "Just gather up your material and meet me in front; we'll find a taxi, and go to the opening session together." What a lifesaver! Agnes was a professor at a prestigious university in Budapest, and she turned out to be a wonderful friend. She had contacts all over Hungary, and she provided insights into Hungarian culture we wouldn't have had otherwise.

My presentation, "Cross-Cultural Communication Exercises for Teacher-Training" went well, and that evening there was an after-dinner "joke-telling" session organized by a British instructor who was a stand-up comic in his spare time. As the evening wore on, the jokes got raunchier and raunchier, as the tellers drank more and more beer and superb Hungarian wine. I was the only presenter from the United States, and toward the end of the evening, I decided to tell the story of John Bobbitt and his wife, Lorena.

"This is a true story," I began. "It may have been reported by the BBC, and maybe not. You can find the moral for yourself. Just a few months ago, a man named John Bobbitt came home from a party involving heavy drinking, and forced his wife to have sex with him, the kind of sex we in the U.S. refer to as domestic rape. Then he fell into a deep sleep. Lorena was enraged; this had happened before. She got up and went to the kitchen to get herself a glass of water, and her eye fell on a sharp carving knife on the kitchen counter. She picked up the knife, went into the bedroom, ripped the sheets off her sleeping husband, and cut off half his penis.

"Still in a rage, she fled the house clutching the penis tip, got into her car and roared down the road. In the car, she realized she still had the bloody piece of flesh in her hand, so she rolled down the window of the car and threw it into a field. By this time she had calmed down; she drove to the nearest gas station and called 911. Cops rushed to the area she described, found the penis tip, wrapped it in ice, and delivered it to the hospital where John had gone by ambulance. Surgeons worked for more than nine hours and reattached John's penis. Doctors were optimistic about his recovery."

There was dead silence after I stopped. While I was telling the story, I noticed that men in the audience instinctively covered their crotches. And then there was a buzz of conversation. Where did it happen? "Virginia." Is that a crime in the U.S.? "I don't know. Do you think it's a crime?" There was a buzz of "Well, can't say as I blame her!" from the women, to "Jeez! That's what I call revenge with a capital R!" No one seemed inclined to cap that story, and by common agreement, we all left for the night.

When we saw Agnes the next day, she laughed and told us that I, the oldest presenter at the conference, had set a bar so high that other presenters would have trouble matching it! She said I had upheld the reputation of "outrageous Americans." I assumed it was a compliment. Then she invited us to join a group that was going into the countryside to have lunch at a small village restaurant she knew about.

Driving through the verdant Hungarian countryside, I couldn't help comparing it to the atmosphere of bleak resignation I had felt in Russia. Here were neat farms, roads without potholes, well-kept houses. Even in the cities, the streets were clean; people were repairing cobblestones, and there was an atmosphere of public connectedness. Hungary had never succumbed to the brutal, totalitarian control of Stalin's Russia. Our lunch was delicious, and we all commented on how well Hungary had recovered from the war. No Hungarian I met acknowledged that she understood or spoke Russian; German was tolerated, but not Russian.

We returned to Budapest by express train, and were relieved to be seated in a comfortable, padded seat car. Arriving on time, we were met by a representative of the IATEFL conference team, which had finally gotten its act together. We checked into a small hotel and called

241

Henry. He arrived with our luggage, and over cake and tea, we talked about our plans. I said I wanted to rent a small apartment, so that Peter and I could cook our own meals; roam around Buda and Pest at our leisure; maybe take a boat trip on the Danube; certainly visit the hot baths and the swimming pool at the Hotel Gellert. I had visited the Gellert in the 1980s and still remembered the swimming pool with its simulated wave action.

Henry immediately swung into action, consulted a map, and came up with a plan. He knew of an inexpensive apartment building located near a tram line, where the manager made a specialty of subletting small apartments for short periods of time. It was a price we could afford, so we said yes, we would take it for eight days.

Once the housing situation was settled, we discovered that there were several schools and organizations that wanted to confer with "the professor from America." Among them was a director of a training hospital who wanted some advice on writing applications for participation in American medical conferences. The hospital had an English language instructor, but he was British, and they wanted American English input. I wasn't sure how a ninety-minute lecture-presentation would help interns and physicians improve their English, but I agreed to try. I figured it couldn't be more traumatic than the three-hour workshops I gave in Russia!

I asked the instructors of various departments to circulate a questionnaire as to the kind of English problems they wanted me to address. These were students with specific ideas; they were professionals who wanted a "quick fix." I decided to use my usual strategy: put them into groups, ask them to create specific questions and rank order them from one to three, try to answer their own questions, and then debrief, with input coming from me. The strategy worked; I left my card and told the instructors I would be available for advice by mail.

Hungarians were the only Europeans I met who seemed to work at several jobs. When the opportunity arose to make an appointment for anything — tea, dinner, a coffee — the Hungarian I was talking to would whip out an appointment book and choose a specific amount of time. Their appointment books seemed to be full of fifteen-, twenty-, and thirty-minute appointments. "Time is money," I heard, many times.

There is a walking plaza in the main area of Budapest, filled with all sorts of small tourist agencies, hair salons, boutiques, and restaurants. We saw a poster advertising Stephen Sondheim's "Assassins" and decided to buy two tickets for the musical. We wanted to find out how accessible an American musical would be, produced in Hungarian. Then we spotted a hair salon which advertised haircuts for men and women, so we went in and made one appointment for Peter and one for me, for the next day.

Unfortunately, we got lost, and we were late for Peter's appointment. We were subjected to a serious scolding by an angry barber when we showed up, who shouted "Time is money" at us, in heavily accented English. He sulked, but gave Peter a good haircut anyway.

The Sondheim musical, sung in Hungarian in a theater-in-the-round, was beautifully staged, and we had no difficulty following the plot, the acting was so good. We had invited Henry and Inez to join us, and they invited a few of the students from Henry's university, so the evening turned out to be another in-depth education in Hungarian culture. They were intensely proud of their writers and musicians, and they always argued furiously over whether Bela Bartok was Romanian or Hungarian. Both countries claimed him.

Budapest is a magical city, which I will never forget. The Hungarians we met were cheerful and pragmatic; Peter and I shared their lust for life. We left reluctantly for Paris to connect with our return flight to Berkeley.

THE SHOCK OF RETURN

Whenever and wherever I traveled, I always tried to enter into the culture of the new place as thoroughly as I could before I left. I studied the language, listened to the music, and went to movies or plays conducted in the new country's language. I read the literature, usually in translation, in order to have as little culture shock as possible. Once in my new environment, I tried to adapt to the mores and food as thoroughly as possible. This meant that when I returned to Berkeley, reverse culture shock was greater than I expected. Coming back from Korea after two years there on a Fulbright fellowship took almost two years to readjust, and, in fact, the impact of "Mask Dance" and Korean brush painting are with me still.

In Korea, I learned the skill of Korean brush painting, and upon my return, built a small studio in which to practice. I learned to wear the hanbok (traditional women's dress) and to sit and walk the way Korean women of my age sat and walked. I had lived in a women's monastery and learned to walk in traditional shoes.

Working and living in a country other than one's own means that the rules of that society seep into your bones. At least that's what happened to me. I lived in a kind of cocoon in Korea. I was in a protected environment, and I had a rigorous schedule at the university, which I did not choose. In fact, all of my choices were limited. The housing officer at Sogang arranged the house I was to live in (I didn't have to pay rent — that came as part of my salary), and as long as I did my job, my free time was my own. I was free to study painting, go to concerts, and take trips into the countryside, as long as university personnel knew where and when I was going. I had my own interpreter, who became my guide to esoteric places and esoteric food.

At home in Berkeley, my life was full of choices. I had to decide what to cook for dinner; whether or not to invite someone over; and to keep track of bills to pay when they were due. There were phone solicitations for charities, reminders of doctor appointments, and decisions about whether or not to renew subscriptions to theater companies. There always seemed to be decisions to be made about everything. In Korea, as in Japan, I surrendered to the advice and direction of my hosts. Being a guest, even a guest instructor, is a lovely, relaxing way to travel.

When I lived in Japan, once again I learned to wear kimono, to walk as Japanese women walk, and I even bowed when I answered the telephone. For some reason, the music, drama, dance, and literature of Japan became deeply embedded in my psyche. On one of my visits home between assignments to Korea and Japan, I went to a language conference directly from the airport. At lunch, my companion introduced me to a friend of hers, and I clicked my heels together and bowed, while my new acquaintance stood there, puzzled, her hand outstretched to take mine. I straightened up, blushing, as I realized my mistake, and took her hand, muttering something about just having gotten off the plane.

My experience in China was just as deep. I felt a strong connection in China, something that went farther back than I can describe; it was a similar deja vu feeling to the one I had in Japan, although I knew I had never been to either country before. Perhaps it was the sense of connection to human beings over a long, long period of time when I visited the caves at Lanzhou and the old city of Kaifeng. Traveling to the country of the Uighurs in Xingjian Province reminded me of China's connection to the Middle East through the Silk Road, and of how, as humans, we travel endlessly through the world.

After I met Peter, our travels changed a bit, but our attitudes did not. Peter was like a chameleon; he took on the look of whatever country we

245

were in. When we were in Moscow, walking through the streets or going to flea markets, people would come up to him and ask him for directions. When he shrugged, and said "Russia nyet, Francois?" he was met with a disappointed, unconvinced look. The same thing happened to us in Turkey and in Greece, while in France, of course, he was completely at home.

I was protected by Peter when we traveled in Europe, and there were two aspects to that travel that eased the shock of return. One was that our trips were shorter — six weeks at the most, rather than one or two years; the other was that the contrast of patterns of life was not as great as in Asian countries. Also, English was much more widely used; music and literature were more familiar, and we were in charge of what we ate and where we slept. We continued to make choices, and therefore the shock of return from Europe was not as great as my return from Asia.

Rhoda in her garden

EPILOGUE

At the end of my first book, I wrote, "The book is finished, but I'm not." Now that the second book is finished, I wonder where I will go from here. Since I change the direction of my life every twelve years, I am now in the final section of my twelve-year cycle, which is supposed to end in 2014, when I will be ninety-six. That's only four years from now, and while my death is certainly possible, it may not happen.

It occurs to me that the process of our journey through life is what's important, not the product. Of course the process affects the product, but we are often afraid of the process, because we cannot control its direction. I notice that people in my age group are primarily afraid of dying, but not of death itself. The dying process is painful, in more ways than one, and I am familiar with the discomfort. I can no longer breathe with ease or walk without support. My joints hurt, and my body often says "NO!" while my mind says, "YES!" Sometimes I listen to my body, and sometimes I don't.

Since it's the process that's important, I have decided that fear is counter-productive. Change is inevitable, and I find myself trying to contemplate that change with equanimity. It's hard. I take palliatives for the aches, say thank you for physical support of friends, and get as many therapeutic massages as I can afford.

I'm in a new phase now at ninety-two, and I'm moving in a new direction. I have decided I want to learn how to write a good play, so I'm going to start at the beginning, as I usually do. I'll sign up for a course, and go as far as I can. I know that it takes at least ten years to become professional at any endeavor, and I will probably not make my goal, but at least the process will be interesting.

ACKNOWLEDGMENTS

To all the people who have supported me through this project:

Rani Cochran

Pat Courtney

Jane DeCuir

Jonathan Furst and Tracy Joy

Bonu Ghosh

Tova Halpern

Jeanette Larsen and David Eichorn

Ruby Privateer

Lilly Rivlin

Tom Wyse and the Guys Upstairs

Made in the USA
San Bernardino, CA
16 August 2019